I0658852

Samantha Lytton

THE DIMPLE STRIKES BACK

LUCY WOODHULL

The Dimple Strikes Back
ISBN # 978-1-78184-695-7
©Copyright Lucy Woodhull 2013
Cover Art by Posh Gosh ©Copyright 2013
Interior text design by Claire Siemaszkiewicz
Totally Bound Publishing

Published in 2014 by Totally Bound Publishing, Newland House, The Point, Weaver Road, Lincoln, LN6 3QN, United Kingdom.

Totally Bound Publishing is an imprint of Total-E-Ntwined Limited.

THE DIMPLE STRIKES BACK

Dedication

To my husband, my love, my fan, my rock. Thank you for always standing by me.

Chapter One

You Can't Spell 'Happiness' Without 'Pain'

No one would suppose, looking at me, little Samantha Lytton, that I am a sophisticated movie maven with an illicit thief for a lover. But that hypothetical lookie-loo would be wrong, and not just because I'm shorter than the average actress and/or gangster's moll.

Outside the oval window beside me, clouds floated by on the vicious air currently bouncing my airplane to and fro. And taking my cocktail with it. "Shit!" I hissed. I swiped at my lap and accidentally splashed the puddle of vodka I'd dribbled there onto my seatmate's sleeve. The businessey dude frowned at me and patted the offending liquid with a napkin.

"I'm sorry," I said. "I hate flying. But I love vodka! And talking when I'm nervous!" A too-long peal of laughter floated out of me from parts unknown. I took a deep breath and fought for calm. "Okay, I'm done now." I beamed him the smile that *Entertainment Weekly* called 'charming and dorky'.

I'd like it noted that they totally put 'charming' first.

My fellow first-classer didn't seem impressed by me. No matter—I was suspended over the ocean, high on Xanax and whatever booze I'd managed to get into my mouth, on the way to London to shoot my very first starring role in a film. A bona-fide *film-film*—not one of those budget shoots where the catering is a Happy Meal thrown at you after filming illegally in an alley while you wear Goodwill clothing all night.

In the last year, *People* magazine had called me 'Clara Bow two-point-zero', and declared me the only entertaining part of my first movie *I Cried Lavender Tears in Paris*. Well, except for the bit when Justin Bieber exploded.

After that, I'd won a small but memorable scene in a Judd Apatow flick, a sidekick part in a Tina Fey movie and a recurring arc on a TV show soon canceled for being too clever for anyone to watch. I was an underground darling in that I was a funny actress who looked like an average woman—with better-than-average teeth. I'd accepted any project offered to me, and as they began coming out, I got noticed by the Powers That Be.

The Powers That Be are a group of male studio executives who base an actress' worth on a calculation that goes something like…fuckability + sexiness * (hilarity + popularity on Twitter^2) + (blonde * 10)

I score highly enough in the tits and hilarity departments—even though I am no longer blonde, but redheaded—that they have taken a massive risk on me with this new movie. Not for the first time, I clutched my stomach, terrified that I'd outpaced my abilities. In a few days, I'd begin shooting *What Could Go Wrong?*, a heist spoof about a down-on-their-luck couple who rob the British Museum with a group of misfits.

Now, Sam would tell you that he was instrumental in getting me this movie. He's my illicit thief lover and yes, I had indeed learned about skulking and running and lying and truly superior oral sex from him. And about how you can drown in hazel eyes whether they're mossiest green or deepest brown.

He also taught me that the dimple is the most savage of facial features, causing everyday ladies 'brain paralysis' so they throw off the shackles of their boring, secretarial lives and embrace an existence on the lam from cops and robbers alike. He'd used me to steal a Picasso. I'd turned the ensuing notoriety into the acting career I'd always dreamed of.

"Yup." I slashed the air with my vodka cup. The dude beside me ducked and cowered. "Life is good," I told him with a pat on the arm. "Sometimes storm clouds assemble and piss rain all over your head, but other times — ouch!"

My other seatmate had woken up. Captain Taco's claw still clutched my ankle, his mournful feline cry echoing throughout the elite cabin. I tapped at his paw until he released me, then I pulled his carrier out from below the seat. My human friend muttered, threw down his *Wall Street Journal* — a paper one! Perhaps he was from the past — and stalked to another part of the airplane.

I stuck my head above the seat, periscope-style, to search for flight attendants. The coast was clear. I released Taco from his prison and took his bundle of feline black fluff into my arms. He actually did comfort me, the little bastard. He was an ex-pet of Sam's, and it had taken some time for us to form a solid relationship, but we had finally meshed. I loved Taco to bits and cuddled him at every turn. He agreed not to murder me in my sleep as long as I fed him. I cradled him, belly up, while he gave me a glare of wild condescension.

The last year had been surreal, going from depressed secretary comforting herself with roller skating and Pizza Rolls—often together—to respected working actress. I considered pinching myself to make sure life was real, but Taco took care of that with a bite to my hand. I hissed and sucked on the already flaming pink wound.

"Ma'am, I'm afraid you cannot have an unrestrained animal out during flight."

I smiled at the polite, frowning flight attendant whose pasty skin reminded me I'd soon be on an island where clouds battled the sun and often won. She offered to help me put Taco away, but I did it myself. No reason for the innocent to be mauled by eleven pounds of adorable rage. I'd given him kitty sedatives, but he didn't seem to enjoy them the way I did.

The lady hung around, a smile creeping into the corner of her mouth. She leaned forward. "I'm a big fan, Ms Williams. Love your new hair color."

Le sigh. "I'm not Michelle Williams. I get that a lot, though."

"Wait—are you the lady from the Tina Fey movie? What was it... *The World's Worst Wedding*? You are! You're so funny!"

She got me on the second try—I couldn't have stopped the grin that split my face if I'd tried. "Hi. Thanks. Hi."

"Meeeewwwwrrrrr," said Taco. My resume left him unimpressed thus far.

She put one knee on the empty seat beside me. "I'm sorry, it's just in case the cat gets free, you know? I don't want her to get hurt."

Taco hissed and swiped. I jerked my leg to safety. "Captain Taco is a he. He's sexist, that's why he thinks being called a girl is demeaning."

The flight attendant laughed. "Can I get you some champagne? Perhaps a magazine?"

I held up the now-slightly-soggy-from-vodka script in my lap. Very professional. "I should probably keep studying this. Although champagne would definitely help."

She sucked in a breath and gawked to read the title page. "Is that the Daniel Zhang movie? Oh, my goodness, he is so unbelievably hot."

"I know! They're gonna pay me to kiss him!"

"Jammy devil!" She giggled more and whipped off to get me bubbly I didn't really need.

I didn't know what a jammy devil was, but I generally approved of both jam and devils. "Am I bovvered?" I asked no one.

"Hhhhhhhssssssss," replied Taco.

"Oh, you're always taking the piss." I settled back, my glittering bubbly in hand. *You're going to be brilliant,* I told myself. *And you'll have a killer British accent any minute now.*

Yes—I felt much, much less terrified. No more fear of plummeting into the cold ocean like Kate Winslet in *Titanic.* Although she'd won an Oscar for her icy plunge. Hadn't she? Leo DiCaprio sure hadn't. Always a bridesmaid, never a golden statue for Leo. Poor Leo. Only his millions to sustain him. I would absolutely win an Oscar, though. Someday.

I blinked away some of my brain haze, pulled up my script and read the title aloud. *"What Could Go Wrong?"* My case of the yawns reached its zenith after the flight attendant handed me even more champagne. I decided to catnap before I studied my script. A powerful yawn overtook me. Yes, I'd already memorized the thing, anyhow. Super professional…yawn…respected actress…burp. "Excuse me," I said before I nodded off.

What Could Go Wrong?
by
F. Langley

Draft 2 – Shooting Script

Int. The British Museum – night
Chase Dakota, *disbarred barrister (played by Daniel Zhang), crouches in the doorway of a dark gallery of the museum and blows powder into the air. Ghostly streaks of laser light appear, criss-crossing everywhere. The way forward is blocked. His partner in crime, unemployed museum curator* Jayde Loving *(played by Samantha Lytton), pokes her head up from where she's been skulking along the floor.*
Angle On: Jayde tucks some of her red hair into her black skull cap.

Jayde Loving: Daniel Zhang, I loved you in *Mission Extremely Difficult III.*

Chase Dakota: Thank you, lesser-known actress from America. I wanted Kerry Washington for your role. You're just so…pasty and short.

Jayde Loving: I know. It's not even genetic.

Chase sneers and turns away from Jayde.

Chase Dakota: Sad. But my star power will guarantee box office success, especially in Sweden. They love me there.

Jayde Loving: Really?

Chase Dakota: Why wouldn't they? You think blonde people can't like actors of Chinese descent? That's racist.

Jayde Loving: What? No, I didn't mean it that way! I just don't know anything about Sweden! Except that they made Alexander Skarsgård which, you know, bravo.

Chase glares. Jayde pulls the script from her back pocket.

Jade Loving: I — I'm confused. None of this is in the script.

Chase Dakota: It's called 'improvisation', you hack. If you can't act, can you at least lose ten pounds?

A shadowy figure slinks in and crouches beside Jayde.

Illicit Lover Sam: I don't think you should lose ten pounds, my love. Your boobs might shrink, and then where would I lick food off of?

Jayde Loving: You can't be here! You're a thief!

Chase Dakota: This film is *about* thieves, idiot. I can't work with this Yankee trash!

Chase storms off set.

The Director: You're fired, you bargain-basement Emma Stone.

Jayde Loving: What? No, I — what is happening?

Illicit Lover Sam: Everything seems to be going wrong.

Jayde Loving: No shit, Sherlock.

Illicit Lover Sam: Remember when you didn't get cast in that episode of *Sherlock*? That was a pathetic day.

They are joined by the executive producer, Captain Taco.

Captain Taco: When she lost the role, she cried all over me. I was licking salt from my fur for a week.

Illicit Lover Sam: Disgusting. Hey, do you have Ms Washington's number? I'd rather illicitly lover her.

Jayde Loving: I thought you cared about me!

Illicit Lover Sam: We are now beginning our descent into London Heathrow Airport.

Jayde Loving: I swear by this tray table, I love you, Sam! Don't leave me!

Illicit Lover Sam: I'm sorry, but you must turn off all romantic attachments in preparation for landing. All penguins to the cockpit.

Angle On: A procession of human-sized penguins begins waddling their way down the aisle of the set, which is now dressed as the inside of an airplane. The last one leans over Jayde's seat. He whispers in her ear.

Giant Penguin: They've stopped manufacturing Cheez-Its.

"No!" I yelled, bolting up only to be whipped back into the seat by the belt. Both my seat mate and the once-friendly flight attendant were grimacing as if I were a madwoman.

"Ma'am, please prepare for landing."

I nodded and shifted from butt cheek to butt cheek, but both were numb as bricks of, well, bricks. My head pounded like a...pounding...lump of...pound cake. I squeezed my eyes shut. Wow—Xanax and champagne do not mix. It was far too early in my career to need rehab—that was the sort of thing you saved for when you slipped to the D-list.

I squared myself away and squeaked as the plane made one of those swooping, steep banks that makes you feel like you're gonna die.

In...out. In...out. My heart rate slowed with my breathing, and I glanced at the script I'd half-crumpled. *I'm okay,* I told myself. Life was heavenly, after so long a struggle. I was a smart, strong, capable woman with bright red hair at the top of her game.

Not a damn thing would go wrong.

Chapter Two

Reunited and He Feels So Hood

I hopped off the plane at Heathrow and grabbed a coffee post-haste. Caffeine was exactly the chemical I needed to counteract all the other chemicals floating around my arteries.

I have come to realize some of the perks of being a kind-of-somebody — one of them is that you can travel with six suitcases and people smile instead of frown at you. What? I was going to be there for two months, and Momma needs her leopard print. My wardrobe used to come almost exclusively from thrift stores, but since I'd made a few bucks, I'd indulged my inner fashion goddess. I am a five-foot-tall lady built like Betty Boop, and it's a truth universally acknowledged that body-con dresses inspire strange men at baggage claim to spontaneously help you.

My passport stamped, and my luggage loaded precariously on a cart, I surveyed the immediate area for a person in a suit holding my name on a card. I spied Hill, Platter and Souphanousinphone, but no Lytton.

I leaned against my vanity mountain for ten minutes. Nothing and nobody, save an attempted pickup by a guy in the Marines. I told him that while I was grateful for his service to our country, no, I wasn't keen on humping him in the airport bathroom. Finally, I took a gander at my phone to see if the travel plans had changed. I saw an email from my studio liaison confirming the cancellation of my pickup. I smelled a rat.

I saw a rat, too. He was the most beautiful rodent I'd ever seen.

"You cancel my ride, and you can't even be here on time?"

Sam flashed a cheeky grin from underneath his shades and truly goofy beige sun hat. With a rush of pure joy, I silently greeted his dimple, only one, on the left side. It was just for me, that damnable dent. I hadn't seen it in a month, and the hole it left felt like a missing limb.

"Samantha Lytton, party of one?" He halfheartedly showed me the pathetic sign he'd made on notebook paper. "Or party of seven? What the hell is all this? God, woman. At least my cat is on top."

"Mawr," Taco agreed, his furry face pushed against the slots of his kitty jail.

I shoved the cart into Sam's knees. He made ostentatious being-hurt noises that I ignored. I clapped my hands. "Come, come, underling. Direct my luggage to your vehicle forthwith." I sailed past him toward the automatic doors leading to Ye Olde London Towne. Or at least the Ye Olde Suburbs. When he followed me into the cloudy afternoon, grumbling profusely, I added, "And stop breaking into my email!"

"On my honor, I would never read your ridiculous inbox. Much, anyway."

"Honor?"

"'Honor among thieves' is a phrase."

I stopped dead in the parking lot, and he tumbled straight into me. Catching his arm as he headed unceremoniously toward the deck, I said, "I think...the entire idiom is 'there is *no* honor among thieves'."

"Well" — he stood and brushed dust off his knees — "everything's bad if you look at the whole thing."

I had to laugh. Selective observation is what made our 'relationship' work.

"Chauffeurs don't wear such tight pants, mister."

He glanced at his painted-on jeans and turned around to present his butt to me. My heart leaped, and my lady parts...let's just say they weren't numb from the airplane seat anymore. I tugged on his hand. Its strength flowed into mine. "Get the car, Sam. I have some jet lag for you to treat."

"How inebriated are you, scale of one to ten?"

I kicked him, and he sauntered off with the luggage cart, laughing, that tight butt promising a delightful evening ahead.

* * * *

Kissing and groping, we fell into the door of my apartment, and subsequently onto the floor. I'm certain my new neighbors were clutching their Queen Elizabeth anniversary tea sets in shock.

Personally, I was delighted — his warm, gorgeous mouth on mine, his hands everywhere at once and my skin on fire for him to devour me. He kicked the door closed and hauled me up into his arms, over his shoulder. Is there any better feeling than a manly man carrying you, consensually of course, to his cave of love—

He dropped me. Okay, he didn't quite drop me, but my butt still smarted from its too-quick meeting with the hardwood floor. And what had caused my lover to suck in a breath, splat me and run away?

"Meowr! Meowr! Meowr!"

Sam opened the carrier, scooped up a freaking-out Captain Taco and rubbed his face in the cat's black belly. I couldn't hear everything, but the words 'wuv,' 'miss my widdle baby' and 'fluffy wuffy stuffy foo' were uttered, to the horror of my ears and all right-thinking people. I leaned on my arms and waited for them to finish, like a mortified college freshman whose dorm mate has brought back a lover to fumble with in the shared space. There were even slobbery sounds as Taco pushed the stupid hat off Sam's head and began eating his hair.

I took the opportunity to explore my new digs, a charmingly-furnished place in creams, browns and mint greens. It was vintage—maybe thirties from the lovely rounded door arches. I rose to explore the rest.

"Where are you going?" Sam asked, the syllables clipped in annoyance.

"Who, me?" I kept going about my business. Ooh! A cute pantry. And the studio had left a gift basket of fruit in the kitchen! How thoughtful, although it's not surprising that they didn't leave me what I really wanted—Pizza Rolls. But starlets aren't supposed to eat fatty foods unless a reporter is present, in order to pretend that they aren't being forced to diet. "Do you remember my name, Sam? I'm the one not named after tacos."

An arm snaked around my waist from behind. "Your name? Your name…" The hand attached to the arm crept toward my boob. I batted it away. My backside still hurt, and he would have to work harder than that. "Is it…the most beautiful movie star in the world?"

I snorted. "Really?"

His lips tickled my ear as he whispered, "In this tight dress, is your name Beyoncé?"

I shivered from the caress and pushed back into him. He was hard. So was my breathing. I didn't remove the hand that now returned to my breast. "You're getting warmer."

"Olivia Newton-John?"

Turning to face him, I laughed and said, "Yes!"

"I missed you so fucking much." He kissed me so urgently it hurt a little, but seeing as I was biting at his lip as if to eat him whole, I didn't care. The near-violence of his mouth, and his cock pushing against me, made me feel powerful, a goddess who inspires lust and groping. He broke the kiss off to throw me over his shoulder once again. My poor brains sloshed in my skull, afloat on leftover liquor and misplaced gravity.

He took off down a corridor with purpose. "It appears you know the way to the bedroom," I said.

He grunted and threw me on the bed. Oh, how I'd missed man-grunts since I'd seen him last. Or smelled him. There may be no single scent on Earth I prefer more than the essence of his skin, of him. Not even cheeseburgers.

Everything stopped. He straddled me and balanced himself on his arms. "Did you just moan 'cheeseburgers'?"

I licked my lips. "I was thinking of you favorably by comparison."

He cocked a brow, his eyes deepest pools of brown in the fading light of the room. "I take it as a compliment if I scored above ground beef."

I laughed. Tears came out. "I'm sorry." I swiped at my face and clutched his white shirt with wet hands. "I missed you, horrible man. Too long."

He leaned down, slowly, and kissed my forehead. "I love you. But you're not allowed to cry more just because I said that." His breath was sweet, and his lips on mine turned me to jelly. One more tear slipped into our mouths. He licked it away and murmured endearments peppered with kisses across my cheeks, eyes, neck. When Sam became ardent, the power of his emotions always flattened me, especially when he held my face in his hands like I was a precious gem. I blinked away another dribble of waterworks, and he said, "That's it. Enough of this mushy shit." He flipped me over.

I was in big, delightful trouble now. He pushed the spandex of my dress over my hips to reveal... "Beige shorts? I do not approve of these."

Laughing, I turned my head and said, "I didn't know you were going to be here. These don't show under the dress."

"Is that supposed to be a good thing?" He tugged at them in a way that made everything from the waist down sit up. "You should be prepared for me at all times."

"Not even for you would I endure a thong on an eleven-hour, overnight flight."

He paused. "I concede the point." His voice seemed to be coming from a mouth now much closer to my backside. My hips squirmed. A quiet, perfect kiss landed on my right cheek. My thighs parted. I could no more have stopped them than I could cease the movement of the sun. He laughed softly and ran a single finger between my lips. I gasped and clutched at the duvet cover. The ache of desire swept through me, and I eased toward his lovely intrusion. He obliged me, sliding his finger all the way inside and scattering kisses across my thighs and ass.

He fucked me with his hand, slowly, my body moving and shuddering against him. Tight at first…and then loosening around his talented fingers that knew me so well. All too soon, I asked him to take me, moaning incoherent words and clutching at him as best I was able while he held me by the neck, his big, warm hand firm and making me wet by itself.

Sam laid his body across mine and whispered in my ear, "I think I'll ride you thoroughly, if you ask me nicely."

My lust far outweighed my pride, and I begged him. Oh, yes, I begged him prettily, dirtily, desperately while he smirked so obviously that I heard it in the nasty way he whispered, "Do you want me, my plucky little starlet?"

"Yes, please, baby."

The head of his cock teased up and down along my opening as my desire turned painful and wonderful both. We'd recently eschewed condoms in favor of clean blood tests, the birth control pill, and trust. And holy shit—did trust feel absolutely amazing in more ways than one. He grunted with the strain of teasing me—even he couldn't take it much longer. I lifted up onto my knees a little and pushed backwards. He slipped in all at once, and we gasped together.

He held there and kissed my neck, the place he knew would drive me crazy. The soft movement of his lips dazzled my senses, my skin drowning in pleasure. The pressure of him inside me eased, and I relaxed more around him with every kiss and flick of his tongue on my back. It had been weeks, and he held his patience until I could accommodate him well. I turned my face to the side. He placed a sweet kiss on my cheek. It was so perfectly chaste, and his cock so marvelously warm, I said, "Move."

He withdrew. Not the whole way, but enough for the delicious slide to make me moan with unadulterated delight. Holding there, just inside the edge of my entrance, he reached around to play with my breast. I wiggled my ass to make him move that yummy body of his, and he swatted it—only hard enough for the slap to echo in the quiet room, and for the sting to drive me mad. But I decided to obey and let him tease me with soft, maddening kisses, caresses, his hair tickling my skin like a feather.

He thrust into me, his hips pressed against my ass, his thighs between mine. Deliberately, slowly, he played with me, sometimes squeezing me, sometimes slapping my bottom as he rode me. And all the while, he breathlessly relayed a never-ending monologue of the beauties of my body, of what he would do next, of how he'd missed this or *this*.

I could have died right then and been as delighted as any woman who'd ever lived.

I said, "I want to see you."

With gentle motions, he pulled out and turned me over. The dimple deep and pleased, he yanked one knee over his hip, then the other. I rubbed my thighs along his, wanting to experience every single inch of his skin. His tongue tasted my mouth as his body entered mine. I kissed his cheeks, his forehead, his eyelids, relearning the planes of his face, one I desperately wished to see so often I tired of it, if that was possible.

He gazed into my eyes and slid home, a contented smile hovering around his open mouth. He loved to watch when he screwed me, and sometimes it was almost too much—those dark irises seeing straight through me, into my heart, my soul, neither of which ever, ever wanted to let him go. I closed my eyes against the force of his and just appreciated his body with mine, playing soft then hard, driving, moaning, wet, slippery, hot, sweaty, on and on until I came on his cock while he never ceased giving me exactly what I begged for.

My body dizzy and joyfully sated, I nipped his ear and whispered, "Lie on your back."

His answering smile dazzled even as he did my bidding. I yanked a pillow from under the covers and fluffed it behind his head. Never let it be said that I am not a full-service mistress. I gave him a long, thorough kiss, so thorough I almost forgot what I wanted do to him, especially when he raked his hands through my hair and held me there. Is there anything better than making out? God, I could've kissed him forever, but that might not have alleviated the urgency currently pressing between my thighs.

I broke away, lightheaded and ever-so-slightly short of breath, and buried my face in his chest hair. I bit along his collarbone while he ran silky fingers down my back. I meandered to his stomach, tickling him, naughtily, just a little. I let my hair tease his cock long before I deigned to touch it with any other part of me. His hips squirmed. *Mmmmmm good.*

I began with a long lick from base to tip. He fumbled through my hair and took a fistful. He tasted like me. I loved how dirty it made me feel.

Lightly, I took him in my hand and ran loose fingers up and down, up and down. The fist in my hair tightened, and he groaned my name. Still pumping him, I put my mouth over the head and started to suck and lick. He fell back against the bed completely, his eyes closed tight. He was warm and slick and wet and I worked him in earnest, my free hand running along his hip, his ass, his balls. He didn't last long, but twisted the bedclothes in his fingers and came into my mouth.

Damn, that was fun.

I flopped to lie beside him, and he immediately took me into his arms, his eyes still closed, and laid my head on his shoulder. I noticed the first traces of misty evening streaming through the open curtains. Good thing we were on the seventh floor. I think that might have been my best performance ever.

A yawn the size of Donald Trump's ego escaped my mouth. Orgasmic tranquility had officially melted my bones.

"Sleep," he whispered. "I'll make dinner reservations for a little later."

He could have suggested just about anything then and I would have acquiesced. He took my hand in his and cradled it against his chest. I fell further into the bliss that was him.

I was home.

He said nothing more, but turned us so that he spooned me until I fell asleep. Just before I fell off the cliff, I panicked that he wouldn't be there when I awoke. It had happened before, when things got dicey for him, and he'd needed to flee the jurisdiction. This time it was me who squeezed his hand to my heart. As if that might make a difference.

* * * *

"You haven't said 'thank you' to me yet," Sam smarmed at me over curry in the amazing Indian restaurant he'd chosen. We sat in a circular corner booth lit only by candlelight and post-connubial felicity.

I took a sip of water—the curry was hot, but Sam looked even hotter. He sat in shirtsleeves rolled up to the elbow, which is the official sexiest arrangement of shirtsleeves, the next being on your floor. "Precisely why am I giving thanks?"

He huffed and scooted closer to me. His hand strayed to my knee under the tablecloth. He inched the black lace of my skirt high enough for me to be glad the tablecloth was long. "I'm certain your auditions for the role of art thief in your movie were successful because of my diligent tutelage."

I removed his hand and dropped it onto his own crotch.

Oh, indeed—the story of how we met is the stuff of fairy tales. He'd used me to steal a Picasso that had hung in my then-boss' office when I was a secretary at the Steak on a Stick corporation. Sure, he'd almost gotten me killed eight different ways, but I'd learned many valuable skills, such as how to deal with two different international art theft organizations, how to lie to the po-po and get away with it and why running in bunny slippers is not ideal.

See? Most fairy tales are bizarre and laced with violence.

I took a bite of palak paneer instead of answering. He didn't seem to require one, but took a sip of beer while his dimple congratulated itself without my help. "Perhaps I got the part because of how talented I am."

"Okay, if *that's* what we're gonna call it." He laughed and squeezed my knee. Somehow this entire exchange burrowed under my pride bone. Resentment pooled in my stomach. I put my fork down, and his arm snaked around my waist. "I'm kidding, Samantha. I'm sure you're going to be wonderful—you always are. Hey." He turned my chin so that I lost my step in his eyes, deep brown in the flicker of candles. "What's wrong?"

"How long are you here?"

All his limbs retreated, and he deflated before answering. "I'm thinking a couple of weeks. If that's okay."

"Of course it's okay," I said in a sugary voice that fooled no one. "When have I ever told you to go away? You do that by yourself."

A thorny silence fell over the table. The waiter came and went with fresh water.

He threw his napkin on the table and said, "Let's have a relationship talk. No, we're going to. You obviously want one. Listen—" He shifted toward me, one knee up on the seat and pressing into my thigh. "I love you. I'm asking you to trust me when I say I'm trying to make things work with you."

Was being a couple this freaking hard for other people? It didn't help that almost every moment we spent together, barring perhaps this one, was wonderful and fun and full of groping. But those moments were not coming any more frequently, even after a year. "So we can spend a month together sometimes instead of a week?"

"God dammit." He distanced himself. He stared at his sweating beer bottle, took a long pull and sighed. "I'm trying, Samantha. Are we really back in the place where you doubt everything I say? When was the last time I lied to you?"

I thought to myself *I don't know*, but had enough sense to understand that that sentiment wouldn't play well to this audience. A tear slipped down my cheek, causing distress-grunts to overflow from my date like an unattended bath. I swiped at my face and said, "I'm just tired. I'm sorry. I want to be in the same zip code as you are."

"Do you love me?"

I jerked my head up. His voice had sounded so sad and needy, but his countenance was a rumbling thundercloud, ready to burst. I did love him. I had, even when I called it 'lorvst', which is lust plus bonus emotions you aren't ready to admit to yet.

He hadn't thought much of 'lorvst'.

"I..." I squeezed my eyelids shut—I never could cogitate and see that catastrophic face at the same time. Objectively, he's a nice-looking, but not gorgeous guy. I, however, found even his pores to radiate beauty. With a stalwart breath, I braved his hazel eyes again. "I do love you, Sam. But I'm afraid you're going to smash my heart sooner or later."

He sagged back against the booth, the hurt etched in his whole body—every muscle tense, his mouth tight. A minute slipped by. I said nothing more, needing to hear his answer without giving him any sympathetic wiggle room. My willingness to let him wiggle had gotten me more familiar with my vibrator than him as of late.

He nodded and a haggard smile appeared. "How can I fault you for thinking that? I just—" He took another drink.

I picked up my wine and followed suit.

"I just wanted you to tell me…that you cared."

Well, that made me feel like a grade-A asshole. My stomach twisted around on itself. I took his hand and held it to my cheek. He immediately began stroking my skin, and I couldn't bear to fight anymore. "I can be patient," I said. "I don't exactly have a traditional job anymore, either."

He swept in for a kiss that nearly snapped my bra off. His lips were hot and desperate, fired up by angst. Pulling back, he said, "You know that I think you're the funniest and most brilliant actress alive, right? You pretty much steal whatever you're in, my short redhead."

What egocentric thespian wouldn't grin after a line like that? "Yes, I'll sleep with you. You don't have to go on and on."

"I know you'll sleep with me. It's my principal certainty in life, besides you crying when I don't want you to. Which is always."

Oh, sure, mock me just because I tear up faster than you can say, 'Look, a Sarah McLachlan commercial about abused animals.'

"Maybe I won't sleep with you," I muttered before polishing off my dinner with one giant bite. I wasn't that easy!

"Yes, you will."

Yes, I was.

He downed the rest of his beer and caught the eye of our waiter. Sam handed over his credit card without looking at the bill. I wondered which alias' name was on it. Sam was definitely his actual, real, birth-certificate first name. After that, things got fuzzy. "Should I be thanking Richmond for my meal, or Bert?" I asked. "Perhaps Ernie?"

He pulled my arm and drew me to him until there was no air between us. His whisper was hot on my ear and danced down my neck. "How, exactly, will I be thanked?"

"Who, exactly, are you?" I finished my wine, my stomach warming to it, and him, and our game. "I'm not familiar with Bert. Perhaps he doesn't like it when I unzip his pants with my teeth."

A small, breathy moan escaped his mouth. It blew across my neck, already over-stimulated. I could swear it blew across my pussy, too. His voice got low and deep, the way it did when he pushed me into the mattress and… "*Everyone* here at Thief Industries enjoys it when you do that. How about this—" His fingers skimmed upward and unzipped my dress a scant inch, and then teased the exposed skin at my nape. I locked my jaws together to stifle my whimper. "Let me take you back to the apartment and convince you that I have the utmost respect for your heart. And for," he nuzzled my earlobe, "a lot of your other places." He tugged the zipper pull up again, one millimeter at a time. "Maybe you can teach me that teeth thing."

I find that most things in life would go so much more smoothly if sexy people suggested them. 'Let's create world peace,' a saucy lady might say, or 'Sheltering the homeless is a capital idea,' says the half-naked male model, and suddenly—boom!—all problems ever are solved because of the worldwide orgy. I guess that's called 'advertising', and was why the characters on *Mad Men* were always raring to get it on.

Sam craned his neck to see my face. "I'm not sure I want to know what you're contemplating, but I believe you're agreeing with me?"

I smiled. "Mmm-hmm."

We rose to leave, his hand in the small of my back and straying lower. I giggled and swatted him away. I did not need a cell phone pic of me getting goosed by an international fugitive. No way was I so famous that folks were stalking me hoping to get a moment for TMZ, but with my ill luck, it would figure.

In the street, he tugged on my hand and led me to the street corner, then farther into the shadows between two stone buildings. He pushed me against one and whispered, "This is a skimpy dress, Miss Lytton. If I pulled your panties to the side, it would be nothing to fuck you right here."

My back protested the sharp stone, but the rest of me was ready to sacrifice my underwear to the alley and get going. I cupped his face and kissed him, sucking on his lower lip as if my lust depended on it. And suddenly he was gone, ripped away from my mouth. "What?" I managed to say before a bag enclosed my head.

Chapter Three

That Old, Familiar Fleeing

I sucked in a panicked breath and stale burlap filled my dry mouth. Two sets of hands jerked my arms in opposite directions, but I pulled against all of them and kicked in front of me. I could tell someone stood there, and he cursed when I connected with whichever part of him. One of my arms flew free. By some miracle, my purse still hung from my shoulder, and I swung it to the right and then the left. My other attacker fell away. I jerked the bag off me to see Sam on the ground wrestling with one guy, another going to his accomplice's rescue and a dude behind the wheel of a black car close by on the street. "Get 'em!" yelled car guy in an American accent.

Oh, hell no. I was way too fucking horny to let my piece of ass be kidnapped. Also, I loved him and stuff.

I unleashed fury on both the dudes pummeling Sam, now bagged on the head, too. I shrieked and kicked and punched, and the guy on top let Sam go to deal with me. Luckily, just then, a stream of burly guys came a-running from the pub next door. Our goons nearly flew into their awaiting car and sped off, a couple of the pub dudes in hot pursuit on foot.

"Sam!" I knelt on the alley ground and burst into tears, like any proper woman in a melodramatic movie from the 1930s. I removed his burlap sack. He blinked and tried to talk, so I kissed him for being alive. I tasted blood in his mouth, streaming from a rapidly-purpling punch mark.

"Thanks for kicking me," my loving lover said.

Whoops. I attempted to sniff my tears back into my eyeballs. "Sorry, I had a bag on my head."

"If I had a nickel for every time you wounded me, I could hire a bodyguard."

I chose to ignore that ridiculous remark. I only ever hit him when he deserved it, or when he startled me, or sometimes in the middle of the night—allegedly, since I never remembered this, and everyone knows that thieves are liars.

"You all right?" asked one of the helpful men who'd saved us.

Sam's brow thunderations increased as he counted the number of potential witnesses. "We need to get out of here," he muttered to me as he steadied himself on my arm on the way to a wobbly standing position. He kept pulling me toward the street, where his other hand was already hailing a cab.

Our rescuer pursued. "Did they mug you? Let me call the police, yeah?"

A horrible growl rumbled forth from Sam, and I took that as a sign for me to say my lines. "No, thank you! We're okay." Sam shoved me into a back seat and yanked the door closed behind us. "Thank you!" I screamed, hoping the friendly crowd could hear me and wouldn't consider all Americans to be ungrateful jerkfaces. I grinned and waved like a mad lady. One gent returned my wave, even as he shrugged confusedly.

I turned to Sam, who was attempting to clean the blood from the corner of his mouth while the cabbie looked askance in the rear-view mirror. "Bar fight," I lied. "Don't worry." I grinned until the driver stopped caring, then gave him the address for my apartment. "Sam, baby, are you—"

"Not here," he replied.

"Well, I'm okay, thanks for asking." I slumped into my corner of the cab and laced my fingers together. They'd begun shaking at some point. His bigger hand came down over mine, the gesture warm and saying the opposite of his testy protestations. I threw myself across the seat to lean on his shoulder, and he held me, wordlessly, as we fled from yet another attack that had rained down upon us no doubt because of him. I wiped my nose and considered that I hadn't been harassed in an entire year.

When a milestone like that was a mark of favor in your relationship, it was a bad sign, akin to seeing someone post 'out of French fries' at McDonald's.

I couldn't stop the fresh tears. We arrived at my building, and I kept my face down through the lobby and in the elevator. My hyperactive fear and relief battled with each other to see which would drain my muscles of energy.

Inside the apartment, I dropped my purse in the middle of the floor and continued into the living room, where I fell onto the couch face-first. Sam swept into the bathroom and washed while I kept shaking like a wind-up toy. Every time I'd try to take a deep breath and tell myself it was over, I'd hear the squish-thud when one of the assailants punched Sam, or feel the scratchy bag close my eyes for me, and begin quaking again.

After a few minutes, Sam returned and sat beside my legs. I twisted into a cross-legged position facing him. Oh, my poor baby—he had a righteous shiner that almost blotted out his dimple. I reached one finger to brush the place on his cheek where it should have been. "Come out, come out wherever you are," I whispered. His brows came together in an expression of such sorrow, I just had to kiss him. Nothing mattered more than making that horrible sadness flee.

We grappled with each other, clothes flying, breathing labored, desperation palpable. He pulled my dress off over my head and wrapped his arm around my waist to face me toward the back of the sofa while on my knees. He held me that way, his chest naked against me, and spread small, sharp bites across my neck while he fumbled with the fly of his pants. His fingers teased my pussy, but almost perfunctorily, a means to his end, and mine.

I spread my knees wider, and he grunted in approval. Not even bothering to remove them, he pushed my panties to the side and slid into me, roughly, knocking the breath from me in a startled moan of pleasure. I braced myself on the couch as he fucked me, thrusting in fast, then pulling out slowly, as if to make me lose my mind. I think I did right around the time he began fisting his hand in my hair to pull my head back. We moved as one, making the couch quake and thump on the wall.

I reached behind me to grasp the tight, working muscles of his ass, so smooth and gorgeous in my hand. It spurred him on, and he moaned, "Fuck me, Samantha," hot and wet, into my skin. My entire body hovered on sensation overload, and I begged him to never stop. Stopping was thinking, and neither of us wanted that.

He eventually did slow and release me. He slumped into the cushions and said, "Come here." I dropped onto his lap, his cock stretching me tight, my body a little sore from his passionate onslaught of this afternoon. But I didn't care, and soon I slid on him without coherent thought. It seemed he couldn't pull me close enough—both arms wrapped around me, his face in my breasts, hair, and kissing me so deep and slow that the sensation fluttered from my lips to my hips. I rode him until I could no longer take in a full breath, until he came and shuddered underneath me, gripping me so tight it hurt, until I finally burst with my own orgasm and fell over him.

"I love you," I said, my breath faltering.

His head on my shoulder, he said it back to me, achingly, full of the emotions I'd tried to release us both from. I got up, took his hand, and we went to the bedroom and dropped into the covers without another word.

I don't even remember falling asleep, but awoke at five a.m. local. I made a trip to the bathroom and watched Sam sleep for a long time, until the sun had come alive. I should have been snoozing, trying to acclimate to the time change, but I figured I'd feel like crap one way or the other.

The conversation I was having with myself, I should be discussing with him. We'd avoided it long enough, believing that love and great sex would carry us through a relationship model that looked like a tightrope walker balancing above a crocodile pit.

"Hey—" said a sleepy voice.

I started and stiffened in my armchair beside the bed. "Hey. You should go back to sleep," I said.

"I've been here for a week. I'm mostly adjusted." He sat up, the sheets bunched around his waist and legs. His skin glowed in the morning light, and his hair flopped in a rumply, sexy mess over his forehead. "You should come here." He patted beside him.

I avoided his eyes and decided it was a great time to pick invisible dust off my robe.

He sighed. "Okay. We have to talk about it." My gaze stayed averted. The ball was so far in his court he was sitting in the line judge's lap. "I have an idea about what's going on."

"Please don't tell me," I burst out. The moment I said it, I understood it to be true. I couldn't know. Knowing things would put me in even deeper boiling water than I already was. He'd destroyed my life one time, and I'd rebuilt it—better, stronger, faster. My new life was pure *Bionic Woman*, and damned if I'd give it up so easily.

"I wasn't going to tell you." After this razor-edged reply, he shifted in the sheets and decided what to say, his mouth pursed and bitter. "Look, I know this is hard. I miss you." His voice broke, just a bit, just enough to shatter my composure. "I miss you all the time. You're like a tick on my skin."

Ah, the romance of a country boy from North Carolina.

He continued his love poem, "And I understand that this situation is untenable. But I've spent quite a few years building a...lifestyle and a means of making money that wasn't above-board. I can't snap my fingers and make it stop. People know who I am. They know who you are, obviously."

I sucked in a gasp. "They followed me."

"Yeah, probably. Not your fault."

Of course it wasn't, but my stomach twisted all the same.

"I'm trying to get out. I've been a straight arrow since the Picasso debacle. Well"—he shrugged and sent the dimple into the fray—"I may have been forced to circumvent local statutes here and there in the interest of staying un-jailed, but—"

His smile did not help. I felt betrayed by the dimple for the first time in ages. Lately, it had told me truths instead of lies. Truths like 'I love your boobs in that sweater', or 'I enjoy giving you the last of my Tater Tots'.

I bunched my hands in my nubby pink robe. "I can't believe I'm going to say a sentence like this, but I have an image to protect now, Sam. What happened last night—it could have led down a road that destroys my career. I'm finally doing what I love. And I'm good at it! People seem to want to watch me doing it, which is bizarre, but fantastic."

"God, Samantha, you have to believe me when I say I don't want to put any of that into jeopardy—"

"But you will. You do. You can't help it." I turned to watch the street begin to wake up into the zip of morning traffic. "I knew this going in."

"Yes, you did."

His bitterness was palpable. I tasted its sour notes, with a finish of…being finished.

I couldn't say the words. How could I say it? I began to cry—the silent kind, where the tears just slip away, but still sting your eyes long after they've gone.

How had an ill-advised lark gotten so out of control? How was it that I was a…B- or C-list movie star? What was my life?

And what kind of stupid, moronic woman chooses the one man she can't take to a public premiere unless she wants the FBI tip line to go nuts? I wiped the tears from my face with my robe in a pathetic effort to feel less pathetic.

He slid to the end of the bed and leaned to grab my hands. My face jerked up to find him searching my eyes. "I could let you go and say it's the right thing to do and be noble, but fuck that. I'm not noble, and I love you. I want you more than I've wanted anything, and I will fight to make this work."

"How?" I shook my head and turned my gaze from his eyes to his chest. But I couldn't look at him there, either. Every last piece of him would undo me, dissolve my resolve and turn it into lust or love or some highly magnetic combination of the two. Lord a mercy, he was human quicksand. *He wants me more than he's wanted anything, but I don't hear from him for weeks on end.* Suuuucccckkkk. *He doesn't want to put me in jeopardy, but* oops lol *kidnappers.* Ssssuuuuuuucccccckkkkkk!

His jaw worked as he set my hands on my lap in a way that was a wrenching combination of loving and angry. He whipped on his pants, his back to me. I didn't want to be thinking goodbye when I watched his butt disappear. We'd had so many swell times, me and his firm posterior. So many well-fitting pairs of jeans.

"I'm going to find out what the hell happened last night." His shirt and shoes on, he paused at the door of the bedroom, his face puffy from sleep and hard from worry.

"Yes, wonderful, the solution to our problems is for you to leave." I stood to try and reach the moral high ground. "How long will you be gone this time, 'figuring things out'? A week? Two? When will I hear from you? Will it be an actual call so I can hear your voice and pretend we're in the same room, or will a dirty text suffice for the all-clear?"

He grimaced in an obvious effort to not hurl expletives at me and sagged against the door jamb. Shaking his head, he said, solemnly, "I'm sorry. And I don't know. I'm not an accountant, and I didn't know you resented me so much for it."

"It's not that fucking hard, Sam! You pick up the phone. You can even track me with mine! Isn't that what you wanted? I guess I should be keeping tabs on you. At least then I wouldn't go to sleep at night and pray for a ghost." I clutched my hands to stop them from reaching out.

"So what is this? Are you dumping me?"

There they went again—the tears, sliding down, like my stomach, like my heart. "I don't know. I'm heartsick from wondering about you. Every. Day. It's not cute anymore."

"I was going to take you sightseeing today, so…" He laughed, the dimple giving a little bow. "Sorry. Again." Standing there for another moment, he waited for me to speak, to beg him to come back and give me kitchen scraps. But I had a stubborn streak as wide as the Mississippi, and I merely nodded.

I'd spent a year ignoring the reality of my relationship with Sam, ignoring that it wasn't a relationship. Or maybe that it was. Ignoring that I wrote 'Mrs Sam the Thief' on my mental Trapper Keeper every day in glitter pen. Now was the time to face things, and to hold fast to myself, and my needs. I'd made lemonade from Picasso, and damn it, I would drink up. *You have to take care of yourself before you take care of anyone else*, Oprah told me in my brain.

My every nerve ending screamed for him as he walked out the apartment door. I sat, frozen in place, for quite a while—not crying, barely thinking. I'd rarely in my life ever felt so alone, adrift on a strange continent.

Nothing to do but sob in the shower then watch *Law & Order* on Netflix until I was numb, like every successful Hollywood player.

Chapter Four

When the Cat's Away, the Mouse Will Be Very
Confused

Ext. Hyde Park – day

Angle On: Our heroine Samantha Lytton *walks along the banks of the Thames.*

Music Score Plays: The new, hit single from the group Whiny Boy Band Popular With Your Twelve-Year-Old.

Samantha takes stock of her life in a touching montage.

Samantha Lytton: I thought we'd be together forever.

Nearby Rollerblader: Are you talking to me?

Samantha Lytton: I'm talking to the romantic comedy gods.

Angle On: Samantha continues her slow walk, past the picturesque trees filtering a dappled sunlight, past the cafe where she buys a seriously large ice cream cone, past the garbage can she runs into accidentally while trying to take a bite of her ice cream, past the laughing group of twenty-

somethings who capture her every move on their cell phones.

Angle On: A wet, spreading chocolate stain on Samantha's white T-shirt.

Samantha Lytton: Oh, my tit! Fucking seriously?

Twenty-Something: Keep filming! It's Michelle Williams.

Other Twenty-Something: Damn, she's short.

Samantha Lytton: I'm not Michelle Williams! Why does everyone say that?

Twenty-Something: Beige American actresses all look the same, innit?

That actually makes Samantha feel better, as she's usually cast in a role labeled 'ugly friend' or 'goofy sister'.

Angle On: She ditches her disintegrating ice cream cone in favor of a drink at a nearby pub. It seems a more suitable spot in which to pause and consider her life choices. After knocking back a couple — FYI, when you ask a blunt-nosed English bartender for a dirty martini, he may give you the stink eye and just pour you a beer — she weaves into the street at three in the afternoon.

Angle On: A police horse Samantha befriends, his magnificent brown hair the same color as the deuce he leaves in the street.

Samantha Lytton: If this were a movie, I'd clumsily step in a pile of horse shit. I'd probably *be* the pile of horse shit.

Pile of Horse Shit: There are worse things, Samantha Lytton.

Samantha Lytton: You can talk!

Pile of Horse Shit: We of the horse shit have many secrets.

Samantha Lytton: Tell me what to do, oh wise, yet stinky one.

Angle On: Samantha lets out a very ladylike burp.

Pile of Horse Shit: Perhaps that smell is the mess you've made of your romantic life. You must decide if you're going to trust Sam. Trust or trust not, there is no try.

Samantha Lytton: You're cribbing advice from Yoda?

Pile of Horse Shit: You're the one talking to a pile of crap in the dirt.

Samantha Lytton: Fair enough.

Pile of Horse Shit: You've fought thus far for your one, true love. Await his call this evening tide and work things out together. Communication is the key.

Samantha Lytton: Thanks, Mr, um, Shit.

Angle On: A copper joining his horse.

Police Officer: Do you require assistance, Miss?

Samantha Lytton: Nope! I wasn't talking to—I mean, I don't like crap. I mean cops. I mean, have a nice day. I'm sure you're very nice. Taxi!

Angle On: Samantha takes a cab back to her apartment. She presses her face to the glass as the city rolls by, reflected in the window. The music swells. Samantha then considers that the window of a cab is probably filthy, and jerks away. Gross.

It took a full minute after waking in my London flat to realize that I'd fallen asleep at seven p.m. the evening before, and that it was now six a.m. the next morning—and Sam had not called. I gripped my cell phone, heart tripping to and fro in my chest, and pressed button after button to check texts, emails and received calls. Nothing. I took a deep breath and hit my first speed dial. It went straight to his voice mail—do not pass go, do not collect the shattered pieces of your love life. Had the men who'd jumped us succeeded in tracking him? I tossed the phone on the bed and squeezed my eyes shut. He'd done this before. Not answered for days and days. "To hell with it."

I shoved every bad notion out of my head and lumbered to the shower. Today at ten a.m. I had my table read for *What Could Go Wrong?* and I intended to look dazzling, perform majestically and be the star I was pretending to be. The star who definitely did not get depressed-drunk by herself and have imaginary conversations with feces. No, that woman was gone, as was her impossibly stained shirt. It was time to woman up.

Shit! Where was the plug converter for my hair dryer?

I collapsed on the floor of my bathroom and cried for five minutes, which might have been an inappropriate response. My insides jumped around even faster than my thoughts, and it took me a while to compose myself, with the help of a crumbled, leftover muffin from my flight the day before.

Luckily, one of my neighbors had a locally-sourced hair dryer, so two hours and a borrowed bag of frozen peas on my puffy eyes later, I hit the streets of London in a fabulous vintage brown tweed dress and red knee-high boots. I looked so damn cosmopolitan I should have been stopped by a style blog.

A woman who looks like this would never be left by her lover. No, indeed, she'd dash into the studio offices, totally on the guest list, and breeze into the large conference room where the table read would take place. And there it was—my name on a tented card dead center along one side of the table. Jayde Loving, Samantha Lytton. Oh, how I loved her silly name. For every ridiculous 'y' added to a character name, she gains ten percent more sexy.

I'd shown up early, which is not a thing the stars of a film tend to do, I'd discovered. But better early than late. I was one of the two major leads of this film, and I could not fuck it up. Just the thought of making an ass of myself and costing the studio fifty million dollars gave me a wave of such anxiety I actually had to sit in the folding chair. I played it off by diving into my bag to search for nothing. Soon, folks were introducing themselves—some of the other actors, the Director of Photography, other technical wizards who would be paid to stare at my face in close-up for many, many hours. I apologized for this to some of them, and they laughed. Yes! I was a functioning adult! I was a fabulous starlet! I was...drooling.

Oh, baby.

He walked in the room. Daniel Zhang, the man *People* magazine had placed third in their most recent Sexiest Man Alive issue. When asked later, I would tell my best friend Ellen that I heard slow-mo saxophone music timed to his long, lean strides. He smiled before he took off his aviator sunglasses, which he twisted off in the hottest move since hip-thrusting was invented. He was so handsome up close that he didn't seem real—warm brown eyes that crinkled at the corners, tan skin smooth and perfect, his hair black and brushed forward gorgeously in the way that only comes from four-hundred-dollar haircuts.

Recently, he'd ended a Tony-winning run in *Hamlet* on Broadway. As Hamlet—the first actor of Asian descent to do so. I sighed. Yes, sighed when he came straight for me and extended his hand down, down, down. At six feet tall, he had me beat by an entire foot.

We'd emailed a little, but he'd been so busy we hadn't gotten a chance to talk. We hadn't even read together, the producers figuring he was so golden that he'd create enough chemistry for six romantic sub-plots and innumerable fanfictions.

With a smile I hoped would mean big box office for us, he said, "I'm so delighted to finally meet you, Samantha."

And at that moment, the first verified case of 'death by unbelievably sexy British accent' occurred.

Almost. I shook his hand, mine cold and clammy, and managed to stutter, "Hi. Yes. Me, too. Mister Zh—Dan—Daniel. Zhangiel."

He laughed. "My friends call me Danny."

I giggled, but in a very professional manner. I collapsed back into my seat while he worked the room, which parted lovingly for him like a pair of overeager female thighs. When he circled around, his ass was so perfectly formed in his brown pinstripe pants that I had to literally think *close your mouth, Samantha*. My disloyalty to the main ass in my life slapped me, and I vowed to not gaze adoringly at strange butts anymore. Well, not overly much. I wasn't dead.

I checked my phone—nothing from Sam, not even in response to the texts I'd sent earlier. I decided to be angry rather than fearful about it. I functioned on angry, but scared just turned my mind into a wad of stale cotton candy. I needed all the brain power possible to perform fantastically at the read. The producers were getting their first real taste of how this film might turn out, and I could be replaced. It would cost them, because yay contracts, but it could happen.

Fortunately, as the next few hours unfolded, the laughs were many and happened in all the correct spots. Danny, as his friends call him, was easy to riff off of, and the chemistry was natural and zinging around the room.

During a break, he came over to me at the snack table. "I'm a big fan," he said.

I looked around. "Of me? Be real—you'd never heard of me before you saw my audition." He was one of the producers, so he would have had to sign off on me. Remembering that flattered me anew.

"That's not true! I watched you on TV, the one about scientists during World War II. Very funny." I'd done an arc on a one-season hit wonder called *Manhattan Projectile*. It was a black comedy spoof about science, inequality and America, which naturally meant that no one in America had watched it. "You have a real spark. I'm the one who put your name on the list for this role."

"Really? I thought that the producers just called in everyone cited in the latest issue of *The Hollywood Reporter*."

He chuckled, a warm sound, friendly. The word 'gentleman' doesn't have much meaning nowadays, but, by my first impression, it seeped from every attractive part of him—and there were no unattractive ones visible to the naked eye. He was kind to the caterers, calling them by name, had a handshake for everyone in the room, and it didn't seem put on. I laughed and stared at my Diet Coke. "Well, thank you. I'm very happy to be here."

"We're happy to have you."

It came out so lilty that I flicked a glance into his eyes and felt myself blush. He extended his arm toward the table, where folks were sitting down again. I rushed to my spot and thought Sam-like thoughts—stealing stuff, fake driver's licenses, Hot Pockets.

I was sure I'd see Sam tonight. I was only lusting after movie stars because of our strange evening last night. And because movie stars named Daniel Zhang were skin-meltingly hot when they tell you how glad they are to have you.

But I'd learned that being had wasn't all it was cracked up to be.

* * * *

As I left the studio, Danny squeezing my hands while his eyes promised unending love—it could happen!—I mentally worked through the next few days of prep. Wardrobe fittings, stunt rehearsals and the like. It would be a busy few days until my first actual set appearance.

I rushed into my apartment to find no one there. I checked my phone for the hundredth time—nothing from Sam. Dammit, dammit, dammit! And damn *him*! Should I be worried? He often went on radio silence when it suited him. "Ggggaaarghh," I growled, picking up Captain Taco for the cuddles I wished his daddy were giving me. The cat grimaced and turned his nose away like he'd rather be anywhere else. Just like Daddy!

A knock at the front door. "Yes! Oh, thank God." I plopped fur face on the couch and ran to the door.

"Surprise!" screamed my best friend Ellen. She rushed in and picked me clear off the ground in a hug. Taller than me, she practically strangled me with love and tiny, yet squishy, boobs.

Her girlfriend, Nicolette, walked in after, a look of bemused resignation on her face. Nicolette was the cop who'd busted the evil art theft ring wide open during the Picasso debacle. With my help, of course. She hadn't liked me since, what with my interactions with known felons, and letting one get away only to return to my bedroom. But I was working on her. This past year, I'd helped Ellen plan Nicolette's surprise birthday party, and I'd brought one of her favorite bisexual starlets with me to sing 'Happy Birthday' to the enraptured, mostly-female audience. Now, if that didn't earn one lesbian brownie points, I don't know what would.

I squeezed my Ellen back and rested my head on her shoulder. We'd been BFFs since high school, and nobody knew me like she did, embarrassing haircuts and all. "What the hell are you doing here?"

Ellen shuffled everyone to the couch, the gracious hostess straddling the worlds of friendship and friends-with-benefits-ship. "We just flew in! You said you'd have a little time before the filming got nitty gritty, and we're overdue for our first official vacation together, so here we are to crash Europe with our awesomeness."

I grabbed her and held her so hard she squeaked. And then I cried on her shoulder. Literally. She wiped the moisture off her button-down before setting me nicely aside, raising her eyebrows to Nicolette and saying, "Let me guess—it's so hard being a movie star."

The Dimple Strikes Back

"Shut up." I punched her and she obligingly rearranged herself between Nicolette and me.

"What's wrong?" Ellen asked.

Nicolette handed me a tissue from her purse. "That is so nice," I said, new tears flowing. Maybe she was starting to warm to me! Nobody is concerned about the snot situation of a person they despise. I cleaned up a little and put on a pot of coffee for everyone. Upon my return to the couch, they stopped making out—whoops—and I said, "So, I have a situation that involves a boy."

Nicolette quirked an eyebrow. Ellen gasped and said, "You banged Daniel Zhang! Good girl!"

"I didn't bang him!" Perhaps I shouldn't have confessed to her the threesome fantasies I'd been entertaining about Danny and Sam. I'd have to learn to keep these thoughts between myself and Colin Firth. Colin Firth is the name I'd given to my Hitachi Magic Wand, because is there any straight woman who doesn't need a little Colin Firth from time to time?

I served the coffee and prepared to recount my sordid tale. Ellen sat up straighter and pushed her brown hair behind her shoulders. Captain Taco leaped onto the couch and danced from lap to lap until he settled on mine. Even Nicolette appeared interested. "I'll begin by saying that I am definitely not talking about a man who ever committed a crime of any sort."

Nicolette's face got pinchy. Ellen grabbed one of her hands and they shared a look I chose to interpret as them being fully in my corner, grimaces notwithstanding.

"This not-a-criminal man, let's call him...Ham."

Ellen grinned. "I like him better already."

"Don't taint my favorite food," Nicolette said.

"How about...Bam?"

"Acceptable."

"Okay, so Bam, everyone's favorite upstanding citizen, surprised me here in London—he picked me up at the airport. Wow." I leaned down to unzip my boots. "Three of you flew all the way to London to surprise me." I sucked in a halting breath and let it out in stutters. "You all l—l—love me!"

"I don't know if I'd go that far." Nicolette turned her amber eyes away and took a sip of coffee.

"No more crying!" Ellen leaped forward, tissue in hard, and smashed it against my nose. She relented after my gasp of pain—my honker was stinging so much, those flying birdies almost made an appearance around my head.

I did not cry any more, but removed my boots quite calmly. "Anyway, if I may continue—"

"You're the one stopping you. Does this story end in time for dinner?" Ellen asked.

"Bam picked me up. We went out for food. We left the restaurant and got frisky in the alley."

"You classy bitch."

I nodded, accepting this honor as my due. I continued, "And then three men appeared from nowhere and tried to kidnap us into an awaiting car."

Finally! Ellen and Nicolette stopped playing footsy and paid attention to the serious matter of Bam and the mystery men. "We got away, and Bam stayed the night here. Then he left yesterday morning, saying he was going to make inquiries about the attempted kidnapping, and I haven't heard from him since."

"You almost got kidnapped!" Ellen yelled.

"Bam is missing!" The outbursts startled the cat, who jumped away and hid under the table.

Ellen crumpled and put her head in her hands. "Once again, Dipshit McGhee misses the point." She glanced up to me. "The *kidnapping* is the problem, Samantha. His disappearance is a mitzvah. Besides, he didn't call or email you for the entire month of August last year, which I remember because I heard whiny updates about it all thirty-one days."

I fumed, angry that, per usual, Ellen had cut right through my lust-brain haze and sliced into the heart of the matter. And I hadn't whined every day of August! Even if I had, BFFs are not supposed to count the small shit that way. I never brought up the fact that for the first four months of Ellen's and Nicolette's relationship, I was treated to exhaustive and detailed accounts of every sexual act via text. Although, in her defense, I had learned a few things, and I'd be much more effective now if I were ever cast as a lesbian character.

"I know, I know." I grabbed Ellen's hand and held on. "I know Sam is probably just...contacting nefarious underworld persons in an attempt to secure my safety."

Ellen put her arm around me. "Yes, he is."

"I mean non-nefarious," I amended, glancing at Nicolette.

"You also mean Bam, not Sam," she replied with a wink. She leaned forward and put her coffee on the table. "Look, girl—is this really so bad? I know you care about him, but," she huffed, "you are an up-and-coming thing right now. Do you need this bullshit in your life? Instead of pining after this mess of a man who doesn't even give you the courtesy of a reply, and you here crying and carrying on, why don't we get a drink, go dancing and forget losers who don't deserve us." She stood, looking fresher after an intercontinental plane ride than anyone had a right to be. Her black hair fell across her shoulders in waves, and her brown skin positively glowed. She was so pretty and confident, it was compulsory to do what she said. Plus, she was a cop. Ellen gaped up at her, enraptured and practically drooling.

Dammit, Nicolette and Ellen were right. "Dammit, you're right," I said, standing as well. "Fuck it. We're in London! Let's go party, eh, mates?"

"You are not good at accents," Ellen said. "This is one instance in which you should listen to your mother." My mother, Suzie Lytton, felt that my stardom was a fluke of nature and that I could ruin it at any moment by being myself. That hadn't stopped her from moving from Vegas to L.A., the easier to surf my coattails and give sparkling interviews to low-level morning TV shows.

In a cringe-tastic Cockney, I replied, "Bugger you in the crikey, ya chit!"

"That's not a phrase people say." Nicolette grabbed me by the shoulders and pushed me toward the bedroom. "Now put on something tight and let's go. We'll find you someone not wanted by Interpol."

This was a side of Nicolette I'd heretofore not seen. Although I had heard about it around the two-month mark via text. My bill that month had been obscene for several reasons. "Can it be a man?"

"Hasn't California turned you gay yet?" She grinned and started going through my suitcases. "That's what my mother warned would happen to me when I moved from Atlanta. Ooh, is this Alexander McQueen?"

"I wore that to my first premiere. I'd never spent so much on something that wasn't a car before in my life."

We all sighed—women bonding over expensive couture that took off five pounds the moment you slipped it on. My two wardrobe assistants settled on a black, halter-neck jumpsuit I'd picked up but hadn't actually had the guts to wear anywhere. Ellen explained, "It's Europe! You're expected to look like a disinterested courtesan."

"How do I do that?"

"Stop shaving your legs." How that would help me tonight in a pair of pants, I had no idea. Perhaps the superior European attitude to beauty didn't need to be seen, just felt. I think *'je ne sais quoi'* means 'fuck you, I'm awesome, and I do what I want'.

Nicolette and Ellen decided to dress and makeup me into what they considered to be an acceptable level of vampiness while we sucked down mid-grade whiskey leftover from their flight. The idea that I might dump Bam caused Nicolette to grin at me like never before. But it could have been the booze.

They both selected garments that fit them more or less—Nicolette a wrap dress that fell to knee-length on me, but was a mini on her, and Ellen a miniskirt and tank top with a leather jacket on top. If there were three hotter ladies in London that night, I'd deny it.

We went to an Italian restaurant with a famous chef's name on the front and drank enough wine and ate enough carbs to power fifty drunken marathon runners. Then it was another bar, a dance club full of sleazy, grabby guys, and another dance club full of respectful, non-grabby ladies. While I doubted I would find my next true love at the all-woman disco, I did get enough business cards pressed into my palm to tell me that my non-hetero fan base was an enthusiastic group.

"I bet you make the gossip blogs tomorrow," Ellen hollered over the din to me as I posed with another fan, this one delivering a gin-ny kiss to my cheek when the cell phone shutter went off. Oooh, that would make my agent, my manager, my publicist and my attorney so happy! Gay rumors for a Hollywood actor meant big trouble, but bisexual rumblings about a woman made her more interesting to some.

Sometime around two a.m. my body started shutting down from lack of sleep, heartache and whatever the hell was wrong with my feet—my four-inch heels had acquired switchblades and were in the process of carving me up like a side of beef. I plopped into a booth—in the VIP section, y'all!—and was soon joined by my compatriots. Thereby began the sloppy 'I love you so much' portion of the evening. You know, the one where you tell each other how beautiful you are despite the fact that your mascara is now gracing your cleavage?

I opened the proceedings. "Nicolette, I think you're so awesome and good and beautiful for my friend, and I'm sorry you don't like me because I screw criminals." I paused to yawn. "Criminal. Just one at a time, because I'm a fucking lady, thank you."

Nicolette put her hand on my shoulder. "You're kind of annoying, but I don't hate you. Especially if you've dumped him. Did you dump him? I don't see why you couldn't date…Ryan Gosling. He seems like less of a turd than most of them."

"No!" Ellen swept into the booth on my other side. "We can't talk about men. It's a rule, for authors, of which I am an esteeeeeeemed one"—she bowed, we applauded—"to have ladies have conversations not about penises. It's the Bechdel test, and no more cock talk." Ellen was a semi-famous YA author—her sophomore effort was punching other *New York Times*-listed authors in the face every day. She must have ordered more alcohols for us sometime in there, because a waitress arrived, and Ellen shoved something pink and frosty into my face. "You don't need a man when you have Colin Firth!"

"Colin Firth is a man," Nicolette said.

I explained, "Colin Firth is my vibrator as well as the most Mr Darcy in the pond." I shoved the drink away.

"Hear, hear." Ellen pushed my cocktail back toward me, but I remembered I had a wardrobe fitting I had to be at to in, like, eleven hours London time — which is like American time, except it pronounces 'aluminum' funny.

"Okay —" I held out my arms. "Okay." It took a while for my mind thoughts to swim through the lake of vodka between my brain and my brain. "I am a professional woman with an important career. I need to worry about my career, right?"

"Right!" Nicolette toasted me and only spilled half her drink on the table.

"This is my first step to world domi — dom — conquer. Conquering. First, I play second banana in a couple movies, and then, next, I play top banana in a Mel Brooks joint!"

Ellen dipped her napkin in some water and dabbed at my boobs. I looked down to beholded that I'd dribbled some accidental drinky there. "Whoops," she said. "Does Mel Brooks do joints anymore?"

"He will for me. It is my destiny and my...future destiny." My head fell to the table of its own accord. And then it stayed there because heads are really heavy, you know? Because my brain is so big and full of cheese. I turned my mouth to the side. "I do not need some stupid man getting me all jacked the fuck up because he can't keep his paintings in his pants and then they kidnap me. That is poor life management." I was finally able to lift my noggin. I held my drink aloft. My righteous bitches did the same. "To money!"

"Mo money!" Ellen said.

"Mo stress!" Nicolette added.

"Mo'Nique!" I finished my pink thing. "I like her."

Nicolette nodded. "She's got a lot of talent." She finished her round and set the glass very carefully upside down. "Fuckers in my department won't promote me to detective. Funny how White dudes are always the most qualified for everything."

I grabbed her hand affectionately, feeling more at home with her now that she'd begun with the potty mouth. "It's because they play golf with each other with their dicks and balls. And then the dude with the smallest pair gets to be in charge because he yells the most."

Ellen burst out laughing. Nicolette slumped farther into the seat and said, "Maybe they take the detective exams with their...members. Maybe magic ink flows out."

"I've seen it a hundred times. Magic ink. They think it's magic. It's mostly just sour, usually."

And that was when Ellen fell out of the booth. She came back up for air and said, "I'm gonna write a movie for you, Lytton. It's gonna be called *Sour Grapes* and it's about one woman's quest to improve the flavor of life."

"No! Let's make a movie about all women. Like after the apocalypse, but only the women are left, but we have science, so there are still babies."

"I want to see this movie," Nicolette slurred very sincerefully. "I want to live it."

"To Ellen! Best fucking writer in the world!" I had nothing to toast with, but I held my glass aloft anyhow. Nicolette joined me, hers upside-down. Ellen didn't seem to mind, for she leaned over me to sloppily kiss her lady. I just kinda sat between, my eyes bobbing like a pool buoy, until the groping began. "Hey, hey—that was *my* boob. Nice grabbing, though. Ellen?"

"Yeah, sorry. You can't blame me, though. You have terrific tits."

I clasped my hands to my mammaries. "Thanks!"

"Hey!" Nicolette sat up and pointed to me, then Ellen. "Have you two ever…"

I said, "Oh, God, no."

"Noooooo," Ellen agreed.

"Fuck, no."

"That's horrible. Why would you say that?"

"I'm not that terrible!" I snapped. Geesh, Ellen had such impossible high standards. I dove into my purse and found a bunch of paper moneys that looked rainbowey and weird, so I set them on the table in the hope that someone else might count them into the required denominations. "Ellen has never tickled my taco."

"Wait!" Nicolette's brown eyes turned as wide as really wide brown eyes.

Wow, was I drunk.

"Wait—didn't your low-rent Ryan Gosling name his cat 'Captain Taco'?"

I straightened my spine. "Yes. After Tito's Tacos."

"I fuckin' love Tito's Tacos," Ellen said with a burp. She set to figuring out the money, thank goodness. I love her.

Nicolette nodded. "Me, too. Anyway, that cat is named after pussy."

"No." I shook my head, and then the whole bloody restaurant joined in the wobbling, even the furniture.

Ellen plopped a hand on my arm. "She's a professional detective. Believe her." Her voice dipped low and serious. "It's a pussy cat."

Nicolette laughed so hard she nearly pissed herself, and we all decided that going home was the best thing. My girls had gotten a hotel room, but in the interest of everyone's best interests, I made them come home with me. We grabbed various of my jammies — which looked like high-waders on my houseguests — and crammed into my queen-sized bed. "I won't be offended if you two want to go to the couch and…and…" I offered magnanimously, my eyes heavy and glued shut like, like, like with glue. Ellen let out a snore in response.

"Turn over, sweetie," Nicolette said.

I would turn over. I'd turn over a new leaf in the life department. I was worthy of love that could take place in public and happen every day of the month and in the same hemisphere as me. Damn right.

* * * *

How I made it to the wardrobe fitting
a) looking alive instead of dead
b) on time and
c) without barfing on any of the sexy cat burglar outfits they squeezed me into is a mystery for the ages. But I didn't regret my drunken shenanigans with my hos. Therapy or the VIP room and bottle service — they cost the same, they help you similarly, but for one, you get to wear badass jumpsuits and pretend you're at Studio 54. I suppose you could have a

drunken dance party in therapy, but your treatment will likely be longer.

Bonus — nobody in wardrobe suggested that I lose ten pounds! Had I become an acceptable Hollywood woman? Or had everyone thrown up their hands and just decided to put my bodacious buttocks in black? Who cares.

They took a bunch of Polaroids of me, and had settled on putting me in another jumpsuit. I was gonna bring them back! It featured a collar and long sleeves, like a mechanic's, except fashioned in some material made by NASA that sucked in my thighs until they almost didn't even rub together. Those genius people could have gone to Saturn, but instead they made advanced science clothing for comedy movies. And to finish it off — a giant zipper from my crotch to my throat.

There had been some debate about shoes. The Powers That Be, i.e. studio execs in suits, wanted me in six-inch spike heels. No, no, no. First off — my feet are merely eight inches and change long. The only performance I could manage in six-inch shoes was a ballet on my toes. Secondly — I was so tired of seeing women in action movies leap about in ridiculous footwear. The military doesn't put its fighting heroines in freaking Jimmy Choos! One twisted ankle and the terrorists win. After my polite, yet firm bitching, they agreed to find something in a lower-heeled wedge, maybe with spikes on it.

I ran into Daniel whilst in my snazzy space spandex, and his eyes got appreciatively wide. Score one for me. The tight black tee and army-green cargo pants they'd poured him into would be fap fodder the world over once this movie hit previews, I had no doubt.

God bless the makers of size smedium shirts, as made famous by Chris Evans as Captain America.

He offered to play London tour guide for the day and take me out to dinner—at least one man I knew had the ability to follow through. I'd told him I'd have to answer him after I consulted with my visiting friends, and he wanted to include them, too! It was shameful how many sighs I'd had to internalize during our conversation. One sigh for his pretty face. Another for his hard, gorgeous, hummina hummina hummina body and a third for not wanting me to ditch my girls.

Shame pricked at me. I'd shoved Sam so far out of my thoughts I'd nearly forgotten his name. If Sam was his name. I believe it was, but he'd given me so many over our time together that I chose to doubt in order to alleviate my wanton lusting. I wasn't a woman who usually juggled men—I'd been lucky if more than one noticed me in the space of a year, never mind at the same time.

Of course, Daniel was a fab-O movie star with a fleet of women on retainer for his sexual pleasure. Probably. He wasn't flirting with me—he was polite. Dreamily polite.

Forty-eight hours since I'd heard from Sam.

And about sixty since I'd been attacked because of him. Again.

We met Danny for a late lunch at an out-of-the-way joint near the National Portrait Gallery with seriously the best cheeseburger I'd ever had. If I admitted that on Twitter, however, I don't think they'd let me back inside America. The grease hit the spot—specifically, the hangover spot.

He charmed Ellen and Nicolette to the point where they decided to ditch us right after, saying they wanted a romantic night in the city. Sure, they did—one for them, and one for me. I could tell how much Ellen liked him by the way she subtly elbowed me over and over again until I had to restrain her because of my rib bruising. As they left us in the street, Ellen made a graphic gesture of sexual encouragement.

That was just silly. I was a professional woman, working on her burgeoning career and interacting with her colleague and oh, golly, he put his hand in the small of my back. "Would you like to visit the portrait gallery?" he asked.

I giggled, which is not a professional response. "Yes. I want to see Queen Elizabeth I, the best monarch you ever had, and a woman who didn't need no man."

He smiled, subtle at first, then it blossomed into something mischievous. "It can be good to not need someone." He led me down the square toward the entrance. "But *wanting* someone—that's the delightful part."

"If they want you in return."

"Sometimes even if they don't. 'A girl likes to be crossed in love a little now and then.' So does a boy."

Did he just quote Jane Austen to me? If he pooped salted chocolate, he might be the perfect heterosexual man. I rewarded his intellect with another giggle. That made two, which was two too many.

I was already crossed in love. I didn't need to be double-crossed.

His face reflected a mix of bemusement and flirtation. Why flirty? He likely flirted with everyone and everything—the world was his oyster, and we all wanted to pour hot sauce on him and lick him up. Or, wait, maybe he was the oyster? Whatever, the licking was the important part.

I paused my libido long enough to take a breath in Trafalgar Square, not quite believing I was here. Not quite believing I was *being paid* to be here. I smiled so hard it began to hurt. I almost had an out-of-body experience, with the secretary me from a year and a half ago peeking in on the future and fainting from dreams coming true. For once, I controlled my urge to cry, and instead swallowed the ball of joy lumping my throat. I turned it into a goofy face for Danny, which elicited a chuckle and a head shake that seemed to say, 'Crazy Americans!' I was their official representative.

We proceeded into the museum, and the crowds parted before us, whispering worshipfully. About him. Almost every person in each room just stopped and stared, and trepidation fluttered my insides. I didn't know if I wanted this level of fame. The constant cell phone pics. The never-ending attention. But this was what came with the paycheck, right? I didn't want to be an ungrateful asshole. Besides, they weren't looking at me, except tangentially. Thank goodness, because I just had to swallow a cheeseburger burp, and I'm pretty sure Angelina Jolie has taught herself not to burp or fart.

I kept my head down and pretended the attention wasn't happening. That was what Danny did, although he plastered a constant, small smile upon on his features. He seemed aloof and accessible at the same time, like the monarchs hanging on the walls around us.

He wound us through the elegant rooms with gleaming wooden floors and skylights that made them seem bigger, grander. Dutifully, he delivered me to the Tudor collection, wherein I visited my queen. I stopped in front of a portrait that featured Elizabeth I standing atop a map of England. Yes. Top of the heap.

Large and in charge. I grinned and nodded up at her, redhead to redhead, virgin queen to non-virgin commoner.

She had the right idea. *I'm the boss of me.*

Danny leaned down to me and, *sotto voce*, asked, "Did you really foil an international group of art thieves?"

My head whipped up, the shock in my face palpable and likely guilty-looking. He put his hand to his mouth to cover a laugh and said, "My goodness, you did!"

"No. That's just tabloid...tabloidery."

"You're fibbing. I read that you testified at a trial." He peeked over his shoulder to spy two teenage girls who'd crept close to us. They squealed and ran away to the other side of the gallery, where they were bolstered enough to begin filming us on their phones. As one, we smiled, waved and left the room to visit Henry VIII. I'd always rather hoped he burned in hell for throwing away wives like soiled tissues, especially when sex selection is made by the male of the species. How beautifully ironic that the best thing to come out of him was a daughter. And maybe a church, you know, depending on your God views.

"Is that why you cast me? Because you think I have practical experience?"

"No, no—that's merely a bonus. I need a funny foil. I've not done a lot of humor, but I'd like to."

My eyebrows shot up. Wow. This guy was an esteemed alumnus of the Royal Shakespeare Company. He'd won an Oscar and several BAFTAs. I couldn't even boast a People's Choice award. And all this while being a man of color. Leading men of Chinese descent were rare in the cinema, and even rarer were the ones who'd never performed a lick of martial arts. "Well, I hope to pratfall gracefully to try and make you look good. Because, you know, it's so hard for you to come off well."

He expelled an offended breath, alleviated by the gleam in his eye. "I'll have you know that I am a terribly respected thespian. One time, Kim Kardashian said that I was, like, totally hot and stuff."

"It's the 'and stuff' that cuts the quality actors from the chaff."

"'Quality' is my middle name."

"Is that Chinese?"

He winked. "After my great-grandfather."

We stopped in front of a painting of young Henry VIII. Danny scooted in behind me. His heat radiated through the breezy maxi dress I wore, giving me *thoughts*. Generally, I find *thoughts* to be wicked, especially the ones in my brain, which embraced the seven deadly sins with great gusto. He got so close to my ear it tickled me straight to my funny-feelings bone. "Shall we lift one of these for practice? Or will we limit our skullduggery to the British Museum, under the guise of 'rehearsal'?"

I nearly choked on my own spit. Did I only attract men with grand larceny in their hearts? I drifted away and flung a smile back over my shoulder. "It's all fun and games until you're frisked by a hardened police officer with cold hands."

Danny opened his mouth to quiz me more on matters I didn't want to speak of, so I went on the offensive. It's a trick I'd learned in Hollywood— everyone loves talking about themselves, and will do so for you gladly when you want to change the subject. Although it did not escape me that he'd read up on me. My ego swelled further under my pushup bra. "So, Danny, how on Earth are you single?"

"Who says I am?" This delivered with a chin swish the likes of spymasters in old movies. "Although I am. Dreadfully so."

I put my hand to my heart, which broke for womankind everywhere. "Too gorgeous for the masses?"

He scratched his eyebrow and blinked bashfully. Weird to see gestures you'd heretofore viewed forty feet high in your local movie house played before you on an intimate scale. "Not by half, I'm afraid. It's challenging navigating what and who is real in this field. You must find that to be true."

Oh, yes—both career-wise and in my personal life. I danced the bullshit two-step on the regular. "I think it's just plain hard to find someone to be simpatico with. And even harder to live day to day without killing the patico." So many things get in the way. Careers, interests, the FBI…

Two fifty-something women stopped us and asked to take pictures with Danny, who obliged immediately. He got in between them and put his arms around their shoulders while I took the pic. They laughed like schoolgirls, gushed at him for a minute or two then left with copious waves.

We toured room after room of famous faces and beautiful portraiture, Danny making witty small talk and maintaining the sort of pleasant demeanor that looks friendly in surreptitious candid photos. Not me. When I sat on one of the benches, the cushion made a fart noise that the entire room turned to gawp at. And then I almost fell on a bored little kid who'd decided to sit on the ground behind me. A smarmy-looking dude got a nice chuckle out of that, and a dynamic picture. I began to stick closer to Danny so I could improve myself in the wake of his glow.

At least I was making a good showing somewhere—Ellen texted me a link to *The Daily Mail* with a spectacular pic of the three of us from our night of revelry, complete with 'Is She a *Lesbian*?!' scare headline. My stock inflated like my ankle currently was.

After a couple of hours in the museum, my heebie jeebies were cranking up in overtime from

a) being in a museum at all—hadn't I once sworn to never look at a piece of asshole art again? Not good, considering that my new job took place...mostly in a museum—and

b) brain-cheating on Sam, with whom I might have been broken up...or not...oh, who the hell knows.

I suggested we take our afternoon elsewhere, and it sounded entirely too sexified. But in my defense, there are only two ways to say 'let's get out of here'—seductively or with terror, as if the aliens are invading.

We walked a little ways to find the bar he wanted to show me—the Beaufort Bar in the Savoy hotel. Holy cow, was this place fancy. I would win +10 *You've Arrived* points with my mother if she could only see it. Everything appeared dark and sexy, black wood and hot waiters. Immediately, we were ushered into one of the golden alcoves at one end of the room—literal golden nooks with couches inside. The shimmering wall curved behind us like a cocoon at Liberace's house. It was all I could do not to wave my hand and declare, "Let them eat cake."

After a gin martini—hair of the dog, what what—and staring too long at Danny's impeccable face with those clever eyes, my tongue loosened. I figured I'd have to talk about it sometime. I ordered another martini and scooted closer to him, which he did not appear to mind. His arm crept around the back of the couch. Ahem, I only got closer because I was about to tell him of trials and tribulations, not because I felt reckless and marooned on a British Isle of doubt.

"About the whole 'trial' thing," I began.

His eyebrows rose like curtains. "Yes?" he led with a half-smile.

"Well—" I swallowed. "I had a day job as an executive assistant, before all this." I laughed. All this still seemed like a dream. "I was bamboozled by some thieves I met at the office, and there occurred a minute amount of"—more swallowing, a drink of martini—"kidnapping, but it wasn't bad."

"It wasn't bad!" He'd begun to regard me with that look of 'you're nuts', an expression more than a little familiar to me.

"I wasn't beaten or assaulted or anything. Just...removed from my life for a few days so that I couldn't tell on them. Anyway, eventually the police found us." This was the extremely abridged and kinda lie-ey version of the events. "And I testified at trial a few months ago. The one criminal they caught went to prison. The end!" I grinned and took the fresh martini. One shouldn't guzzle Bombay Sapphire on an empty stomach, but it'd been a guzzle sort of week.

His eyes narrowed in 'I detect bullshit' mode. Or so it seemed to me. "So you encountered an art thief at work in an office?"

I nodded.

"And he kidnapped you."

I nodded. I drank.

"Then you got away and got them...him arrested and were the hero?"

Hey! I liked the word hero. I smiled and nodded.

"Astonishing."

Astonishing—even better. I shook my head. "No, no. It coulda happened to anyone." Anyone with a weakness for dimples.

"You leveraged it into a successful career, though." He scooched closer, just a wee bit. "The thieves—what were they like? I mean, what does it take to do that?"

For a moment, I couldn't find a way to answer. Sam wasn't bad-bad, merely…morally relative. He'd gotten very insulted when accused of being evil. "Thieves…adapt. If they want to be successful, they're calm. Smart. Flexible."

Danny considered that, smiling as I watched him mentally work it into his character. When I offered no more, he asked, "Were you in Los Angeles to try and break into film?"

"Yes, but failing. I couldn't even get auditions." The soul-crushing defeat of those years haunted me. My chest tightened. "I wasn't pretty enough to be the girl next door. In LA, a 'girl next door' is always a model. I tried to go for the 'quirky sidekick' sort of roles, but there were a billion of us average-looking sorts of ladies with acting degrees we still had to pay off and few roles to nab. Being shorter than hell didn't help me."

Understanding washed across his face. "It's so difficult for women in this business. You get, what, perhaps one role out of four in a script?"

I laughed. "If that. And we're usually only there for the hero to hump, so she's got to be a babe. What else are we good for?"

A wry grin. "I can't think of one thing."

"And I'm a White lady—I benefit from the gross fact that so many role breakdowns specify Caucasian only."

Bitterness drew his brows together. "Asian men are either kung-fu masters, takeout delivery guys or funny, sexless clowns. In a few years, I can play an *old* kung-fu master, dispensing clichéd wisdom to a new generation."

"Lucky you."

He stroked his chin. "At least I'll get a fancy beard." Staring into his Scotch, he said, "A couple of years ago, the RSC put on the Chinese equivalent of *Hamlet* with an almost all-White cast. Because, you know, there are so few good Asian actors. We can't even get cast in our own works."

I didn't know what to say. I knew what the smack of sexism felt like, but his racist experiences much have been enraging, disheartening, dehumanizing—to say the least. I squeezed his arm, as if that would erase the degradation.

"If I hadn't lucked into *The Silent Forest*, and if it hadn't somehow blossomed out of the arthouse circuit, I'd probably be selling shoes or something now."

"Can I gush over you in that movie? I was in college, and it was me and my friends' favorite sob-fest." I clasped my hands over my heart. Yes, it was that kind of film. "When Chyou died in your arms?" My voice ended in a squeak and my lip fluttered.

He laughed at me, his eyes crinkling at the corners. He was probably a dozen years older than he'd been in that three-hankie film, but even more handsome with maturity. "Do I need to find the smelling salts?"

"No, no—" I held him at arm's length dramatically, "I'll be fine...someday. No, I won't. I'll never get over that movie!"

"You're too kind." He leaned back and turned inward. "My parents were so gutted when I wanted to do that film. The language. The nudity. My mother." He shuddered. I guess the horrors of a mother's shame are universal in any culture. "I'm first-generation born in the UK, and let's just say they probably would have preferred that I do anything but wiggle my arse on camera."

I covered my mouth to disguise my smile. "My mother probably wouldn't let them put my bare ass on camera. 'Are you sure you want to do that, Samantha? Think of how many glorious heinies have been filmed. Yours can't even crack the top thousand, I'm sure. Never mind your face!'"

His guffaw held the stench of pity. "Ouch. My mum has come round—now she brags about her son when I bring her to award ceremonies."

"Aw, I'm glad for that."

"Me, too. Odd how becoming rich makes your choices seem smarter."

"Amen, my friend. Amen."

Oh, but I was having entirely too lovely a time right now. Two martinis in my tummy and no dinner. There must be something about the cloudy British air that turned me alcoholic. "I should go." I set my drink on the table and gathered my purse to me while trying to ignore the disappointed fall of his shoulders. And ignore the thrill that came with it. "I have to try and pretend that I'm not an idiot at stunt rehearsal tomorrow."

"How many days do you have?"

"Just the one. I have to jump off a height, and punch a couple people. You have so much more than I do."

"Yeah." He scratched his chin and gestured for the waiter to settle the bill. "They're fun for me—the stunts. I've rebelled against doing any martial arts, but just plain kicking arse is thrilling. As far as the production insurance will let me." He barely glanced at the tab, doubled it by way of a tip and handed it back to our obsequious server. When we were again alone, he said, "May I take you home? Rather, not *take you home*, but walk you, or..."

A flush crept up his face, and I knew I had to say, "No, thank you. I had a late night, and I'll probably just cab it."

Deep breath in, deep breath out. Oh, but I was an evil woman. What sort of lady wanted to jump a new dude right after maybe breaking up with another? I told myself that inner existential turmoil often led to confusion in the clitoral area. Especially when you met a super-hot fellow who was so kind, and human, and *normal* — and performed a job you could tell your mother about. "Thank you for this. It makes me feel less nervous about the whole film to have gotten to know you a little."

"Me, too."

"What? How can you be nervous? You're *Daniel Zhang*." I said it as if reading off a marquee forty feet high.

We wound our way out of the hotel and onto the sidewalk. "I'm not *Daniel Zhang*. I'm Daniel Zhang. I get zits." He pointed to his cheek, but I damn sure couldn't find a flaw.

I stood on my tip-toes and pressed my lips to the imagined blemish.

Oh, I shouldn't have done that.

My regret punched me in the gut with a fist the size of Texas. He smelled like sexy, woodsy cologne, with a vague undertone of man.

Oh, I shouldn't have smelled that.

My mouth dry, I rocked onto my heels and smiled to cover my mortification.

He bent the long, long way to my face. His lips parted softly, and I meant to back away, I really did, and I put my hand to his chest to keep him at a distance. His pecs were hard and warm and *oh, no, why was I kneading my hand there*? Mayday, *mayday*!

He kissed me, gently, firmly and with just enough pressure to make my blood zing and cry *more, more, more!* My body from the waist down had somehow melted into amoral slush. Pulling back, he smiled, hopeful and sweet.

Oh, good Lord, baby Jesus and all the saints. My insides flailed and I tried to form actual words with my mouth, which was paid to make words and say things, but nothing spluttered out. I waved my hand goodbye like a toddler and bolted to the cab stand. Yup, running away with great, clomping steps was the only thing to do when kissed by a movie star.

I waved again from the window as we pulled away. He returned it, his entire demeanor relaxed and easy and sexier than a sexy man who sexes and *oh, shit fuck* what have I done?

* * * *

As per usual, I discussed my shame with food, which never judged me. My Indian takeout told me that *he* had kissed *me*. A very important distinction for the guilty. And that it had been one hundred percent friendly. Like a friend. I'd given him a chaste smack on the cheek—why? whyyyyyy had I done that?—and he'd reciprocated in the more worldly European fashion. I wasn't in Puritanical America anymore. This continent had told the Puritans to screw off so that everyone still left here could kiss each other on the mouth like buddies. That's a history fact right there. I bet Daniel kissed everyone goodbye—pals, women, men…

And then I spent three minutes daydreaming about Daniel kissing a dude as my food got cold. And then I spent twenty minutes downloading that film he'd done in which he played the gay lover of an equally-hot football star. And then I spent thirty shame-filled minutes not watching the movie while I unpacked my suitcases finally and thought nice thoughts about Sam, still my boyfriend, maybe, and who'd brought me so much joy. And copious frustration. But more joy.

No, I would definitely *not* watch that sexy movie. I'd go to bed early to make up for the jet lag and the drunken fiestas, er, self-care I'd been indulging in for days.

Sleep overcame me—about twelve hours' worth—and I awoke feeling like a new person. Ready to kick butt at stunt work. Ready to handle my men, er, man situation like an adult! Ready to open my email…

I read the note, sent from a Gmail burner account, twice through before I nearly dropped my laptop on my foot. I collapsed onto the floor of my bedroom and stared at the picture they'd sent until tears blurred my eyes so that I saw no more.

It was a picture of Sam, clearly used as a punching bag and tied up, holding this morning's newspaper—the date was legible, even to me, although I didn't recognize the language of *Het Laatste Nieuws*. Dutch, likely.

Because the note told me to travel to Bruges, or he would die.

Chapter Five

I Do My Own Failed Stunts

Int. Sleazy Hotel Room, Bruges, Belgium — day
Angle On: Samantha Lytton *grapples in the dark with an* Unknown Assailant, Assumed To Be A Jerk Thief. *Samantha grabs the scumbag by the arm, twists her body nimbly and flips him across the room, where he falls to the floor.*

Samantha Lytton: Cough him up! Where is Sam?
Unknown Assailant, Assumed To Be A Jerk Thief: Sam who?
Samantha Lytton: I don't know!

Angle On: Samantha lunges at the bad guy. He jumps to his feet and dashes across the room, clearly trying for the door. She trips him by whipping out one sexy leg, and he collapses on the dingy carpet next to the bed. She grabs him by the front of the shirt.

Samantha Lytton: I know you have him. You told me to come here. Dammit, tell me where he is!

Unknown Assailant, Assumed To Be A Jerk Thief: Why do you want him back? He's a liar. Once a thief, always a thief.

Unknown assailant has an Irish accent. It's a clue! Or maybe it just sounds pretty.

Samantha Lytton: But…I love him.
Unknown Assailant With The Nice Accent: I guess you shoulda told him that more often.

Unknown Assailant sits up, cradling his busted head which has been very effectively pummeled by Ms Lytton, who is a total badass.

Unknown Assailant With The Nice Accent: Haven't you been a little withholding? You can't blossom in a relationship by assuming the worst. Love requires a leap of faith with both feet.
Samantha Lytton: I made a real commitment to Sam! He's not in jail, is he? That's 'cause of *moi*.

Samantha indicates herself by pointing both thumbs at her chest, in case the Unknown Assailant doesn't understand French.
Lying by omission to the cops? That's love.

Unknown Assailant With The Nice Accent: Yes, I know you've made some real sacrifices. It's hard being away from your partner all the time.

Samantha plops down cross-legged next to the Unknown Assailant.

Samantha Lytton: It is. Always wondering if he's okay. Or just plain missing him. I have needs.

Surprisingly Insightful Unknown Assailant: Of course you do. You're a vibrant woman at the top of her game. And he should respect that he's not meeting your individual desires.

Samantha Lytton: That's all I'm saying!

Unknown Assailant puts a gentle hand on Samantha's shoulder.

Surprisingly Insightful Unknown Assailant: You two must hash through these things openly and honestly. It's the only way for love to grow into a mutually beneficial life together full of faithful trust.

Samantha nods, knowing that the Unknown Assailant is right.

Samantha Lytton: So…do you know where Sam is?

Surprisingly Insightful Unknown Assailant: Not really. I'm in charge of kidnapping wayward drug dealers, not art thieves.

I had no choice but to attend my stunt rehearsal, so I threw my entire body and soul into pretend-clobbering the character in the museum gang who turns on the rest of us. I tossed him across the room and faux-punched him in the face, all the while fantasizing that he was whoever had taken Sam. It only helped for as long as I moved. The moment I took a break, hell broke loose in my brain.

I ping-ponged between terrified worry about Sam and palpable anger. Rage jettisoned through my veins and brought with it a sapping of my energy, a deflation of my spirit. My body hurt from a hurricane of emotions.

I'd forgive Sam anything if I'd only find him and we could walk away together, safe.

Until the next time it happened.

My entire life seemed like playacting. During the day, I masqueraded in front of the camera, and at night, Sam and I impersonated June and Ward Cleaver. I'd left it to my beaver, and thinking with my lady parts had gotten me into his messes from the very beginning.

After today, I'd have a couple of days off, plus the weekend before I needed to be back at the studio for rehearsals. I could do a trip to Bruges and back if nothing went wrong. Not knowing what else to do, I'd replied to the nasty email and told them I'd be in the city by tomorrow morning.

"Ha!" I said out loud.

Bruce, the guy I'd just faux-roundhouse-kicked, took my laugh as a sign of high spirits and replied, "Yeah! You're pretty awesome for a wee thing," in his adorable Irish accent.

I managed an almost-human smile and retired to the edge of the dance studio to find my phone. After wrestling all day with whether or not to tell anyone about my situation, I knew I had to tell Ellen. I was supposed to meet her and Nicolette after work anyhow—no way could I hide such a thing from my soul mate. Two different people had asked me if I was sick today based on my Gollum-like complexion. Danny had been shooting concerned glances my way, but at least my gross appearance kept further kisses at bay.

Only one more sequence to go through before I finished for the afternoon—Danny did his own stunts, but I was quite happy to let my stunt double, Missy, earn some cashola. Somehow, after fighting actual, bona-fide bad guys in reality, the fake version didn't hold as much appeal.

I mopped my glistening brow with a towel and plopped on the floor to text Ellen.

Urgent situation. Pick me up at Trafalgar Dance Studio in an hour for a council of war.

An almost instantaneous reply shot through time and space to berate me.

WTF? I will kill that stupid thief of yours! I thought we'd dumped him! I have a nice girl all picked out for you. She enjoys eighties music…

I actually managed a giggle at that. A head-swirling amount of relief nearly knocked me over to know that I always had one friend on my side.

Not that I wanted to expose more people to danger. Shit! Shiiiiiiiiit. I slumped against the wall and replied.

Someone may kill him for you. Just swing by – I need more brains to help me decide what to do. But I don't want Nic to do anything…police-like.

You can't see me, but I'm rolling my eyes at you.

Don't hurt yourself.

I finished the day and, by the close, had performed with such dedicated vigor that the stunt coordinator cited me as a model student. While the friendly, joking group gave me a round of applause, I tried not to barf on the bouncy dance floor. Danny asked me if I wanted to join everyone in a drink nearby, but I begged off, using my friends in town as an excuse.

Dammit! I'd love to bond with my cast, but you know how it is — maybe-boyfriend being held prisoner by mysterious thugs. After giving everyone a hug, I bolted out the front door and ran straight into Nicolette.

I righted myself and said, "I need a drink and a quiet place to talk. But mostly a drink."

* * * *

We held the council of war at a pub near my apartment in case my place had been bugged. The suggestion that my flat was being monitored earned more of Ellen's patented eye rolls. By the time the evening was over, poor Ellen's eyes might pop out of her equally-aggravated skull. And then fly across the room to slap sense into me.

"Personally, I vote to leave him there to deal with the consequences of his life of crime," Nicolette said. Ellen began to raise her hand to agree, but I kicked her under the table.

"Ow!" My BFF rubbed her calf and shot more lasers from her peepers. "You can't really go to Bruges and what…kick down the door with guns blazing?"

"I learned how to kick in a door today, thank you."

"Sam—"

"I'm going!" I slammed my beer on the table and pulled my sweater around me. This Cali girl was not used to sub-seventy-two-degree temperatures. Or perhaps my blood had run cold. "I'm just wanting advice about what to do. And no, I can't call the police—I don't know exactly where he's wanted or why, but I have to assume it's everywhere and for everything. Ugh." I put my head on the mostly-clean table. "Nicolette, please tell me we're off the record here."

It was Nicolette's turn to be kicked under the table by Ellen. The cop chewed on her lip then said, "Fine. I was never here. We never talked about this. I don't know who you are. I wish I didn't know who you are..."

"Thank you." I peered up at her with eyes full of tears. "That means a lot to me."

"You're bonkers. You understand that, right?" She took my hand and patted it. "I urge you to contact the Belgium authorities. Him in jail is better than the two of you dead."

"I'll have them on speed dial." I squeezed her hand and ignored the commentary in my brain, which was residing in the Land of Denial, on the Continent of LaLaLaICan'tHearYou. "But I'm hoping I can meet them publicly and offer money, or something. I mean, I have cash now, not that much, but some. I ain't Tom Cruise."

Ellen sucked down half a beer, wiped her mouth with the back of her hand, burped and said, "This is stupid. So I'm going with you."

"What?" Nicolette burst out.

"What? No!" I reached across and grabbed at her arm. "No fucking way. This is my problem. I—"

"I can go where I want!" Ellen pronounced this with such vehemence the two opinionated ladies with her actually quieted. She lifted her eyebrows in a 'so there' way and continued, "I just looked it up on my phone. Eurostar will get us into Bruges in three and a half hours. We go tonight, we trick the bad guys...somehow, and then we tour the city. I read that it features the most photographed place in Europe."

Nicolette plopped her forehead on the table. It was a common gesture for this particular evening. "I'll go," she said, "but only to guard Ellen." She whipped her head up. "Your boy is your problem."

Guilt, fear and anger swirled in the cauldron of my stomach as if stirred by a witch named regret. I butted, "But—but—"

"But me no buts!" Ellen pointed in the air majestically. "I do what I want to do—I love you, and I'm going to help you. The three of us are smarter than some douchebag art thieves." Nicolette quirked one eyebrow in doubt. "Well, at least two of us are." She let that dangle. Of course, she meant me and herself.

Of course, she meant herself and Nicolette. I was the moron charging into danger for the sake of a criminal, when I could be meeting a nice lesbian who enjoyed terrible eighties hits. But I already had one of those, God bless her crazy self.

Into the fray! My only hope was that the heroines would not piss their pants in terror.

Oh, and not die.

Chapter Six

Belgium? I Hardly Know Him!

With a hastily-packed suitcase and a slump in my step, I boarded the train to Bruges, connecting through Brussels. The scenery probably would have been lovely had it been daylight, or had my eyes seen anything but worry and Sam's face. I sprang for the first class car, and we sat at a foursome of seats facing inward toward each other. We situated ourselves as far away from the other passengers as possible. The only plan was to get there, rush to the little hotel Ellen had spontaneously booked for us then email the bastards again to find out what to do next. I figured the possible scenarios were as follows.

One. The rat bastards wanted money, and I'd be able to supply it. They'd give Sam back to me.

Two. The rat bastards wanted me, and I'd walk into a trap. They'd demand money from the movie studio. Studio would pay for me, then fire me. I'd never work in this town again.

Three. The rat bastards wanted me, and I'd walk into a trap. They'd demand money from the movie studio. Studio would not pay for me. The story of my disappearance would make a fabulous *Lifetime* movie.

Four. The rat bastards wanted me, and I'd walk into a trap. They'd kill me and Sam. Ellen and Nicolette would take a beautiful picture in the most scenic spot in Europe.

The odds were not in my favor. I was Katniss Evermess.

About an hour into the journey, a woman plopped down beside me, scaring the bejesus out of us and causing me to scatter my bag of potato chips. I gritted my teeth, as the chips were the only thing keeping my anxiety at acceptable levels, i.e. not barfing in public. She was an Amazon, six foot at least, and Nordic-looking, as if she could carve a boat herself and sack England with it. "You are famous actress Samantha Lytton, yes? You match picture in magazine." She showed us an English tabloid. "I am big fan." She stated these things in a flat, accented voice—the most underwhelmed fan encounter I'd ever had, and that included the countless times someone had thought I was Emma Stone and only realized the mistake up close when they saw my wrinkles.

"Yes," I replied. I gave her a smile as half-hearted as her enthusiasm. "How are you?"

"I am have gun and you say nothing or I shoot you friends."

Well, that woke up the table.

She peeled back her coat to show us the gun. Ellen appeared outraged. Nicolette went calm—cop mode, I guessed. I took a deep, shaky breath and laughed.

"What funny? Why you laugh?"

"What accent? Why you talk like?" Really? I was being kidnapped—fucking *again!*—by cartoon Natasha. I couldn't believe anyone actually spoke like that but, then again, I was a stupid American who only spoke one language. My mangling of French likely sounded as idiotic to the entirety of the Gauls.

The lady whipped out the gun and held it under the table. "I am here to watch you. I am take you to meeting place in Bruges. Give me purses."

We complied. The kidnapper glanced around to make sure no one was paying attention, then proceeded to go through our stuff and remove every piece of electronics.

"Great," Ellen said. "Do you have a name, stretch?"

"My name is not stretch. I am Dina."

"Dina…" I leaned back to see the gun. It was pointed at Ellen. Oh, God. "Let my friends go. Please. I'm the one you came for."

"No. You all come with me, even Blacky."

Nicolette's eyes nearly bugged out. "Did she just call me 'Blacky'?"

Ellen grabbed her girlfriend's hand and pulled it into her lap.

"And why 'even Blacky'? Like it's my honor to be kidnapped with the White folks? Like I need to be sent to the back of the kidnap bus?"

"Quiet!" Dina nearly yelled this and pushed the gun into my side. I hissed out the remainder of my breath and retreated to the window as far as I could. Not far enough. At this distance, there would be little difference between 'blew her head off' and 'blew her neck *and* head off'. I mouthed 'I'm sorry' to Nicolette, who nodded and pulled Ellen closer. How pathetic I was — apologizing for the ignorance of our kidnapper.

Why? Why'd they come with me? What was I even doing here? I'd landed an amazing job! I had good hair!

Cosmo had lied to me. The world told me that if I were rich and successful and lost ten pounds, everything would be okay. Everything was most certainly not fucking okay!

We spent the next ninety minutes staring at each other in silence. I'd never wished I was an X-Man so much—capable of telepathy, or of making some ignorant woman's head explode with my brain.

Impotence became my new best friend. I couldn't do anything to Dina—if I did, Sam would likely die, and they'd probably find me all over again anyhow. How easy it was for them. My vulnerability made my armpits sweat. This must be what testicles feel like. How did men live like this every day, wondering when a swift kick would come? And why do we pretend that balls are much stronger than a nice vagina? Vadges take a licking and keep on ticking!

At Brussels-Midi station, Dina ignored Ellen and Nicolette and kept close to me like a large, Russian skin. I kept my sunglasses on inside, eager to not be spotted by friend or foe, although that last part was too little, too...whoops. We boarded the next train, which would take an hour to get into Bruges.

Being kidnapped on a train was nothing like they make it out to be in the old movies. No Gene Wilder to be seen. No madcap porters. Just the numbing anonymity of modern-day hurry up and wait, with a side of heeeeeelp!

As tour guides go, Dina performed at a C- level. We hurried out of Bruges Station and into the Belgian night. A white van awaited us, and I reared back for a moment before a decisive shove from Dina sent me sprawling. Nicolette helped me to my feet with a reassuring arm squeeze. Her presence simultaneously flooded me with confidence and regret. I didn't recognize the driver of the transport, a blond guy, but the creepy white van itself reminded me of another that had picked me up as I fled on roller skates. Jane had orchestrated that particular kidnapping.

So many snatch-and-grabs. If I were kidnapped twice more, would I get one for free?

Jane. She was supposed to leave us alone. Such was the mutually beneficial bargain Sam had struck with her after I'd saved her from certain death by being highly functional in the aforementioned skates. She was Sam's ex-thief-boss, and we'd parted ways by promising not to tattle on each other. Sophisticated, elegant and smarter than hell, Jane reminded one of the great Black supermodels at Studio 54. I simultaneously wished she'd give me life lessons, and that I would never see her again.

I got neither of my wishes.

We arrived at some part of the old, medieval city — tall rows of houses with gorgeous façades of brick. The streets of stone glittered in the evening sprinkle of rain. Between the darkness and the mist, the city appeared to have been unchanged by the past six hundred or so years. The fresh smell of precipitation lingered strangely in my fearful nose — it was too comforting a scent. A canal sparkled besides us, beautiful for an instant before they hustled us into a door beside a chocolate shop. Up a narrow stairway we went and into an apartment. Dina pointed to a brown 1970s couch, and the three of us sank into it simultaneously.

My psychic instincts were four steps behind, naturally, for in breezed Jane, resplendent in a white pantsuit. Relief almost flooded me because Jane wouldn't want our brains or blood splattered all over that designer masterpiece.

Then again, Dina looked as if she accessorized with vile substances all the time, and she still pointed the gun at us.

Nicolette said, "Lady, your racist associate here could do with some education."

Jane whipped her head toward Dina, currently gnawing on her fingernail. "She's local help. You'd think Europe would be more advanced than America, but unfortunately…"

Well, at least no one would die because of skin color, or sexism. One step forward…

"Jane," I began as nicely as I could manage, "to what do I owe this latest unwilling, yet charming, visit with you?"

"I'll let Sam tell you, so that you understand this is his doing."

The blond dude brought in Sam. I clapped my hands over my mouth to see him bound and bruised, his face blooming in shades of black, blue and a charming reddish-purple. He squeezed his eyes shut at the sight of me, and swore when he took in Ellen and Nicolette.

"The feeling is mutual, asshole," Ellen snipped.

Sam grimaced at Ellen, but turned his attention to Jane. "Jane, why the hell are you doing this? We had a deal."

Jane ran her hand across her short, stylish white hair. "You broke it, not me. You went to the Feds."

He blinked, shades of confusion, not denial, shaping his face. "Neither your name nor your…anything has been given to any law enforcement."

She laid her best 'you're full of shit' look on him. "Hedging at its best. Care to elaborate?"

Blond guy let Sam go, and he nearly fell into a dirty upholstered chair beside the couch. Sam glanced at me, and his dark, dark eyes held such sorrow that my terror redoubled itself. His gaze was the sort you give to your beloved when they tie you to a post about to be set aflame. In this metaphor, I was pretty sure I was the kindling at his feet.

Sam closed his eyes, one of them only partway because it was already pummeled half-shut, and said, "What are you going to do with us?"

"I'm going to kill you all unless your story is very, very good."

I gasped. Jane wasn't the murder-y sort! What the fuck had Sam done? I grabbed Ellen's hand, to my left. I saw her grab Nicolette's hand on the far end. I squeezed Ellen twice, the signal.

We were not going down without a fight.

I bolted off the couch and launched myself at blond guy. Ellen slammed into Jane, and Nicolette had the joy of going after Dina, closest to her.

Blondie was a lot bigger than I was, but I had surprise on my side, and my head butted him smack in the solar plexus. He went down like the Titanic, except cussing in a language I didn't understand. The hiss of the curse word is universal, however. It stopped when Sam kicked the guy in the head.

Ellen had belly flopped on Jane and stayed there, and the older woman twisted on her back like a turtle. I grabbed the gun from Blondie's pants and pointed toward everyone still fighting. "Stop, or I'll shoot!" I yelled in an original fashion. Jane sighed, elaborately, but stilled herself. Nicolette didn't need any help. She'd forced Dina into some sort of awesome wrestler chokehold from behind and appeared delighted to not let go. I'm pretty sure I heard, "How you like my ass now?" muttered.

"Ellen," I said, "grab this and shoot anyone not on our side if they so much as frown at you. Where you shoot is up to you. Feel free to be creative. I'm going to untie Sam, and we'll search the rest of the place for more bad guys. Good?" Everyone nodded, and I handed Ellen the gun.

Sam started to talk to me and I said, "Not here," and pivoted him around to see a zip tie binding his hands. "Damn, I'll need scissors or a knife. Nicolette, kick Dina's gun over this way." She did, and I caught it mid-slide on the wooden floor. "Okay, we're going to search now. Sam, have you seen more of them?"

He shook his head. We set off in the direction from which he'd been dragged. Just a kitchen with a table, chairs and a lot of empty cupboards which yielded nothing to help cut Sam free. We crossed through the living room, where my ladies had everything under control, and into the single bedroom and bath. There we found Jane's handbag with a Tiffany Swiss army knife inside. If you're going to stab, do it in style.

I sliced through the plastic and he rubbed his wrists. The tie left an ugly red welt in its wake. Pity overcame me — then I remembered why we were here.

I avoided his gaze and examined the room. "Ah-ha!" Vertical blinds. I cut the long cords used to lift the blinds and used them to tie up Jane, Dina and He Who Curses in Dutch Maybe. My stomach finally dropped from its temporary home in my lungs once everyone was bound and sitting on the couch where we'd been.

"It worked!" Ellen whispered to me.

"I love you both. Nicolette, I know I'm not in your top ten people, but you are a righteous friend."

She shrugged, but spared me a small smile. "If you would just date an accountant or something..."

Laughing, I said, "I tried. Holler if you need help." I went back to have a chat with Sam. I pulled his arm so that we stood in the corner farthest away from the rest of the group. "Talk. Everything. Now. And I swear, if you lie to me in this moment, it's over. Forever."

His lip curled, and he stared at his feet. Hard breaths thundered through him, making him shudder. "I'm sorry," he began.

"Later. Get to it." I needed to bark orders like a drill sergeant—he was a heartbeat from losing his shit completely. "Do you need a doctor?"

He shook his head. "I have not gone to the police giving up Jane."

"Okay."

"However"—he swallowed—"I have been talking to the Feds." I gasped. Holy crap! A thrill of hope spluttered to life in my heart. "It's obviously gotten out, which, thanks a fucking lot, Uncle Sam." I started to ask a question, and he took my hand. "Here's the deal. The only way I can really be with you is if we're not afraid I'm going to be arrested at any moment. But neither did I want, well, this to happen—every damn person I've ever broken a law with coming after me. And you." He squeezed his eyes shut and ran a hand over them. "Can I sit, please? I hurt...everywhere. I haven't slept in I don't know how long."

I nodded, love glomming my throat. I helped him to the sun-bleached carpet and sat opposite, waiting for more, my breath coming quick. I took his hand—it was filthy, a little bloody. Hopefully he'd gotten at least one punch on whoever'd beaten him up, probably the blond guy.

He said, "You don't think about leaving the criminal business when you enter it. I guess that's what makes most of us so dumb." His laugh was dry and brittle. "I knew I couldn't implicate any of my accomplices. It's simultaneously dirty and suicidal. So I tried something different, something I hoped was smart.

See, there are quite a few fakes in the museums of the world. Say for example a painting goes out to be cleaned, the art restorer could use some cash, and then someone like me helps to supply a stellar copy, while the real one is sold underground."

"That sounds like the movies!"

"You would know." He flashed his first real smile, and the dimple infused me with an odd sort of comfort. "I decided to go to the museums, anonymously, and tell them I knew which of their pieces were fake."

"Why not the cops?"

"I'll get to that. Some of the museums, big ones, didn't contact me. They thought I was a hoax, I guess, or maybe they'd rather stay ignorant. If the copy fooled them, and they're never going to sell it, why bother? But quite a few did respond. I told them which pieces were fake, and that I knew the locations of the genuine ones."

"You do?"

He shrugged. "Some, yes. The buyer is the last criminal in the string, you know? I told the museums that if they wanted their real art returned, to put pressure on the authorities and demand they make an immunity deal with me. That way, my function wasn't to put my accomplices away, but to have millions and millions of dollars of art restored to its rightful place, and the buyers would be the ones on the hook."

I sat up straighter. "You didn't care about giving up the buyers?"

"If there weren't buyers, there'd be no theft. I don't steal shit for my health. Besides, the buyers don't know me from Adam. They can't take it out on me, and the Feds will safeguard my anonymity."

"And the government went for this?"

"In the case of several taxpayer-funded museums, yes." He chuckled smugly. "Especially after I said I'd tell the press about the fake stuff sitting in the world's most prestigious museums if they didn't."

I shook my head, flabbergasted. "So...you have an immunity deal?"

He nodded, the ghost of a smile highlighting the tiredness of his face. "Yes, for the United States, the UK, a few other countries. Nobody was happy about it, but the arrests have already started. The thing is" — he leaned forward—"the hardest part was getting everyone to agree that I wouldn't give up any other of the thieves. But the museums were critical to that part, because they wanted their stuff returned. That's why I approached it the way I did. Money is what matters."

I searched his smashed-up face. "And you did all this for me?"

He scratched his head, then sucked in a breath as he found an injured spot. "Yes. And for me. But now..." His eyelids closed. They were dark, and his whole face sagged so much I wanted to weep. "Now I guess word is out that I'm giving up accomplices. Which is bad. Very bad."

"Very bad, like even generally nonviolent Jane wants to get rid of you?"

"Yes."

We sat holding hands for a minute or two. "What do we do about our prisoners out there?"

"Fuck if I know. You—you guys came in here with a plan?"

I grinned, and laughed, my mirth tip-toeing the edge of hysteria. "Yes. At the signal, we decided we'd each attack the thug closest to us, hoping, of course, that there wouldn't be ten of them."

"I can't believe it worked."

I laughed and threw up my hands.

"We've also been audio recording everything since we got on the train in London. Voice-activated, battery-powered flash drives."

"What?"

I pointed to the sloppy, teased-out bun on my head. "My hair is big because it's full of secrets."

"Nice reference."

"Thanks." Even at a time of terror, I can call forth the spirit of *Mean Girls*.

"If you use the recording you will, of course, edit out anything where I definitely didn't admit to any sort of knowledge about..."

"I'll do it if the dimple tells me to."

He smiled and swept me into his arms. It was a beautiful, touching moment, except for his smell, which touched me in a bad way. I pulled away as soon as I could without wounding his pride. "We still haven't solved our Jane problem."

"Uuuggghhhh." He slid down the wall and splayed onto the floor.

"I'll just go check on them."

I went into the other room, where our prisoners were behaving, and Ellen and Nicolette were whispering amongst themselves. And then it hit me, like a flying house in a tornado. "That's it!" I said triumphantly. No one else seemed impressed.

I zipped back into the other room and told Sam my idea. He nodded, obviously so sick and tired that he thought me handling the denouement was a clever idea. I told Ellen and Nicolette, who gave me a proper enthusiastic response.

First thing we did was grab everyone's personal belongings. We got our own phones back, and promptly took pictures of our bad guys huddled together, which made Jane frown like I'd accused her of wearing jewelry from Wal-Mart. She'd been the only one smart enough to not carry any sort of ID on her person. Dina's real name was on her passport, tucked in a backpack, and the blond guy was named Jan de Boer. We took pictures of their identifying information—all three of us, in case one phone got busted or whatnot. Then, we took selfies with everyone in the background. Finally, we announced that the three of us were emailing these pics to different people.

Deliberately, and in front of Jane, I handed Ellen my phone and said, "Jane, please come and speak with us."

She rose from the couch elegantly and followed me into the bedroom, where Sam had propped himself against the wall again. His skin had taken on a horrifying gray cast, and I blazed hot all over. I squeezed my hands into fists, but didn't punch anyone. I was the good guy, dammit.

Sam smiled at Jane and said, "Ain't she something?" while pointing at me. His hand fell limp to the floor. "Please sit. I can't look up at you. Your dude out there is gonna make my chiropractor rich."

"Your dude Jan de Boer," I supplied.

"What do you want to talk about?" Jane got to the point in Jane fashion. She swept to the floor and sat cross-legged, as nimble as I was.

I began. "Jane, Sam has told exactly no authorities about you. So your actions here of planning to murder all of us are premature at best, and super mean at worst. Really!"

Jane sighed.

"Janie, we had a deal, and I've stuck with it." Sam shot her a look so sincere, puppies should take notes.

"That's not what's being said."

"So you just decide to go on a murder spree?" He winced and pushed up straighter. "Shooting an internationally-known movie star is a fabulous idea? How many video recordings exist of Samantha on the train, in the station, all with your stupid Dina out there? You think no one will put that together?"

Jane ground her jaw and snapped, "Movie star?"

"I know, right?" I grinned. "Who'da thunk it? By the way, my agent now has a picture of you with me."

The elegant goddess of a woman uttered a word I never thought would pass her lips. She recovered nimbly into a blank, professional face. "Perhaps I overreacted. But there was an arrest recently—"

"Yes, the arrest of *a customer*," Sam finished. "He probably won't spend a day in prison. The rich rarely do."

"Hm."

"Call your dogs off, Jane, please. I really don't want to see you in jail. And it's not because you'd rat on me, it's because I have genuine respect for you." He leaned forward. "There are plenty of millionaire buyers in the sea. This has to stop, though. Next time you pull shit, we'll sing songs about your misdeeds at trial. I don't suppose you could reassure the rumor mill that I am not a snitch? I'd greatly enjoy not being slaughtered."

She cracked a small smile and nodded. "I'll do my best."

She rose to leave, and I said, "By the way, this entire adventure has been audio recorded for posterity. Have a nice evening."

We let them all go, with protestations from Nicolette duly noted. She and Ellen, armed, promised to follow the baddies back to the train station and watch them get on trains headed out of the country. This left me and Sam alone in the romantic, medieval city of Bruges. "I want to fall over and die," groaned my dreamy lover.

"No dying, but our hotel is somewhere in the old part of the city. I'll let you collapse once we get there."

He agreed with a grunt. I mapped the address on my phone, and we happened to be only a few blocks away. I wondered what the ancient denizens of this city would think about my magic pocket-sized device that called forth any piece of information. They'd burn me as a witch. And all my roles in plays would have been portrayed by dudes. Nope, modern-day miracles were a blessing. Birth control separates us from the primates.

I half-carried him out, but after a few minutes of my groaning and sweating, he limped on his own while complaining about dating such a shorty. The quaint hotel Ellen had booked soon appeared.

The manager was not pleased to behold Sam in his bloody glory. We were shooed out of the lobby and into the tiny, two-person elevator to our floor. Rustic charm and a big, soft bed greeted us, and Sam fell into it immediately. Well, onto it. I had to move him onto one half with a series of butt pinches, and finally just plain ass slaps until he shifted sufficiently to give me room. So tired was I that I didn't even mind his stench. Adventure movies never mention the body odor, but Indiana Jones' manly pit stains come with a terrible price, and I don't mean Nazis.

* * * *

I awoke the next morning to find Sam sitting on the small balcony adjoining our room. He'd showered and looked adorable, except for the rainbow of bruising on his face, some of which had begun to turn green, and his clothes, all of which were unfit even for rags. I offered to go out for coffee, which he accepted with more joy than he'd displayed when seeing me. But who could blame him? There were some days I'd probably kick my mother for coffee, but then I'd have to hear about how my kicking was weak, and if I just went to the gym once in a while, I'd be married.

Coffee and some truly amazing chocolate pastry in hand, I joined him on the deck. His aura had such a tint of doom to it, I just sat there inhaling chocolate and awaiting the downpour.

"Is someone watching Captain Taco?"

"No, I left him to starve because that's the kind of person I am."

"Funny. They pay you to do comedy, right?"

His sourness rubbed off on me like cheap shoe dye. "I made quick friends with my neighbor and asked her to look in. Hopefully she's not a thief. Har de har."

He took a too-fast drink of coffee and hissed when he burned himself. After a moment, he said, quietly, "You should keep him."

"I am keeping him. I have been..." My heart doubled its speed as it began to take in the meaning of what he said before my brain did.

"I'm breaking up with you." He refused to look at me, but focused on the orange tiled roofs shining in the sunlight of Bruges. What a perfect day to be let go.

He actually managed to ruin chocolate, damn him. I set my breakfast aside and said, "I thought I dumped you in London."

"No, you didn't."

"Yes, I did."

"Dammit!" He turned fully toward me. "This isn't a joke. Jane was the nicest person I ever worked for. If she's gunning for me, then..." He let it dangle, the horrible end to that sentence. I pictured him running through the streets, a mob of lowlifes chasing behind with torches and pitchforks.

I stood, the better to yell at him. "A couple of days ago, you said you loved me too much to be noble. Or was that a lie? Or, are you too noble to lie, and that's why you're dumping me, because you used to be a liar? Ugh!" I kicked the metal railing, but I didn't have any shoes on, and my toe screamed in pain. I fell back onto my chair and held my foot. At least I could be dignified when my world was crumbling. "Fuck everything! I just want to be a normal couple who watches TV in Snuggies and has weekday sex and argues about who has to clean the litter box! Which should be you, because you're obviously related to poop."

He laughed. I said a bad word and stomped inside the room to repack my overnight bag. Dump me? Doesn't he know who I am? I'm a middling actress who's dieting all the time! And why the fuck can't I get Pizza Rolls in Belgium? Stupid jackass!

Sam tiptoed in from the balcony. I threw a pillow at him. He ducked, but not fast enough, and it bounced off his ugly, fart face head. "I'm doing this for you," he explained feebly. "I'm trying to do the right damn thing for once. We've gotten so lucky, ducking my enemies. But this has to be the last time. I can't put you in danger anymore. Besides—why are you even mad if you thought you'd dumped me?"

"Because I love you! I was content with lorvst and casual sex, but then you crept in my brain and made me want things I can't have!" My face overheated, like a car sitting in the Florida sun. "You gave me a cat, you bastard."

"Samantha, I'm sorry—"

"No! Don't you dare mush out on me. I wanna fight. I want to be mad! I want to be angry at you and your asshole thief buddies. I want to be furious at—at—everything! So call me a name or shut the fuck up!"

His face crumpled piteously. "I don't—"

"Gaaaaaaahh!" I threw my bag to the floor and slammed my hands on my hips. "I put on cute underwear for this rescue. I had plans for us! Do you see?" I stretched out the neck of my black T-shirt to show him a lacy red bra. "I was hopeful. I leaped into the fray for you, in pretty lingerie, and I demand that you drool over this underwear." Suddenly, I desperately needed a screw. A breakup screw.

"Baby—"

"Now. And don't you 'baby' me. *I* have been *dumped* by the *criminal*." I said 'I', 'dumped' and 'criminal' with such outrage I actually spat them. Was it backwards day? I wiped the spittle off my chin.

"*The criminal*? Nice. I've always been on the lower rung of this relationship, haven't I?"

"Oh, what a marvelous martyr you are." I scanned the room for anything I'd forgotten. "I don't want any tender bullshit from you anyway. What's the fucking point?" I would not cry.

I would *not* cry.

I shrugged and said, in a delightfully mild tone, "Fine. I'll just go back to London and bang the first movie star I see."

That made him mad. The parts of his face that weren't beaten up turned red. "This is mean. You're being so mean." His voice broke, and he suddenly sounded like a little kid.

I steeled my heart. "Then it's good you're getting rid of me."

I finished shoving my stuff into my bag and began stomping around to find my purse. His voice was pathetic and small when he said, "I didn't want to part badly."

My turn to guffaw. "How else was this going to end? Jesus, and I thought I was the one living in fantasy land." I plopped ten Euros on the nightstand for the maid service. "You know what I won't miss? That stupid dimple. You only have one—what is that? You're lopsided!"

He growled, actually growled, and returned, "I won't miss your temper. I won't miss your compunction for hitting me."

Good. Now we were really fighting. I wanted a cage. I wanted a net and a trident, *Star Trek*-style, with dramatic violins shrieking my heartbreak, because it couldn't just be over because we said so in a no-name hotel on a beautiful day. At least we were in Europe. Breakups in LA happened over vegan fro-yo, which is wrong on so many levels.

I took a step toward him. "I won't miss your being pissy in the morning. Like this morning. I bet Daniel Zhang is pleasant first thing in the morning—he's such a gentleman. Maybe I'll find out."

He didn't take the bait, but stayed where he was. God, what did a girl have to do to get some breakup nookie? My desperation for one last bite of him nearly yanked a scream of frustration from my bowels. I clenched my teeth to rein it in.

He snapped, "I won't miss your friend bad-mouthing me at every turn."

"Aw, did mean old Ellen hurt you in your fee-fees?"

He kicked the pillow I'd launched at him and crossed toward me, steam practically coming out his ears. "Do you think this is easy for me?"

"I don't care! Why did you even bother with me? This could have been a fling that hurt no one!"

"No, it couldn't!" He swept into the last few inches between us. "You stomped on my heart the minute I met you."

"The minute you manipulated me to steal that Godforsaken Picasso, you mean."

"Stop putting words in my mouth!"

"You're a fake and a phony, and I wish I'd never laid eyes on you!"

His lips flapped for a moment, outrage momentarily freezing his vocal chords. "That's a line from *Grease!*" He shoved a finger in my face. "Which I only know because I watched Olivia Newton-John movies with you because I was a good boyfriend."

"Oh, yeah. The two days a month we spent together were some real quality time. I saw the McDonald's drive-thru more often than I saw you."

"If I were a Big Mac, you'd never dump me."

"You. Dumped. Me!" I turned to leave the room, and he caught my arm. And finally, finally he kissed me. I held on so tight I probably hurt him, but then I wanted to, and I didn't. I just needed to feel his lips and never stop. To taste his sweet breath consuming mine. We were practically snarling at each other, biting and kissing, tossing away clothes and shoving aside the covers on the bed.

He crawled backward across the bed, challenge in his gaze, which splintered into olive green shards, ready to destroy me. When I began to climb on top, he hauled me the rest of the way across his chest. He buried his hands in my hair and kissed me with such fervor, it was almost as if he didn't want to take in air that wasn't mixed with mine. I had no need for foreign air. I'd get a lifetime of that when he left me.

I got on my knees to the side of him and took his cock in my hand. He groaned and sagged back, his eyes squeezed shut. His flesh was hot, and he pumped his hips, using me as leverage. My heart swelled with pain at his lovely body—the subtle swells of his chest, the cords of his neck, his hand clutching at my thigh. I'd never known a lover who'd filled my heart with such beauty, who'd made me feel so beautiful. Perhaps it was the combination of us that perfected us.

"Don't you do that," he said, sitting up. He lunged across me, and I fell onto the mattress as he covered me. "Don't turn soft now, or I won't give you what you want." His hand snaked up to hold my breast, then down to trace my waist, cup my ass and flick between my legs. He swatted my thighs away from one another and settled his fingers in my pussy, playing there, in, out, tracing every millimeter of me. The soft, wet caresses were maddening. I held his hand there so he wouldn't stop.

While he teased me, mercilessly, delightfully, he worshiped my breasts. He danced across each nipple, seducing each one with licks, whispers, making me arch up for more…then switching to the other one. Frustration twisted my hips and tossed my head. He seemed to enjoy my suffering, a damnable, evil smile adorning his face—the dimple commanding one final performance to punish me.

"Do it," I begged him. He pushed a finger inside me, maybe two, for he stretched my flesh, and the pressure…the maddening slide, oh, God, this man. I would have agreed to anything then, and I pressed my lips together to the point of pain to stop myself from begging him for the table scraps of his time, no matter how dangerous. I actually laughed, I was so pathetic, my need for his skin and his cock beyond all pride. I fucked his fingers, pushing them in deeper. This seemed to rip the resolve to torture me from him, because he only thrust his fingers once or twice more before he replaced them with his rock-hard dick.

He moved into me, until he could go no farther, and stopped there, his breath held and his mouth falling open to moan. The breathy little sex sound was too much for me—him moaning because of me always broke my good sense. I arched up to meet that dirty, open mouth with my own and kissed him. I traced the inside of his lips with my tongue and he made the sound again. The delicious smell of his flesh consumed my senses, and I bucked against his hips.

With slow, lingering thrusts he made love to me. I lost sense of time while we drank in each other's bodies like an illicit drug. I traced every inch of him I could reach—I needed my hands to remember him. The mole on his right hip. The silk of the hair on his thighs. The pressure built and built in me, but when I was close to climax, he'd pull back, stop, plant kisses on my temple and laugh in my ear.

Oh, he gave me what I asked for, all right. On and on, until I couldn't have recited my name if asked. The room warmed with the coming of the day, and made us even more fevered.

I rolled us over so I could look at him while I rode him. His hair rumpled everywhere—I'd done that. He smiled up at me with a face so full of love I couldn't take it anymore. I lowered myself on him, and he held me close, hand across my back and cupping my ass when I came in an explosion that short-circuited my entire body.

He turned me over and stayed close to me for the delicious minutes he continued moving inside me until he, too, succumbed. He looked so beautiful in his ecstasy, I had to close my eyes.

I held his head, and his back, and his shoulders. He smelled of sex and man, and I never wanted to move away. I hated him just then, because I loved him so much. You dream of love from the time you understand what it is, not knowing what it is to have your heart ripped out whole when it's gone.

Blinking the tears away, I gently moved him, got up and put my clothes back on. I couldn't look at him.

God, I really had been mean to him. He wouldn't miss my nasty streak.

He didn't stir on the bed at all while I got my stuff together. At the door, I said, "Bye, Sam." He sat up, but I couldn't meet his eyes. I walked out the door and closed it behind me.

My emotions were threatening a full-scale revolt, but I couldn't remember what room Ellen and Nicolette were in. With shaking hands, I dialed Ellen's number from my cell. The moment she heard me, she told me her room number, and I ran there on stumbling feet. I made it to the hall outside their door before I fell on the carpet and sobbed. My best friend opened the door, and I heard Nicolette call from inside, "Did she dump him?"

Ha. Nope. He'd done the right thing for the both of us, the rotten, no-good bastard.

* * * *

Nurse Ellen knows how to treat any illness of mine. She whisked me and Nicolette to the town's picturesque Market Square, where an outside café supplied us with coffee and waffles. Belgian waffles, naturally, and eaten traditionally without syrup. The delicacy was so buttery and rich and perfect that I almost forgot about Sam's perfect, if not buttery, skin. The jaunty sunlight reflecting off the medieval splendor shined a harsh light on the dark state of my soul. Would that it were raining on my head, the way it rained in my heart. I told Ellen this, and she took my waffle away from me until I promised to be less Taylor Swift-y.

I recounted the story of how he'd been noble and let me go. How we'd had a dignified discussion, like adults, then I'd packed my bag and sailed out of the room, head held high, dignity intact. Grace-Kelly-like, actually, except with hair a fiery red not found in nature.

"You mean," Ellen said, "after you banged him."

I swallowed the last of my waffle and searched for the waiter. Circumstances called for a second waffle, and for the cute waiter who supplied such. "After...I banged him. How did you know?"

"You have sex hair."

My hand flew to the knotted mass at the back of my head. Between my slept-in clothes, streaked makeup and matted hair, I appeared to be stuck in the 'before' part of a romantic comedy. But there'd be no LOL-worthy 'after', because my hero had kicked me to the Belgian curb to wallow in my own dejection. And *after* I'd rescued his sorry ass! My neck still hurt from head-butting that giant blond guy. How do you explain that to the doctor?

"Why did you even want to have sex after he dumped you?" Nicolette asked.

"Sometimes a girl just needs the D, okay?" I swiped a fresh tear away and looked from one to the other of them. "Or the V. I mean, don't you ever think to yourself, in times of trouble, like, wow, I really need some succulent lady flower right now?"

Nicolette quirked an eyebrow. "No. Literally no one in the world has ever thought those words to themselves."

Ellen put her hand over her mouth, but her shaking shoulders gave away her laughing.

I burst out laughing, too, and more tears plopped onto my plate even as I chuckled. "Y'all don't call them 'lady flowers'?"

Nicolette broke down and smiled at me. "I prefer 'magic beaver', myself."

"There is no kind of magic beaver I don't like," Ellen agreed.

"Seriously, though..." I grabbed the nearest hand of each of them and said, "Thank you for helping me rescue him. You put yourselves in danger to save someone you don't even like." I swiped a tear away and turned to Nicolette. "And you compromised your morals to assist and let him escape, although he says he's been pardoned by the US." I'd told them everything, of course.

"We didn't do it for him." Ellen handed me a napkin for my mess of a face. I'd given up and offered myself over to the rain of sorrows turning me into a puffy depression monster.

Nicolette said, "That's what friends do."

"Are we friends?" I ended the question in a squeak, so overjoyed I was to hear her say it.

"Ugh, not if you're going to keep crying on my hand. Stop that!" She snatched her arm away, but came right back again to pat mine. "I guess you're okay. But no more of this putting her in danger." Inclining her head toward Ellen, she continued, "I do like roller skating with y'all. You nerds know how to party, in kind of a sad way."

They managed to put a smile on my face, one I bravely tried to keep up as we walked around the pretty brick and stone town. The most photographed place in Europe contained a bridge, a canal and a beautiful tree gently bowing to the sparkling water. They called it the Quay of the Rosary. It was the sort of place a couple ought to take their picture to frame. I couldn't even act myself into a decent photograph, so Ellen kicked me out of the shot and I acted as photographer for my friends.

Bruges held a preponderance of chocolate and lingerie shops. Not together, although we did purchase the chocolate boobs we found, because, like, duh. Both the candy and the underwear made me think of Sam—licking dribbled chocolate off my boobs was an activity that happened shockingly often, as he had a love for licking and boobs, and I had a love for inhaling yummies sloppily. Soon my moping got the better of my fellow tourists—we gave up and took a cab to the train station.

I stayed quiet on the return trip to London, knowing that my mouth couldn't help but ruin everyone's good time. Ellen even offered to find us a roller rink in London to cheer me, but I declined and sent them on their way to have fun. I was a soul-sucking vortex of ickiness, bound and determined to find the worst in everything. Everything but food. Me and my two dinners had a lovely night—and by lovely, I mean lugubrious.

Chapter Seven

So Many Men, So Few Brains

Ext. Hollywood Boulevard – day
The year is 2017, and the earth has been conquered by the zombiefied undead, woken from their slumber because they drank too many diet drinks. Yes, that fake sugar was as bad as your annoying health-nut friends thought. Even so, no one who's left really wants to hear their yapping on about freaking kale or whatever.

Angle On: Samantha Lytton *is one of the few left after the apocalypse. She stands on the wall the survivors have built around the city of Los Angeles. The divide is made of old set pieces from zombie movies, although the irony is lost on almost everyone because this is LA.*

Angle On: Samantha lifts binoculars to her face and peers across the desolate landscape of a broken city. Dating in this place was a disaster even before all the cute boys wanted to dine on your brains. As always, she is on the lookout for a male survivor who enjoys long walks on the radioactive beach and talking about feelings until one or the other of you dies from malnutrition, only to return and slaughter the other one. You know, kinda like relationships in the old days.

Cut To: A Studly Stranger stumbles across the desert that used to be Hollywood Boulevard. He is stopped by a zombie wearing a dirty Spiderman costume, but the lone wanderer doesn't have a buck to pay Spidey for a picture, so the zombie gets pissy and huffs away.

Cut To: Samantha, hopeful that this stranger isn't a zombie, and that he might enjoy her rom-com antics. Her brow creases in worry, for her constant tripping, adorkableness and hilarious bad hair days have not been appreciated in all this time. Plus, damn, sometimes a girl just needs the D!

Samantha Lytton: Will my loneliness last forever? Shall I just accept my hapless fate and become a zombie? Maybe they have sex before they eat each other, like praying mantises...

The newcomer approaches the wall, but keeps his distance.

Studly Stranger: Are you a zombie? Blink once for yes, and twice for no!

Samantha Lytton: I could just say, "Hello," since zombies can't offer much beyond a grunt.

Studly Stranger: I've been searching for the living for months now! How strange to find them in Los Angeles.

Samantha Lytton: Our gym-going prepped us for the endless days of running in terror.

Samantha whips out a clipboard and pen.

Samantha Lytton: I'm just going to have to ask you a few questions before we let you in the great wall here... Okay, how old are you?

Studly Stranger: Thirty-eight.

Samantha Lytton: Ooh, that's good! There are way too many teenagers in here. And are you straight, gay, queer, pansexual, bi, trans, asexual, poly-amorous or prefer not to say?

Studly Stranger: Why...why does that matter? I haven't eaten in three days! Please help me.

Samantha Lytton: Question three. Have you ever been convicted of a crime? This one is super important.

Studly Stranger: No! I'm no danger to your town. I'm a refugee from Vegas—that city has been completely destroyed by the zombies. It's hard to tell, though, because they just sit at the gambling tables all day.

Samantha Lytton: Yay! No criminal record. Do you prefer short women, tall or in-between? FYI, the answer I'm looking for is 'short'.

The stranger falls to his knees, barely able to continue on.

Studly Stranger: Short, yes—I prefer whatever you want me to prefer. Why won't you help me?

Samantha Lytton: I'm sorry, but I'm a crazed heroine in a romantic comedy. All I care about is dating—no matter what! Now, on to question five...although I have taken off points because you haven't answered some of my other ones. You're not helping your situation. I mean, you seem to be straight, because gay men in rom-coms are always snapping and giving fashion advice, but you could be pansexual, or—

Samantha refers to her clipboard.

Samantha Lytton: Oh, wait, no you can't be—that sort of multifaceted characterization isn't allowed in

LA. Question five. How do you feel about Valentine's Day, the most important holiday of the year?

Studly Stranger: My vision is fading. I'm so...so cold.

Angle On: The studly stranger falls over sideways into the dust. A zombie limps across the landscape and preys upon him.

Angle On: Samantha sighs and rips the sheet off her clipboard.

Samantha Lytton: Why is it so hard to find a decent man?

I spent the day following our return from Bruges in bed, inhaling macaroni and cheese, staring into space, feeling too zombiefied to even be comforted by Colin Firth.

Plus, I started my period, because God is a *hilarious* dude. While my uterus tried to claw her way through my belly button, I pressed my heating pad on my abdomen and gave myself over to the Break-Up Wallows. Every hour or so, the BUWs would be accompanied by the FASs, a.k.a. the Forever Alone Sobs. To round out the day, I experienced the I Hate My Fucking Ovaries Stabs of Pain.

But for the first time in my life, even though my romantic outlook was as desolate as a post-apocalyptic landscape, my professional life was still the stuff of dreams. Tomorrow, I'd go back into a couple of days of rehearsals, followed by the switch to nights for the actual shoot. My job still filled me with joy, and what a balm it was. My heart had been kicked around my rib cage by steel-toed boots, but I yet possessed a reason to get up in the morning.

I'd never experienced both the unbelievable grief of losing the love of my life and the unsurpassed joy of my ultimate career. Maybe you can't have it all, but having something was better than nothing. I was still an insanely lucky woman, and, in my better moments, I held onto that. In my worse moments, I screamed, cried and wrote embarrassing poetry.

I gave myself the day—one day to be greasy and so pathetic that even my cat pitied me enough to stick close by for pettings and desperate hugs—and the following morning I showered, put on makeup and blow-dried my hair like an actual adult. I slipped on some stretchy jeans and a long, loose T, for while I was a fabulous actress ready to do fabulous acting, I still suffered from the IHMFOSoP.

Often I'd entertained the notion that God or the Being or whomever was a woman, but in times of excruciating period pain, I figured that no female deity would have designed so faulty a plumbing system.

Yet another reason to shake my fist at males.

Although bleeding for seven days and emerging victorious was a badass thing to do.

The next few days were fun as the cast began to gel and riff off one another during rehearsal. I allotted myself time to grieve Sam and worry about him, out there, hounded by the Ghosts of Criminality Past, but I kept my emotions separated from Competent Samantha, who kicked butt at acting.

On the warmish evening before the shoot would start, Danny came over to my rental apartment to chat through our characters, and to rehearse our scenes in a relaxed way. This was a professional meeting, so I wore a dress that revealed only half my cleavage.

The premise of the film was that a group of poor, down-on-their-luck work colleagues from a failing company decided to commit a robbery. They had pretty much nothing to lose — Danny and I played a divorced couple drowning in debt, and the others in the den of unprofessional bandits included a father who needed money to put his four kids through college, a computer geek — a *lady* computer geek, thank you — who wanted a challenge and a woman who must pay for senior care for her mother and father, as well as keep a roof over everyone's heads.

Feelings came to me easily while we rehearsed, but fear gnawed at me that I wasn't being terribly funny. I took a deep breath and dove into the scene we'd gotten to, in which the repressed lust between the ex-spouses came to a boil. The plan was for the thieves to wait in a closet tucked away in the public part of the museum, a place they'd observed to be unused most of the time. Then, once the place closed, everyone would emerge from hiding and rob the joint. I'd wanted to ask Sam about the feasibility of this plan, but I'd forgotten in our most recent kidnapping. Oh, well. Nothing in the media was realistic, just made up by a bunch of dorks in sweatpants pounding on computers, and thank goodness for it.

"You're far away tonight," Daniel said, whipping my brain back to the present.

I tried to laugh it off, but my smile was as tired as a mother taking six kids to Disney. "Sorry. I—" While I struggled to concoct a feasible lie, the truth spilled from my mouth like a too-big pile of spaghetti. "I broke up with my boyfriend and everything sucks!"

Oh, good. I was now crying in front of him. The lump in my chest tightened and squeezed. It took me a moment to control my halted breathing and to stop the faucet raining on my face. I needed to take Successful Human Being classes, because everything I did was the opposite of whatever they'd teach.

He scooched closer on the couch and put a warm arm around my shoulders. "I'm sorry. That's the worst." Rubbing my arm in a manner that made me think ungentlewomanly thoughts, he continued, "This man clearly doesn't deserve you."

"Nope, I'm perfect and amazing." I blew my nose and tossed the tissue in the waste basket I'd moved into the living room for this express purpose. I had emptied it of four hundred snotty tissues and three empty Cheez-It boxes before he came over because I'm not a sad person.

The concern creasing his handsome face touched me emotionally, and also dirtily. "Would you like to talk about it?" he asked.

I did actually crack up at that. Oh, yeah—I'm sure a mega-movie star wanted to hear about my feeeeeeeeelings. "No, that's okay. Thanks for the offer, but I'm doing you a favor by declining. I have a bottle of vodka that's serving as my therapist."

He blinked his brown eyes at that one. Guess he was too together to ever consult with Doctors Grey and Goose.

I blurted, "Let's rehearse. Work is a fantastic remedy for all ills."

He gave me one more arm squeeze and turned to his script. Oh, but I was a nasty whorish slut lady, ready to jump guy number two's bones immediately after guy number one had dumped me.

Hold up, though…

I'd been dumped.

Me equals dumpee.

Moi was the wronged party in the first degree.

That surely negated the Rule of Respectable Waiting Time Before Banging a New Dude, right? And what of my Overwhelming Urge to Screw Now That I Don't Have a Designated Penis Handy? It was like drooling over a potato on the first day of a low-carb diet. These urges could not be ignored—I might rupture my clit or something. I had my health to think of!

My real smile shined through the confusion in my psyche. I too grabbed my script, even though I'd memorized the dialog. My hands needed something to occupy them, as adorable Danny did not yet realize that he was going to be my super-hot rebound lovah. I would boink him on behalf of dumpees everywhere, and they'd probably erect a sculpture in my honor.

Ha! *Someone* would be erect, *bom chicka bow wow*.

"What are you laughing at?" asked innocent Danny innocently.

"You'll find out later."

Oops—that sounded entirely too seductive. I needed to be smooth and cool, like a cigarette marketed to ladies. "Shall we begin on page seventy-two?"

He nodded and swallowed. His casual outfit of a cashmere sweater and jeans made my dirty thoughts sweat. I angled my knees toward his until all four bumped in a sensual collision. Without looking at the page, I said my line. "This was the worst idea you ever had, and I'm including the day you asked me to marry you."

"Really? I counted my worst idea as the day I met you."

"I count my worst idea as...you...also!"

"Say it a little louder, Jayde—we're not in prison yet." Danny leaned forward, in full fight mode now. His intensity robbed me of my breath. Or maybe I was just panting for fun. "But it is lovely to be reminded how everything in the world is my fault. I really missed that since our divorce."

"Oh, don't worry—I've blamed you for plenty since then."

Danny broke character and laughed. I smiled, flattered, and flipped my hair. "A little professionalism, please?"

"So terribly sorry." He purred it in his accent, which made my dial go to eleven.

"Harrumph." My mouth said 'harrumph', but my hips said 'hump'. I leaned in closer. What? It was in the script! I continued the scene. "If we go down for this, I'm putting it squarely on your head. Your failed business is the reason we have no money to begin with, and then your only solution to our money woes is to rob the most famous museum in the world."

He grabbed my forearm and yanked me until we were only inches apart. His warm breath spilled across my mouth like a Caribbean breeze—the kind that makes you want to strip off your clothes and skinny dip. "I did everything possible for us! As if anyone could make you do something you don't want to do."

"I didn't want to end up penniless, thirty-five and divorced—but it still happened!"

"I worked hard."

"So did I."

"Well, sometimes things just happen."

"I know that!"

"Then why did you leave me?"

I gasped and sat back. My heart leaped from its perch on my sleeve and wedged itself in my throat. This hit me much too close to home. I said, softly, "You didn't seem to want me there anymore."

Pain and regret creased his forehead and tugged at his mouth. Damn, he was a great actor. "I couldn't stand watching you wallow in stress and disappointment. I thought you'd be better off without me."

I set my script down, the better to fight properly. "I never said that, Chase."

"You didn't have to."

I sagged backward, letting my character's tense frustration and head-splitting confusion flow through me. This part of the job seemed like magic sometimes — stepping into another skin, putting your own emotions on an overlay with theirs. Experiences may be different, but humanity is universal. We all know what loss is, and I'd been having a brutal affair with the feeling as of late. The painful helplessness of ugly circumstances flowed through my veins as steadily as blood. I continued quietly, "So that's why we divorced? Because you thought I wanted it? I thought you were eager to be rid of me, the five-foot anchor weighing you down."

"Who knew anchors could be so noisy?"

"Who knew men could be so...so..."

"Handsome, sexy..."

"Arrogant, deluded..."

"Awesome, good at football..."

"Argh!" I threw my hands up, inspired by the smug look sliming across Danny's face. "Why didn't you ever talk to me about what you were feeling?"

"Because we were better when we weren't talking." His stopped short, and his eyebrows rose. This was the point in the script in which he was supposed to pull me into his rugged arms and kiss the bejesus out of me.

The new spark in his eye told me he'd broken character, wondering what to do next. He grinned and looked at the coffee table. I should have been roiling in embarrassment—I'd never really been in a romantic role that required this sort of thing—but he'd done it lots of times. His shyness made him all the more attractive. Sam's face swam in my head, but I took a firm hand and squished it somewhere between memories of having the flu and being yelled at by my mother, then piled it under some traumatic events from eighth grade for good measure.

"I guess we shouldn't rehearse any further," I said with a coyness so faux it was practically screaming "liar, liar, pants on fire." My pants were on fire, and Danny was the hunky fireman sent to rescue me.

"Let's save the awkwardness until we're in front of fifty people." He leaned forward and squeezed my knee. I stared at his hand. He stared at his hand. The cat stared at his hand. "I'm so terribly sorry." Danny snatched his wandering digits back while I made "it's okay" noises.

But it wasn't okay—the squeeze should have been at least ten inches higher on my thigh.

I sighed and accepted my fate as a lonely spinster lady. I already owned a cat, so check mark in that box. Did they carry boxed wine in England?

We began the scene again, this time standing, my mind a whirlwind of unanswered questions. Had Sam and I really talked it out completely? Were there feelings he'd hidden from me on purpose? Perhaps he hadn't seen a clear path for us, so he'd chosen no path at all. Everyone chooses the easier, less painful road sometimes. Cowardice or self-preservation—the line is a fine one. The thought made me heartsick. My stomach curdled like bad milk.

I dove into the scene with a fresh sympathy for both — fictitious — parties. Danny and I fought with the bitterness of seasoned lovers used to whipping out their baggage and boarding the train to Blametown at a moment's notice.

"Arrogant, deluded..."

"Awesome, good at football..."

The intensity grew, swirling around a point no one was quite sure how to find. The anger in his face rendered it all the more sharp and painfully handsome. His brown eyes almost pierced through me, searching for more than I was ready to show. Searching for more than my *character* was ready to show, I mean.

I took a step to him without thinking first. He followed suit. "Why didn't you ever talk to me about what you were feeling?"

"Because we were better when we weren't talking!" He grabbed me by both arms and pulled me close. I held my breath. His mouth opened and he leaned down to close the space between us, fast. An inch away from me, he halted and a furrow creased his brow. I laughed a little, barely above a whisper, disappointed and glad both that he'd stopped what he was about to do. He flicked up to gaze into my eyes. My anxious smile widened. His lips softened into amusement, a *what the hell?* sort of smirk.

He kissed me.

I wasn't at all prepared for it. I'd never dreamed he'd actually do it. Who the hell was I, anyhow? Nobody from nowhere! I thought of Sam, of guilt, of obligation, of professionalism. Finally, I thought, *Samantha, you are the biggest idiot in the entire freaking universe.* A hunky movie star is laying a fantastic liplock on you. Kiss him back — for America!

Danny was clearly talented at this kissing thing, as he'd been schooled by dozens of beautiful actresses — at the least. And he'd obviously taken his sexy training as seriously as his acting training, for his mouth played warm, firm yet soft, and definitely tried to coax mine into naughtiness. I wound my arms around his neck. His body felt solid and muscly, his hips angling against me in a slow, rhythmic way that made certain of my places respond as if we were already naked.

His hands crept to my waist and pulled me closer, if that was possible. He abandoned my mouth to kiss my neck, and I whimpered my approval.

My constant state of befuddlement broke through the haze of sex, and I put my hands to his shoulders to push him away gently. He took the cue, ever the gentleman, and eased his lock on all my throbbing areas. His eyes registered the same conflict that I'm certain was reflected in mine, but before I spoke, a knock sounded on the door.

Sam!

Who else could it be? I stepped back from Danny like he was on fire and nearly somersaulted backward over the coffee table. He caught me with a laugh that only mocked me a wee bit. "Thanks," I said. "I have no idea who that is."

"Our savior, I expect. I'm sorry."

"No, don't be. You're quite sexy." He grinned. "I mean…oh, whatever."

"Please stop being so appealing. I obviously can't control myself."

God, this guy really was trying to melt my brain, wasn't he? What even was my life right now? Two different sexy men…international jet-setting…people paying me actual money to do what I enjoyed… I wasn't prepared for this. I needed a pamphlet from my guidance counselor entitled *So You're Not a Loser Anymore.*

He gathered up his things and said, "I think perhaps we have the conflicted ex-lovers aspect of the film settled."

I laughed. "Yuppers."

The door-knock thudded again.

"Have a good evening, Samantha." He hurried to the door, then turned with his hand on the knob. "Are you certain I haven't offended you? I shouldn't have kissed you."

"I didn't exactly shove you off." I walked to him and gave him an arm squeeze. "We just got caught up in the moment. That's what they pay us for."

His eyebrows jumped to attention. "*That's* what they pay us for?"

"Oh, be quiet and go away!"

He smiled, thank goodness, and gave a gallant bow before opening the door. My muscles clenched, terrified of what Sam would say to being greeted by Daniel Zhang at his ex's place at night.

But it wasn't Sam. A woman I'd never met before filled the doorway. "Samantha!" the tall, lovely chestnut-haired woman said. "It's been too long!" Too long? Yes, I guess 'forever' is too long. She breezed into my place, and Danny waved before disappearing down the hallway.

Leaving my door open, I followed the crazy lady a few steps. "I don't know who you are."

"No" — she plopped onto the couch — "but we have mutual friends." Her accent sounded like one of those generally-European jobs, at least to my ignorant Yankee ear, and she wore what appeared to be a vintage 1950s dress of mustard silk, an expensive one.

My eyes darted until I found my cell phone. I needed to call nine-one-one. Or the British equivalent. Dammit, jet-setting was hard.

I grabbed the phone and pointed it like a weapon. "I'm calling the cops unless you leave." Perhaps in a different life, I might have given a strange lady in my apartment the benefit of the doubt, but nowadays it seemed smarter to jump straight to "Ack, she's trying to kill me!" mode.

"You're not calling the police. Is she, Sam?"

Her eyes shot to the front door, where he stood, easy as you please, his hands in his pockets. The bastard smiled at me and closed my only means of escape behind him.

Just when I thought I was out…they pulled me back in.

Chapter Eight

The Word 'Breakup' Is Not Meant to Be Literal

A vortex opened beneath me, and it sucked my soul into the depths of hell and also made my tummy hurt. Here we go again—I fell down the rabbit hole so often I needed to take out a time share with the Mad Hatter.

"Okay, Sam...strange lady who probably wants to do me harm...out with it. No flamboyance, no niceties. Just go ahead and threaten me, please." I slunk into the armchair and crossed my arms, waiting.

"Was that Daniel Zhang?" Interloper Lady asked.

"Yes."

Sam finally said something. "Why was he here?"

"Because how else am I to screw him?" I delivered this lie with a shining smile. He heard it with tight lips and flared nostrils. Ha!

Interloper leaned back on the sofa, holding court. "Oooh, I like her, Sam."

I said nothing more. At least Daniel had gotten a look at her. He'd tell the police about her after I disappeared.

"I'm Valerie. I'm an old...friend of Sam's. And a current one!" She laughed after this—a musical sound in the key of villainess.

"That was fast," I said to Sam.

"I could say the same."

Poor man—he sounded bitter. I smirked viciously and awaited more bombs.

"I want us to be friends, Samantha," said Valerie.

True fact—no one who ever says "I want us to be friends" is a person you should become friends with.

"You know what? No." I stood up. "Fuck your friendship." I turned to Sam. "Fuck you for fucking her, and fuck the both of you for blackmailing me, or whatever it is you're here to do. Just say it, already! Or, or...ne'er darken my doorway again!" Yeah! That was an awesome speech. About my ex betraying me. My heart sank all over again. It wasn't supposed to do that—I'd been riding high on a cocktail of denial and braggadocio.

Valerie crossed her legs and flapped her foot, clad in a stiletto, natch. A pair of back-seam stockings hugged her long, slender calves. I do not have long calves. I have short chicken legs that teeter between 'sorta-slender' and 'robust dock worker'.

"Actresses are so dramatic!" Valerie flapped her bird-like arms in Sam's direction. "Tell her what she's going to help us with, darling."

"I'm gonna get myself a drink." I started for the kitchen.

"I don't think so!"

Sam blocked the way at Valerie's bidding. Damn it! Both the liquor and the long, pointy knives were in the kitchen! I required one, then the other, then the first again.

I shook Sam's hand off me and crossed my arms. He couldn't meet my eye and took a step backward. "You're going to help us steal something from the British Museum."

My heart stopped. When I could find words again, I wiped my sweaty hands on my dress and said, "And why will I do that?"

Valerie laughed and batted her false eyelashes. "Because I'll kill you if you don't."

Finally! A little forthrightness is all I require in a villain. My heart started again, but irregularly in protest, like a fish flopping between my boobs. The knot of fear that had left me after Bruges tightened anew. "You think you can just kill a celebrity"—I shuddered when I said it, okay?—"and no one will notice? I have a movie to film."

"Well, I'm not gonna do it *now*." Her smile never wavered. I believe the phrase 'creepy as fuck' was inspired by her.

"Why are you doing this?" My voice got squeaky, shrill. "And you," I spat 'you' toward Sam as if the word was a venomous spider launching at his head, "you're gonna help her hurt me?"

"No!" He took a step toward me, jerked his head over his shoulder to see Valerie's disapproval and retreated again. "I'm here to help you perform the theft. I'm the expert. You're the way in."

"There are a million things to steal in a million places. Why this museum, with me, right now?"

Valerie shrugged. "I thought you wanted the abridged version?"

"Ugh! I'm getting a drink, whether you want me to or not. Kill me or get the hell out of my way." I shoved past Sam, giving him a solid punch on the shoulder as I whooshed by. Aw, I'd missed hitting him.

Memories... I retraced my steps and smacked him again for old time's sake. And because he'd brought a woman who wanted to kill me to my house. Mostly the latter.

Sam followed me into the kitchen, where I splashed some water on my chest. Another hot flash racked my body. This horrible man was actually sending me into early menopause. At least I wouldn't need the pill anymore. Because I'd be sexless, and also dead.

As soon as we were out of sight, I rounded on him. I slapped him across the face, the sting in my hand infusing me with utter delight.

He ducked down and put his forearms up between us. I pinched him, and, when he recoiled, I kicked him in the shin.

"Stop that!" he gasped.

"Not until I've gotten to your rotten, lying balls!" I readied my knee. He scurried across the floor like a cockroach. I laughed and dove toward the butcher block, full of delightful knives. I didn't really want to cut Sam, but that damn, tall Valerie woman...she could stand to lose a few inches. Up top or below— didn't matter.

"Do you think she won't do what she's threatened?" he said while pressed against the fridge.

"Why are you helping her? How else would she find me?"

He rolled his eyes, which I thought presumptuous, considering the circumstances. "She had you followed, which is not difficult. You're the easiest mark in the world—I've never met anyone who puns so loudly...and so many places..."

"Fuck you." My façade finally broke, and I started to cry. I couldn't find an ounce of energy to care anymore. "This is never gonna work. Why don't the two of you just be done with it? Kill me now. Put me out of my misery."

"No!" He rushed forward and gripped me by the shoulders. "Let me help you, and we'll be fine."

His voice hitched between the words "be" and "fine." That didn't instill confidence. Was my lying liar losing the ability to lie lie-ingly?

I searched his eyes. "*We*? Is she blackmailing you, too?"

"No, of course not. I'm perfectly happy to see you killed."

I shoved him away. "You're perfectly happy to see her banged."

"What?"

"You're banging that evil whore!"

"Are you two talking about little old me?" Valerie's voice sailed in from the other room, light as a feather, stiff as a knife.

A dark cloud rumbled across his face. The dimple hid in shame, nowhere to be found. "You're screwing your co-star. It's been less than a week!"

"And you dumped me. Did you think no one else would want me? I'm short, sexy splendor, asshole, and everybody but you knows it!" I grabbed the entire bottle of Scotch and stomped back into the living room. If ever there was a time to be drunk, this hour, this day, this week was it.

Sam the bastard hadn't even denied taking out the Eurotrash!

"I taught Sam everything he knows," Valerie vamped after I sat back down again.

"I don't need to hear about your sexual exploits." I took a swig of Scotch.

Sam sat beside the ruinous harpy. "She taught me how to *steal things*. A long time ago."

Valerie lovingly caressed his thigh with long, pointy red nails. I drank more Scotch. "I also taught him how to—"

"Okay, here's the plan," Sam said, loudly, pulling his leg away. "I'm your brand new personal assistant. I will accompany you to the set and, with a little preparation and when the time is right, we'll lift the target."

"And what's the target?" I raised the bottle to my lips, but he darted forward and yanked it from my hands.

I shot him a look of pure, stinking, bedbug-filled anger. He smiled and whipped a phone from his pocket. After a moment of poking at the screen, he turned to face to me. "We're stealing the Mold Cape."

Even I had heard of that. I grabbed the phone. "The ancient gold...um, mantle thing?"

He nodded.

My mouth suddenly the Sahara, I gaped at the small picture on the phone. It appeared to be a capelet for the shoulders and bust, but made entirely of gold. The website said that it had been discovered in 1833 in a place called Mold in Wales, hence the name. It dated from somewhere about 1600BC—its value must be incalculable.

They were out of their ever-loving minds.

"How the hell are you gonna sell this?" I asked both of them. "It's one of a kind, and hella famous."

"I already have a buyer." Valerie smiled at me as if I were a simpleton. She was maybe...forty? With the body of a twenty-five-year-old. Not *me* at twenty-five, but someone who'd actually gone to the gym. In a few years, she'd be aggressively reedy and probably so thin it aged her, but for now, gorgeous. She leaned forward on the couch and flipped her blown-out hair over one languid shoulder. "You'll be able to get anywhere in that museum—"

"It doesn't work that way!" I laughed a laugh of pure panic at the idiocy on display. "You think there'll be no security because we're filming? Do you know how many hoops the producers had to jump through to get permissions? How much money the production donated?"

"You are the star. Act like it. I'm not interested in excuses. You get me that cape, or I'll get you." Tee hee hee!

"Why?" I held my breath for a moment to tamp down on the fear threatening to erupt from every pore. "Why me? Why this?"

Valerie laughed and flipped her hair again, this time in Sam's direction. He ducked backward to avoid a fistful of follicles in the mouth. His eyes narrowed in rage for just a second before his face fell into studied lines of neutrality. She said, "Sam wanted to show me his loyalty, and he's happy to use you to do so."

Sam kept his gaze glued to the carpet, but his jaw was working like a hooker on Saturday night. This couldn't be his idea. Likely Valerie had gotten wind of the same spurious rumors about Sam that Jane had heard. But, in a one-up on Jane, Valerie decided she'd use Sam's connection to me to score big before she killed us both.

Because that was the way this misadventure would end, right?

I closed my eyes, so tired the room had begun to spin. Only one thing to do. "Fine. It's not as if I have a choice anyhow." Valerie nodded and grinned at Sam. I took a deep breath. I reached into my pocket, where I'd hidden a paring knife. She was only three steps from me, maybe two if I moved fast. Which I did.

I rushed forward, my knife coming up. She turned too late, but Sam saw me coming. He jumped across her and shoved me backward onto the other end of the couch. "Drop it!" he said, right in my face, his hand squeezing the tendons of my wrist. With a cry of pain, I did as he bade, disappointment rushing with blood through my veins.

"Damn you to hell!" I struggled with him, just needing to lash out at anything or anyone.

Click click.

I was now familiar enough with the sound of a gun being cocked that I froze. Valerie loomed up beside the two of us, the gun pressed against the back of Sam's head. Somehow, that terrified me doubly. The room seemed to go very still.

He smiled at me, small and bitter and chagrined. I held my hands up and said, "Sorry. I'm—okay, you win."

"I always do." She lifted the gun, and Sam scrambled off me. When he sank into the couch, he dimpled up at Valerie, but wiped sweaty hands on his jeans. How in cahoots were they? Was he in danger or not? Perhaps I should request an org chart of the criminal network.

Valerie asked, "When do you start filming?"

"Night after tomorrow."

"Fine. Sam will be in touch." She shoved the gun into her adorable, cherry-print purse. "I'll be watching. If you even begin to approach a cop, and I'm including Nicolette Fitzgerald, it's over."

My head whipped up. She smirked. I should punch myself—how long had I been followed? This threatening business became her. Some goons just came right out and explicitly told you what harm they intended to do you and your loved ones. Valerie simply smiled with perfectly glossed lips and left your imagination to fill in the horrific blanks.

I nodded, not wanting to talk to this person anymore. I couldn't even look at Sam. Whatever tender feelings I'd been nursing about him were smashed, obliterated, withered and many other similar verbs.

"Lay off the booze," Sam advised me, oh so helpfully. I flipped him the bird, which amused Valerie terribly, her laughter tinkling like stale piss all the way out and down the hall.

I leaped up and slammed the door behind them. I locked it, but why, right? Locks were toys to them, a cute distraction on the way to ruining someone's day.

I sank down the door to land hard on my butt. A tear slipped onto my cheek. Not only was I heartsick, now I'd been betrayed and threatened with death as well.

Meeting Sam had led me to this charmed existence of professional success, but I seemed to be paying for the honor over and over again in the worst ways. Did Meryl Streep have to deal with this sort of thing? No one had even asked me if I wanted to make a deal with the devil — somehow I'd put my name in his book without realizing it. I should have gotten to dance naked in the woods first, at the least.

Ellen and Nicolette were set to leave for Paris tomorrow, thank goodness. I felt like I couldn't warn them they were being followed, and no freaking way would I bring them into this morass. Was my phone being monitored? Probably — Sam had done it before. My chest tightened, and I slunk all the way to horizontal to release my fear and anger.

I'd never, ever felt more alone. Hopefully, if I accomplished this ridiculous task, Valerie would only get rid of me.

The bright side was demonstrably dim this time around.

After wallowing for the allotted amount of time, I managed to fire up my laptop—time to learn about the stupid, cursed Mold Cape.

I really have a hate-hate relationship with museums.

Chapter Nine

The Beatings Will Continue Until Morale Improves

Int: A Dark Basement Torture Cell

Angle On: Samantha Lytton, *bound hand and foot to a wooden chair. The dank room reveals no clues as to who her captor is, but it reveals a lot about his/her personality. As in – they watch too many TV crime procedurals. There's a wall covered with her headshots and red string, an unrolled leather pouch filled with knives and other such scary pointy objects and a stair machine.*

Angle On: Samantha rearing back in horror, especially at the exercise equipment.

Samantha Lytton: What sort of monster could conceive of such intricate tortures? Help! Someone, please help me! What is this place? I don't remember auditioning for *Law & Order: SVU*... Hey, maybe I'll get to meet Ice-T...

A faint, musical giggling sounds through the metal door of the basement. Samantha sucks in a breath as she suddenly realizes who has imprisoned her. Valerie the Evil Ex *saunters into the room on her evil ex long legs. She appears fresh as the springtime, while Samantha sniffs and notices that she herself smells like a cow.*

Valerie the Evil Ex: Hi! I'm totally going to hurt you for banging Sam. And also for fun because I'm an evil ex. It's in the book.

Valerie whips out a book — Being a Bitter, Vicious Ex for Dummies. *Samantha pulls against her bindings, but they hold fast, unlike her nerves.*

Samantha Lytton: Help! Heeeeellllppp!

A voice answers through the dark, open door.

Sam: Samantha? Is that you?

Sam dashes into the room and stands between Valerie and Samantha. He places his hands on his hips manfully, and his butt is perkier than a morning TV show host.

Samantha Lytton: I knew you and your wonderful bottom would save me!

Sam crosses to Samantha and strokes her hair. She leans in to his touch, her soul flooded with relief—

Sam: You smell like a farm animal. Valerie, I thought you were going to put those little shocker things on her nipples.
Samantha Lytton: What? No! You adore my boobs.
Sam the Dirtbag: Valerie's are better. They're so…thief-y. I always knew I'd return to the dark side of the Force.

Sam rounds on Samantha.

Sam the Dirtbag: Being good is just too hard—plus, those Jedi robes are scratchy as hell. Who wants to dress like a freaking Jesuit?

Valerie the Evil Ex: Look, Sam—her stupid little feet don't even reach the ground!

Sam the Dirtbag: She's so short is why. Short people are stupid. There's a whole song about it.

Valerie begins singing the mean short people song. Samantha holds her head high. Well, as high as she can.

Sam the Dirtbag: Let's feed her before we electro-shock her.

Sam leaves the room and returns with a take-out container. Samantha's stomach rumbles. A lady of good taste simply can't endure electric nipple clamps on an empty stomach.

Sam the Dirtbag: Here you go, darling.

He opens the box to reveal…

Samantha Lytton: A salad? No!

Sam the Dirtbag: With fat free ranch dressing.

Samantha Lytton: Noooooooooooo! What is the point of that useless crap? Full-fat dairy is my only reason for living, now that you've gone full Darth Vader.

Sam the Dirtbag: I'm not James Earl Jones Vader—I'm the new one. *Hayden Christensen.*

Samantha nearly collapses from the sheer terribleness of it all. Sam and Valerie laugh and laugh, and not in the nice way, but in the way that sounds terribly witchy.

Valerie the Evil Ex: Now we're going to put on clown outfits and have sex in front of you while we force you to exercise. Follow my laser pointer as I demonstrate all the sexual intimacies I taught to Sam.

Samantha finally, mercifully passes out to the sound of Valerie eating the crummy salad.

My brand new assistant Sam greeted me on set the first evening of shooting after a day and a half of sleepless worry and fear. When I did manage to sleep, I dreamt of Valerie and Sam torturing me in the most insidious of ways. I don't know why they always turned into clowns at the end.

I probably didn't want to know why.

Thank goodness there were professionals available to eradicate my puffy eyes and bloom my pallid cheeks. It only pays to look like a zombie if you're playing an actual zombie. And not even then, really, if you're a woman.

"Thanks for getting me on the set," dimpled Sam by way of greeting outside the security trailer. "Remember to call me Zack."

I shrugged and continued inside the museum's employee entrance. "I'm not calling you by yet another name. Why should I make any of this easier for you and *Valerie*?" I said her name like it made me sick. And so it did — my tummy gurgled in protest. I'd been so freaked out that even my favorite comfort, food, proved no help whatsoever. At least I wouldn't bust the seams of my tight costume jumpsuit.

Sam yanked on my upper arm to make me stop walking three steps ahead of him in a lonely, behind-the-scenes corridor. "I have to get to set, *assistant*," I said, frost shooting from my lips.

"None of this was my choice," he said. His face held anguish and, for the briefest of moments, I wanted to run to him and squeeze forever. I took control of myself and removed his grabby hand.

"And yet here we are. Again." I thrust my chin up and said in my haughtiest tone, "If this is to be my last film, I really need some freaking Maybelline. You see, some assturd has threatened my life and betrayed every trust I ever held, so I require the wonders of eyeliner to pretend to be normal."

"I haven't threatened —"

"Samantha!" Around the corner came Daniel Zhang, looking satisfyingly mouthwatering. If I would die soon, I'd at least torture Sam first. And then I'd haunt him. Forever. That man would never again have sex without a cockblocking, screeching ghost from the netherworld pointing at his dick and laughing. If Valerie thought she would out-evil-ex me, she had another poltergeist coming. I smiled, both at the notion and at Danny.

"Hi, honey!" I laid it on thick. I was a fine Southern lady from North Carolina, and we know how to bullshit no matter the situation. "Don't you look gorgeous enough to commit a robbery with?" A tight T-shirt and jeans was never a bad choice on a body that ripped. A faint growling emanated from behind me. It sounded like the protestations of a scum-sucking rat, ha ha! "Do you want to help me pour myself into costume?"

Danny's eyes went from *ooh* to *la la*. "How could I possibly say no to my ex-wife?"

I chuckled and trailed one hand across his bulging bicep, then into the crook of his arm. Thus entwined, we took off down the hall. Danny glanced behind us. "Who is…?"

"Oh, that's just my assistant, S—Zack."

Zack smirked at me in victory. Not for long. I continued, "But his American nickname is Loser. That's what he enjoys being called. It's a long, funny story." I turned my head slightly. "One he won't waste your time by telling or refuting."

Holy crap, Sam glowered murderously in the first degree. "Nice to meet you, er, Loser," said polite Danny. The redder Sam's face got, the more I giggled.

Hmmm. This might actually be a little fun.

* * * *

Flirting outrageously with Danny made the night zip by, even as tired as I was. I seemed to feed on Sam's existential despair—*I am siren, hear me screech.*

Every time I received a break and stepped away from work for a moment or two, Sam would try and pull me aside to speak with me privately. Nope, too bad, so sad, Loser. He'd had many opportunities to *not* turn my life into a waking nightmare of terror and frustration—he didn't get alone time. But Danny did. When Sam would attempt to corner me, I'd call to Danny and take lunch with him, or retire to his trailer for rehearsal or hanging out. Closed-door, thank you. This went on for several evenings. The more Sam scowled, the more I flirted. And Danny, well—he was a nimble dance partner.

Ah, the schadenfreude tasted thick and delicious on my tongue. I lapped it up instead of lapping up a man—boo male persons—or fried foods—pants still too tight, damn it.

And then Sam called my bluff.

I'd accidentally tripped Sam on the way to Danny's trailer one evening—hey, that's my story, and I'm sticking to it. Two minutes after I'd sat down with Danny to go over our next scene, a banging knock shook the door.

The Loser lurketh.

"Samantha," said Sam breathlessly as he whipped the door open. I'd briefly entertained the notion of forcing him to call me Ms Lytton, but decided that it would make me look like an asshole more than it would make him feel like one. "Samantha, there's an urgent phone call from your mother."

I scooted closer to Danny on the couch, raised a flinty gaze to Sam and replied, "I'll call her back."

"But she's so ill," said Sam, a better actor than the rest of us combined. "You never know when it could be the last time you ever speak to someone." His eyes glinted ominously. I almost stood and applauded.

"Oh, no," Danny said. He turned worried brown eyes to me. "I don't mind—please, go chat with your mum."

I gritted my teeth and acknowledged Sam's small win with a nod. "I'll be right back." I rose and shined a beaming smile on Danny as I exited the trailer and took the steps.

We started toward my digs. "Should I even look at that phone? Because I'm pretty sure my mother will outlive us all, and then write an obituary about me saying how weak I was for dying."

He took me by the elbow. Heat zinged from his hand through my arm and down places where I determined zings from him simply *would not go*. I mentally yanked the zings and plopped them back where they belonged.

"We need to talk," he said, low and angry. "I'm getting pretty fucking tired of being run around."

Ah, yes. I'd taken to sending him on long, annoying errands, and always doing it within earshot of several people so that there was never a good way to deny me. One time I'd sent him to fetch my dry cleaning from a chain store, but hadn't said which one—a discovery he made after the first wasted trip. And then I couldn't remember which one I'd taken my items to! Silly me. The fourth location stood the farthest away, and they were closed, anyhow—and I'd been so sure they were twenty-four-hour...

Oops.

After that, a wild craving for a British snack food called Chippie Chaws overcame me. I batted pretty fake eyelashes at him so sweetly, asking if he could please get me some. If the British crew who overheard looked askance at my request, it's because Chippy Chaws do not exist, and definitely not in the elaborate red and purple bag I told him to search for. But that didn't stop Sam from scouring every corner market in a five-mile radius for them before he figured it out.

Oops.

We settled at craft services and sat beside one another on a bench. "No more errands," he hissed at me.

"You are my employee. I have the right."

"I'm gonna dry-clean your..."

I giggled. His face reddened with disbelief. "You deserve every punishment I can concoct!" More laughter spluttered out of me, in waves and waves, and I flopped my head onto the table until I recovered. It was the first real laugh I'd had in days, and I finished feeling forty pounds lighter. Sure, my cast and crew were fun, but I hadn't been my usual sunny self when the cameras stopped.

When I peeked up at him, he'd relaxed and was actually smiling at me. The dimple winked in due obsequience to my masterful gambits. His eyes sparkled with an intensity that was only for me. That look made my breasts tingle, heaven help me. Uuuunnnggghhh, he was always his most seductive when being clever.

"You never get to call me the liar again, okay Miss Chippie Chaw?"

I bit my lip to stop smiling—too late—and stood. "Let's send my mom some flowers, shall we? Put it on your card, and I'll reimburse you." After I lobbed my parting shot, I sauntered away, knowing his gaze followed me.

Or at least followed my butt, which is good enough.

The fifth night of the shoot, I had time to spare. The film business is a glamorous, sweaty, uncomfortable game of Hurry Up and Wait. So I wandered the darkened rooms of the museum.

Truth be told? I was hiding from Sam, who'd manufactured a limp as a way to deflect my errant errands.

The cast wasn't supposed to stray from where we were filming. Right now we were shooting the actual heist itself, which meant faux-liberating the contents of the "Coin and Medals" room. The upper floor lay completely open in the center, so one might see over the railing to the rooms below. Wandering past the history of Britain, I ducked a security guard—it's easy to hide behind displays when you're a Hobbit—and continued on. I'd better practice eluding the authorities if I was going to steal the...

That was when I saw it, the object of my frustration. He stood in front of the Mold gold cape.

Sam turned, startled when I approached. His eyes, dark gray-brown, narrowed, but he said nothing and moved aside to allow me to admire the cape. Although 'admire' seemed a tainted word—how could I consider any object beautiful when I would probably be killed for it?

My downfall was truly amazing to behold— intricate, with small geometric patterns beaten into the gold in rows, all connecting together to make a mantle any living person would want to wear, and probably an ancient god or two. At least I would be smited on behalf of priceless beauty, which didn't make me feel better in any way.

Next to me, Sam sighed and put a hand over his eyes, as if they hurt. For the first time in days, I took a moment to really look at him—awful. Sunken cheeks, uneven shaving, eye bags you could pack ten people's vacation wardrobes in.

He was so beautiful it made my breath hitch, and I forced myself to turn away. I shouldn't have to stare at pretty emo things I couldn't own.

I began to leave the gallery when he caught my hand, gently. "She came after me," he whispered. "Had a gun to my head before I even knew what hit me." He gave a soundless laugh. "She wasn't violent when I was stealing for her. Not at the beginning, anyway."

"Or sleeping with her?"

"Is that worse to you?"

I smiled in spite of myself. "Of course."

He came closer. Close enough for me to smell the intoxicating man smell of his skin. As if a scent should be allowed to reach into your soul and tug. He wore a button-down with rolled-up sleeves—ugh, what that does to me. My already squishy insides turned full jelly. "I'm not sleeping with her," he said.

"What do I care? You dumped me." Oh, but I did care. My brain leaped into a dance of happiness, or at least of less-depressed-ness. "Besides, the whereabouts of your dick is not my biggest problem at the moment."

His voice dropped even lower. "Can't discuss that here."

"There's nothing to discuss! I've done my part." I stared at a smudge on his shirt. The force of his will urged me to look up into his ruinous eyes, but I wouldn't. "If you can find some way out of this for me, I would surely appreciate it."

At least he didn't lie to me—didn't say things like, 'She won't kill us'. Once upon a heist, I'd believed in pleasant fibs. No more.

He still held my hand. His thumb traced soft circles into my knuckles. A million spiteful words flitted around my head like angry bees, but I couldn't seem to line them up long enough to form a sentence. So close. He kept inching toward me. I could get on tip-toe right now and kiss him. He'd let me. He wouldn't let me go.

I'd never wanted him more than right now, and I'd wanted him enough before to do some pretty stupid things. "I have to go," I squeaked, my breath coming shallow.

His hand tightened on mine. "I would die before I let something happen to you."

Oh, God, the tears in his voice... "Let me go, please."

He did. I swayed on my feet, dizzy. His mouth opened to say more, but I fled, unable to keep my cool. If I cried half my makeup off, I'd have to explain why when they fixed me. I ran through three galleries before I collapsed against the wall of a fourth and willed my eyes not to spring forth.

He'd never be safe with me.

I'd never be safe with him.

How easy that made things. Especially once we were dead. Ta da!

I took out my phone and watched panda videos for a few minutes until I no longer remembered the way his neck smelled, or how his hands felt tracing my ass. Panda videos are an acceptable cure for adult-onset icky emotions.

I meandered my way back toward my trailer. Just when I reached the steps, a PA named Sophia ran up to me. "Ms Lytton," she began in a charming Scots accent.

"Samantha is fine. Or just 'Shorty'."

"I can't call you 'Shorty' — I barely have an inch on ye." She smiled and cocked her head. "Your other assistant is here, but I don't see her on the security list."

My eyes bulged. "Other assistant?"

I froze. She froze. Now we were just staring at one another with the same quizzical expression. I blinked and tried to smile. "I mean, yes, let me go meet her. I mean see her."

Sophia took off in the appropriate direction, and I hugged my arms around myself, wishing I had a sweater in the crisp evening air that suddenly chilled me. Who the hell was this woman?

… Of course.

I gritted my teeth until they hurt. The idea that Valerie would invade my private work space at *my* house sent me into a vortex of demonic rage. I actually stopped walking and closed my eyes until the bitter haze left my vision. I didn't know how long I could resist slapping the shiny hair right off her. You don't threaten to murder me and also have slept with my love before he met me and expect to get away with it!

That was when I decided that I would definitely live, if for no other reason than to royally. Fuck. This. Woman. Up.

Chapter Ten

Bad Help Is Easy to Find

I arrived at the security trailer outside the back entrance ready to chew up Valerie whole and spit her onto the ground and then stomp on the Valerie-goo with my foot.

But it wasn't Valerie.

"Are you Samantha Lightbrite?" asked a total stranger in an American accent. Cute woman in her twenties—medium height, red hair and covered in freckles from her hairline to her ankles. She wore a hoodie and sweat shorts, and the blank expression of disenchanted boredom I'd often worn at my old day job.

"Hi, I'm Samantha Lytton." I reached my hand for her to shake it. She pulled a trail of bubble gum out of her mouth and stared at it. Eventually, she turned her attention me. She mashed her gum into her mouth and extended the same fingers toward me. I yanked my arm back and awaited her response.

She chewed.

I raised my eyebrows.

Finally, the mysterious, elegant lady spoke. "I'm Shelley." 'Shelley', the way she said it, possessed four syllables. "The agency, wait, no…your agent sent me." Her voice fell flat, like a limp sheet. She rolled her eyes into her head trying to remember what she was supposed to tell me next. "I'm your new mon-sore."

"My new what?"

She reached out and mimed graspy gestures with her hands. I shrugged. She burst into a frenzy of chopping motions with both forearms.

Ah ha! "You're my masseuse?"

"Yeah." That word contained three parts. *Pop, snap, pop!* went the gum. "Your, um, *agent* knew you were real stressed out, so she sent me to help." She glanced at the head of security, who was currently riveted by this bizarre exchange.

FYI, no one would accuse my extremely hairy agent Bruce of being a 'she'.

Sh-e-ll-ey continued, "You'd better let me help. With your…stuff. Or else you're gonna *be in pain.*"

Wow. Well, I guess somebody has to graduate Undercover Thief school with a D average—not everyone can be the valedictorian. Yet her dull, monotonous voice actually made her threats more compelling. I swallowed.

In a few moments, I'd worked things out with security to give Shelley no-last-name access to the set. My heart thudded and sank as I led Shelley to my trailer. When I arrived there, Sam awaited us on the steps, already giving my 'masseuse' the evil eye. We went inside and formed a three-way standoff.

"I'm Shelley," said Shelley.

"Why are you here?" Sam demanded, giving her a once-over that was in no way sexual, but definitely ominous.

"To make sure she steals the thing." *Snap, pop!*

I plopped onto the couch. "What thing?"

"The...art thing."

Sam turned to me. "That narrows it down."

"Good thing Valerie sent an expert."

Shelley flopped onto the other end of the sofa. "You're stealing it, not me. But if you don't steal it, you'll deal with me. That would be bad."

Not just 'bad', but 'baaaa*aaa*aaaad'. Shelley took out her phone and began ignoring us. "This game is haaaaa*aaa*rd," she said to no one.

Sam cocked one eyebrow and jerked his head toward the bedroom end of the trailer. I nodded and followed him. Shelley made no effort to stop us.

"Who the hell is that person?" I asked the moment he shut the door.

"I don't know. She wasn't on the payroll when I was on Team Valerie. I think a lot of things have changed." He pursed his lips and looked me in the eye. "I guess we really have to do it now."

"Who's we? And didn't we always?"

He sighed and leaned against the door. His brain was forming strings of possibilities behind preoccupied eyes, like one of those old machines that spit out stock ticker tape. "This is fine. I'll steal the cape and try to keep Genius in there away from you."

"Thanks so much."

Squinting at my sarcasm, he took a step toward me. I automatically took one step backward and fell onto the bed, suddenly hyper-conscious that we were alone in a room together with a mattress. Not a comfortable mattress, but beggars can't be spontaneously slutty.

We both blinked shifty eyes everywhere but toward each other. "Well, that was a great Blackmailed Anonymous meeting." I stood to leave. He didn't move. I sat back down and pulled the zipper of my jumpsuit a little higher. "So...when are you going to do it?"

"In time."

"Oh, good. Time. Excellent unit of measure. And so specific."

"You want me to get specific?"

"No, let's be obtuse some more." My voice dropped. "The eagle poops at midnight, pass it on."

His green eyes glinting, he leaned down to my height and said, "Specifically? That tight, black spandex looks so damn hot on you it should be illegal."

I gasped, my mouth dry and watering all at the same time. Oxymoronic reactions were the only kind appropriate for him—heavy on the moronic.

What is a girl to do when her ex says something insanely sexy, and also completely true?

a) Throw him on the bed and make him prove it.

b) Throw him on the bed and make him prove it while reciting Byron to you.

c) Tell him that NASA made your outfit. And then pretend that you were the only two space people on Saturn, so you must get busy and repopulate the planet.

d) Run away.

I chose the path of least resistance—I ran away. Well, after I'd wormed my way around his hot, muscular body, and his warm, lusting gaze, and the giant, tawdry hands reaching for me and—oh, Lord. I eventually escaped.

In the next room, Shelley was still stuck to her phone like her palms were made of suckers. She and Sam deserved each other. I slammed open the door and proceeded down the steps.

Shelley bumped into my back at the bottom. She nearly lost a flip-flop. I nearly bit it in my fancy, spiky boots.

I righted myself with minimal disgruntlement and walked a few paces. She followed. "I have to get to set," I said.

"Yeeeeaaaahhhh."

I walked a few more paces. She followed. I rounded on her, my hands bunched in fists. "You don't have to come with me. Nothing is going to happen right now except me working."

She chewed for a moment while confusion rippled between her brows like wake from a particularly stupid jet ski. "But I'm your massacre."

"Yes. Yes, you probably will be my massacre." No recognition flickered across her blue eyes. I shoved my frustration and rage a bit further down into my intestines and kept walking. It hurt a little, truth be told—if I bottled up any more emotions I'd need an antacid drip. Or a massage.

No doubt the *massage* Shelley would give me would have dire consequences, and, now that I 'employed' a 'masseuse', I couldn't receive an *actual* massage from an actual professional without it seeming weird. So not only was I massage-less, but I would stay that way! Oh, the indignity of it all when a semi-famous person couldn't get her every whim catered to! This was the sort of gross injustice that led to a person saying, "Don't you know who I am?"

I chuckled to myself as I hopped around the lighting technicians to avoid getting in their way. I'd never experienced a massage in my life until about six months ago, because of being poor. Anyone who tells you that money doesn't lead to happiness is a rich asshole hoping you never find out how much they're lying, you plebe.

* * * *

Around dawn, the production packed up and moved so the museum could resume normal business. I waved bye to cast and crew and dragged my tired bones out of the palatial building and toward my trailer. Both Sam and Shelley dogged my steps, as they'd done all freaking night long. Mine was the worst entourage since the TV show *Entourage*. Their eyes glinted from the dark while I worked, their hands bumped into mine at the catering table, and their desire to follow me into the bathroom really went too far, although Shelley had given me a panty liner. But I swore — the next time someone got between me and a bag of buttered popcorn, there would be hell to pay.

This time of morning was the best. My body sank with exhaustion from giving it my all the whole night, and the promise of dinner and sleep loomed bright.

Plus neither of the back-stabbing burrs followed me home.

Danny caught me up while I was on the way to gather my things. He stopped and grinned at me, and I cannot pretend that his regard, which had gotten more and more intense, left me unfazed. I couldn't help returning the smile, even though it sent Sam into some sort of muscle spasm.

I pulled my co-star aside, away from my gang of thieves. Sam made an immediate move to follow, but a bunch of burly grips began carting equipment between our groups. Danny put his arm around my shoulders and squeezed. "You okay? You seem preoccupied." He yanked his hand back. "You're fantastic on set, of course! I didn't mean that."

"Thanks a lot, Danny." I punched him on the shoulder—jokingly, gently. Not like I punch Sam, who deserved regular beatings. "I'm dealing with some...family drama." I.e. crime family. "But I'm fine."

"Come out for breakfast with me. I know a lovely place that serves mimosas. Since it's our 'five o'clock'."

My soul burst forth and sang. Silently, though, or else that would no doubt alarm him. "Mimosas sounds wonderful. I'm in!" I'd given up drinking since we switched to night shoots, as slugging whiskey alone in your apartment at eight in the morning makes one feel even ickier than coping with real life sober.

"Mimosas?" piped up Sam in the cheeriest voice I'd ever heard him use, except for maybe when promised a sexual act or watching sci-fi. He zipped between two moving lighting towers to join us. Shelley hadn't seemed to notice the conversation and began to wander away, presumably to stare at her phone in privacy until the radiation made her eyeballs fall out—she never bothered with trailing me except on set. Sam continued, "Who doesn't love orange juice?"

Danny's face crinkled as he tried to concoct a polite way to disinvite Sam. "Oh, hello..."

The bark of laughter flew from me before I could help myself. My hand flew to my mouth too late. I recovered and said, "It's Sam."

"It's Zack," Sam snapped.

"Loser is what you were thinking of," I told Danny, now peering from one of us to the other as if we were quite, quite mad. We were all mad here—me, Sam, Zack, Loser...

"Sorry, mate," Danny said. "We, um...well..."

"Great! I'll get my stuff!" Sam jogged off to my trailer lickety-split.

Kind, gentle Danny was no match for the devious wonder of Sam, Official Piece of Cockblocking Shit. Two is a party, three is a mess the likes of which could rival the Exxon Valdez disaster.

* * * *

The Princess Margaret was so English a restaurant it looked like the set of a sitcom called *Tea and Crumpets, What What, Paul McCartney*. Rough-hewn stone walls surrounded us, tamed only mildly by the dark wood paneling on their bottom half. The window shades had been thrown open and the bright light of morning awoke me, just as it was designed to. My poor body still fought the jetlag, and now the switch to night work left my spine a giant question mark.

We three grabbed a booth in the back. Through some sort of dark wizardry, Sam arranged it so that he sat between me and Danny in the curved seat. As he bumped my hip to scoot in next to me, he smiled, grim satisfaction in his tightly-set mouth. I remembered I'd told him that me and Danny were doing the hump-de-hump. I smirked at him with a challenge of my own. He thought he would separate me from my international movie star, whom I enjoyed for good reasons and not because it irritated him?

Oh, was he wrong.

So, so wrong.

We settled in, dispensing awkward, pleasant smiles all round. A middle-aged, cheery waitress took our orders of three full English breakfasts, with mimosas to start. I wasn't sure those things went together, but when in the Princess Margaret...

And when you're sitting at one point of an actual, physical love triangle...

Never in history had three people reached for champagne glasses with such speed. Danny bounced the ball and launched the first volley. "So, Zack—how long have you been Samantha's assistant? Are you enjoying London?"

Sam settled back and spread out his arms. His fingers crept toward my shoulder, but I leaned sideways to search for something pretend in my purse. "I've worked closely with Samantha for a little over a year now. I like to stay on top of her." He chuckled, and I snapped my head up. "You've got to ride these artist-types, or else they go off, half-cocked. Know what I mean?"

Danny played with his napkin, clearly having no idea what Sam meant.

"He's been to London before," I added to shut Sam the hell up. "I thought today went really well. We made up for some of the scenes we got behind on last night."

My adorable co-star winked at me adorably. "It helped that no one tried to destroy the museum tonight."

"I did so try! I may be clumsy, but I'm not a quitter." I'd had a bit of an 'oops' encounter with a Plexiglas box containing Roman coins while suspended above it by a crane. There's a steep learning curve to high-wire flying. Could happen to anyone.

Leaning forward on the table, Danny said, "They really ought to find a way to secure your zipper. If it continues sliding downward when you run, we'll be making soft-core porn."

I giggled and tossed my hair. I can do it, too, stupid Valerie! "It's so gentlemanly of you to avert your eyes, the way you do sometimes."

His chuckle curled around us, warm and soft, and caused Sam to utter a sound like that of a wounded moose. Sam tried to cover by draining his drink.

"Did you hear about that fifty-car pileup in Edinburgh?" Actual crickets chirped after Sam said this.

"I'm going to visit the ladies' room," I announced, as thoughts of peeing were preferable to giant car accidents. I scooched out of the booth and gave Danny a cheery, obvious shoulder squeeze on the way. The moose-gurgling noise haunted me all the way to the toilet.

Upon my return, I enacted my plan. I headed straight for Danny and sat on the few inches of booth on the end beside him. "Care for some company?" Quick as a horny bunny, he moved to let me in. Now the three of us jammed together in one-half of the booth, for Sam refused to move. Since we were so close, I put my arm around Danny's shoulders and began recounting a funny thing our director had said today. Sam's eyes glowed like molten darkness, and he inched away from us without breaking his hostile regard.

Victory!

A fresh round of mimosas arrived, thank goodness. Danny didn't even seem to think that me being so cold to Sam was weird, for he stared at my ex as if he were leprous, or perhaps suffering from a disease of the brain. I'd never seen Sam so awkward—he could normally win a charm competition from two counties away with one dimple tied behind his back.

Sam took a deep breath, drained half of his fresh glass and said to Danny, "What's next for you, Daniel? After *What Could Go Wrong?*"

Ah, an actual thing a human being might say! He was fighting dirty now.

"I'll shoot a film adaptation of *Midsummer Night's Dream* next year, but I think I might take some time off the latter half of this year. Reconnect with real life." Danny glanced at me ever so briefly. "Remember what's it like to see friends, relatives. Maybe even date a little."

"That's just crazy enough to work," I said.

"I hope so."

A whole mess of subtext rippled beneath those three words, and a wave of guilt washed over me. I had exactly no reason to feel guilty, but the raw, pained lines on Sam's face and the tense cords of his neck made my innards recoil. A full minute of silence descended. Danny bit his lip and shot me a warm look, which I returned. It wasn't his fault that Sam and I had enough history to fill a college textbook.

The food arrived, smelling wonderful and large enough to feed, well, a ploughman. Holy crap, these English could embarrass even an American breakfast—there was sausage, ham, hash browns, eggs, tomato, mushrooms, beans and something black and circular. "What is that?" I asked Danny.

"Black pudding. It's good—try it."

"What's it made of?"

Sam cracked his first real smile of the day. "Don't tell her until she tries it."

I froze. "Now I'm afraid."

"Don't be." He leaned in and locked onto my eyes. "You'll like it. You like anything having to do with meat." The way he imbued meaning into 'meat' made me straight-up blush. My entire face heated, and the fire spread south until I tingled in a way that no lady should at breakfast.

To conceal my overheated everything, I was forced to try the mystery meat. He'd practically dared me, anyhow. It tasted salty, crumbly—a richness on my tongue that lingered. "Mmmmmm," I offered to all and sundry. This pleased both men greatly.

"It's congealed blood," Sam said.

I stopped a fresh bite halfway to my mouth. But then I thought...is blood any different from meat? The second bite tasted better than the first. I fancied I could detect the tang of blood. It made me feel...metal. Powerful. As if I were a queen who devoured my enemies' hearts and washed them down with champagne. And then went home to her castle to find her two husbands awaiting her. One with a dimple, and the other with an honest smile that warmed the heart...

Perhaps I read too much into pudding.

I couldn't help my laugh at Sam getting my goat, and he cocked one eyebrow at his win before he tucked into his own food. When I turned to Danny, I found him watching me hazily. I blushed anew.

Why couldn't I just have both? I decided I needed to find myself a romance novel that ended with a duchess and her two stable boys living happily ever after. Perhaps I'd produce the movie based on the book...

My breakfast grew cold while I was woolgathering dirty thoughts. Not the first time that had happened.

We made small talk as we ate. A refreshing semi-ease broke through the tension covering us like a humid day. Sam visibly refused to smile at Danny, though, and his jealousy—oh, God, his jealousy—made me hot and foolish. My face bloomed even redder—I felt it roast inside and out. I experienced the same thing when I exercised, and my blood certainly pumped pit-a-pat right now. Even my lips tingled, just a little, with every bite I took.

Finally, I could take my own thoughts no more, and I blurted the first thing that came to mind, "So, Danny, what are you doing after breakfast?"

"Going to bed."

His deep voice almost destroyed me. I managed not to drop my fork, but barely.

I was a wanton harlot who would burn in the fires of purgatory. Already the flames had begun—sweat actually trailed between my breasts.

"Anybody lucky going to join you?" asked a new voice.

I snapped my head up so fast I became dizzy. Valerie. Like an ointment-resistant cold sore, she was back. And wearing an old dress of Ethel Mertz's.

"Hi, Mr Zhang. I'm Veronica, Samantha's European publicist."

Veronica. Well. I was so important my on-site staff had grown from zero to three in a week. If only my paychecks tripled in this manner.

Valerie plopped down on the other side of Sam, giving his cock a squeeze as she sat. Oh, wait, maybe not his actual member, but so far up on his thigh it was difficult to tell the freaking difference.

The wraith began speaking. "Zack told me you guys were here, and, well, to be perfectly honest"—she paused and simpered to Danny—"I really wanted to meet you! I'm such a huge fan."

Danny nodded to the compliment and proffered his most amiable smile. And that's saying something. He's such a sweet man, he'd invented three new types of graciousness.

Valerie clawed at Sam's leg some more. "I also have some things to go over with Samantha, so I'm mixing business and pleasure."

Pleasure because of how much she'd enjoy eating pudding made of my blood, no doubt.

This was bad. Very, very bad. We'd morphed into that most fearsome of geometric horrors—the love parallelogram.

Sam had gone rigid the moment she'd appeared in a puff of witch smoke. Why the hell had he told her we were here? Screw the both of them. I said, "I'm afraid I can't today, Veronica. I'd asked Danny about his plans because I wanted to talk to him after breakfast about tomorrow's scene." My turn to lay a gentle hand on Danny's knee. Not his crotch, because I have some fucking dignity.

"That's absolutely fine. My pleasure," he immediately replied. He flicked his gaze to my hand, still on his leg. One corner of his mouth turned up.

Sam was now also staring at my hand, his jaw working and his poor teeth no doubt gnashing. Such are the stakes in the Game of Parallelograms.

My nemesis darkened, too, as if a cloud had passed over her own personal sun. "I'll have to catch you this evening then, Samantha."

I didn't bother to reply. I knew I couldn't put her off forever. My score surged ahead only temporarily.

"I guess I'll have to settle for making Zack walk me back to my hotel." Valerie faux-pouted and pushed her perky rack at Sam. "Pretty please?"

Sam didn't smile so much as raise a grimace just enough to pass for one. "My pleasure."

He'd said he wasn't sleeping with her. But why did I care? I did care, dammit! Okay? I did care. I loved Sam, and I lusted Danny, and I hated Valerie, and who gave a flying fart about any of it because I was going to die as soon as this movie wrapped, anyway. Panic swelled in me, desperate and breathless, and it took everything I possessed to approximate calm for public view. I continued to secretly sweat.

I leaned in and aimed a toothy smile at Valerie's obnoxious face. "Have fun, you two," I drawled.

"Oh, we will," Valerie snipped.

"Good."

"Fine."

"Excellent."

"Wonderful!"

I wanted to hunt her down in the jungle, skin her and wear her carcass as a warning to other enemies. But mostly I needed to avert my eyes, because if that harpy got one millimeter closer to Sam's junk, I was going to set her ugly shoes on fire.

My hand burst into the air, and our waitress hurried right over with a portable credit card swiper. I paid for the meal and soon tugged playfully on Danny's arm until we were out of the restaurant and in the brilliant sun. A moment or two passed before I saw past my rage to recognize the beautiful day.

Danny slid on a sexy pair of aviators. "Your place or mine?" he asked.

I tilted my head. "Yours. If you don't mind. I'd love to see your place."

"Of course." His mouth twitched. "How nice of you to invite yourself over."

"I think you technically invited me."

He raised his eyebrows in a cavalier way that Jack Nicholson might have envied. "Americans have the most interesting manners."

Ooooooooh. Danny was starting to give me shit. Always a lovely development when a man does that.

"Bye," said Sam, loud, right behind me.

"Goodbye for now," Valerie corrected him with haunting undertones.

Good riddance for now.

I did not peek over my shoulder to watch Valerie and Sam walk away from us. No, indeed. I may be a silly woman who collects vintage Olivia Newton-John tour shirts, but my dignity is still intact.

Besides—I couldn't look without Danny seeing me do it.

The air of doom that had haunted us at breakfast lifted, and I let freedom envelop me for the first time all day. We walked in silence, both of us tired and content enough to not have to fill the space. A few blocks away, I stopped him. "Danny, I didn't really have anything I wanted to talk to you about. I just didn't want to deal with Valerie tonight."

"Who is Valerie?"

"Vanessa. Veronica?" Shit!

Danny laughed. "I guess she really winds you up if you can't remember her name."

I covered my face with my hands. "I'm sorry—my brain has no idea what time it is. Even if it did, the time *zone* is still a mystery. Yes, she's new to me. Jeez, I sound like an asshole."

"No, no. I'm afraid publicists are a necessary evil."

"How do you think I'm doing?"

"What?" He pushed his sunglasses up.

I squeezed my temples—*what an idiot I am*. I hadn't meant to ask him that. "I am...very tired—that was a stupid question."

"Do you mean in the film?" We were in people's way, so he pulled us under the awning of a shop. "I think you're brilliant. Funny, likeable. The audience will be rooting for you the most."

Erp, there it went. Hot face again. "That'll be you."

"Hopefully, both of us. Really—you are holding your own very well. The camera, it loves you. Honestly, it's hard for me to focus on anyone else when you're in a scene." He reached out a hand to touch me, but stopped mid-way and snatched it back.

My head spun from his compliments. Below my layer of bravado and bad jokes, an undercurrent of doubt always bubbled, toiled and troubled. I was convinced that at any moment someone would snatch me from this life and scream, 'It's a lie! She's nothing but a low-rent loser with no talent and bad taste in knick-knacks!'

"Do you have the next couple of days off? I do."

And lo, the heavens opened up, and God smiled upon my mess of a life. I'd completely forgotten that I had some time free. "Yes."

He shuffled his feet and stared at them, and the adorable gesture blitzed me like a basket full of kittens. "Have you been on the London Eye?"

"The terrifying, tall, wheel thingie that looks like it's going to fall off its post and roll down the Thames, killing everyone trapped inside?"

His mouth fell open. "That's not exactly how they market it."

I reached out to touch his arm. My hand fell on his pec by complete accident. Also by accident, I concluded that he spent as much time in the gym as a movie star is supposed to. "I have a bit of a fear of heights. But I have leftover Xanax from my plane ride here."

"It might be better to take you on a date you don't have to be drugged for."

"Some Hollywood player you are."

His eyes crinkled at the corners. Mmmmmm. I said, "So, you want to take me on a date, huh?"

"I want to take you on fifty."

I laughed—a peal of girly giggles that practically erupted from my mouth covered in pink glitter. "We're working together."

Why the hell had I said that? Stupid, stupid Samantha!

"You're right." He sighed and put his sunglasses back on. "I shouldn't have asked."

"I'm glad you asked. My ego is growing like Pinocchio's nose." I removed my sunglasses and plopped them onto my hair. The sun created a halo around his perfectly-formed head. I took his hand and said, "Look, here's the honest deal. I just experienced a breakup. It was"—bizarre, soul-sucking, causing one to listen to far too much Alanis Morissette—"confusing and difficult. You deserve someone who gives you her complete attention."

"Love, only someone who would treat me well would say something like that."

"Argh, stop being wonderful!"

He swooped in and laid a kiss on me. His sunglasses bonked against my face, so he whipped them off with an "I'm sorry," and dove back in, this time with a yank of his arm around my waist. Suddenly I was covered in a warm wall of man—a state of being that I highly recommend. My every hormone emerged from hiding, gleeful to be feeling an emotion besides fear, heartbreak and angst.

Lust was the great equalizer.

We enjoyed the sort of kissing karma that made it good with no practice whatsoever. His fingers slipped ever so slightly into the waistband of my jeans, while his other hand cupped my neck. Fast and firm, his lips played with mine as if he wanted to nibble me whole.

Mmmmmm—he smelled like expensive sex. Like a cologne made of lion glands they only sell to men who can wet panties with a ninety percent success rate. He began to slow down, tasting me, lingering. His tongue brushed my upper lip, and I nearly lost my balance.

I heard a giggle, and we broke apart at the same time.

Sometimes I'm a little psychic—because I had a sure feeling that the teenage girl filming us with her iPhone was about to come into some tabloid money.

Danny plopped his glasses back on, grabbed my hand and we took off at a fast, but not running, pace. Nobody followed, and a few blocks away we ducked into a coffee shop. We sat and stared at one another. After a moment of his handsome, earnest regard shining upon me, I burst into laughter.

He began chuckling, too. "I hope she funds university with the proceeds of that video."

"We can't be that important."

"I'm Daniel Zhang, baby," he said in his most smarmy tone.

"And me without my genuflecting pillow."

He slumped back into the wooden chair. "It'll be good publicity for the movie."

"As long as it's a decent movie."

"Let's hope so."

I didn't know what else to say. I'd even run out of stupid jokes.

"If everyone thinks we're dating, we might as well date," he said, casually, his fingers drumming on the small table.

"So are all your relationships dictated by the public?"

"Why do you think I was briefly engaged to Justin Bieber?"

"Oh, my God." I banged my head on the table just enough to hurt and also feel good. "I'd tell you to stop being funny, but then you'd kiss me again."

"That's preposterous. Go on—try me."

I glanced up to find him laying a very, super sexy smirk on me. I think if there existed a Samantha Kryptonite, it would be a very, super sexy smirk. The man who can convey dirtiness and humor at the same time is a rare man, and to be coveted.

But your Kryptonite is a dimple, said my annoying internal compass.

We have chosen to have a lurid rebound affair with the world's most awesome movie star in order to gain publicity! I replied.

Ha! Take that, stupid conscience.

"Dinner tomorrow night?" he asked.

"Do you mean…dinner tonight?"

"No, I actually meant tomorrow night. This evening I have a previous engagement with my family. Grandma's birthday."

Of course he loved his grandma, the perfect jerk. "Tomorrow night it is. And then we can do…night things." I grinned. He grinned back.

Oh, shit—'night things' sounded like sex! I wasn't prepared to commit to the nitty-gritty already. Some boob action was all I would consider.

Unless the boob-play went well, then I reserved the right to increase the Official Slut Level from yellow to orange.

"I mean...you know, 'night things' as in...it's a date. At night. Because we're a bizarre variety of nocturnal animal called 'actor'." After I delivered this nonsense, I burst forth with an unexpected yawn that originated in my toenails.

"It's a deal. May I show you to a cab?" he asked.

I nodded, overcome by such gallantry. I was jealous of his grandma all the way back to my place.

Chapter Eleven

Step Right Up and See Samantha, the Human
Punching Bag

*Int: Our Heroine's Diamond-Encrusted Bedroom on her
Yacht in the Mediterranean — night.*

Lady Samantha Lytton *lounges in her sumptuous bed,
her cat,* Viscount Taco, *purring beside her. She wears a
satin bed sheet of pale blue silk — it ripples around her like
she's Venus rising from the Beautyrest. She wears no
makeup, yet is flawless even so, the way women are
naturally supposed to be. Except for a little mascara,
because come on.*

Angle On: Husband One, Danny *enters the bedroom,
dressed in buckskin trousers so tight he sways from lack of
blood flow, and a puffy white shirt tucked in, yet still
unbuttoned. He rushes to the side of the bed to kneel at Lady
Samantha's kitten-heel-clad feet.*

Husband One, Danny: I am back from my duke
meeting, The 737th Annual Sneer-A-Thon and Poetry
Slam, where we studied duke-ly things such as the
newest modes of cravat-ing, how to appreciate smart
young women who buck society's norms via obscene

stamp collecting and which words rhyme with 'soul'. How I've missed you, my beautiful *foal*.

Lady Samantha: Duke Danny, these last three days have been a torment! If I didn't have another husband, well, I might have noticed you were gone and been very sad.

Husband One, Danny: My greatest honor is that you notice me now, fairest of them all. Is your hair even curlier than before?

Lady Samantha: Duh. I'm a romance heroine. If it doesn't improve its own unruliness by five percent a day, I get bumped down to 'amusing and/or thick-ankled sidekick'.

Angle On: Duke Danny rushes the bed and rubs his throbbing manhood on Samantha, who also throbs.

Angle On: Husband Two, Sam *enters by swinging on a rope through the balcony and into the bedroom. He is dressed in rough, black trousers so tight we can see what he ate for lunch, and a puffy white shirt tucked in, yet still unbuttoned. And an eye patch. He rushes to the side of the bed to kneel at Samantha's kitten-heel-clad feet.*

Husband Two, Sam: Why exactly, in this scenario, am I Husband Two? I totally got here first, yo ho.

Parrot on Sam's Shoulder: Squawk, totally got here first! And by 'here', he means —

Lady Samantha: 'Tis true, Pirate Sam, that you were my first throbbing member. Well, maybe not *first*. What is this, 1950? 1750? Seriously, what the hell time period are we supposed to be in?

Angle On: The duke and the pirate shrug in the soft glow to the yacht's electric lights.

Lady Samantha: But, darling Pirate Sam, you were definitely the first to plunder the depths of my...soul.

Husband Two, Sam: I love you from your perfectly-dyed red hair to your non-hairy mole.

Husband One, Danny: Gadzooks! I'm the elegant one who's supposed to rhyme things with 'soul'. I took an interactive seminar and everything. For example, 'stole', for Samantha stole my heart long ago.

Angle On: Danny shoots a dirty look to Sam.

Husband One, Danny: Perhaps you *should* be husband number *one*, if we're counting eyes.

Lady Samantha: Now, now, boys. I enjoy both even and odd numbers of eyes. Let us all get along, and by 'get along', I mean—

Parrot on Sam's Shoulder: Squawk, she means 'gang bang'!

Angle On: The two husbands gaze hopefully at Samantha.

Lady Samantha: I do mean gang bang.

Both Husbands: Huzzah!

Lady Samantha: But Sam—no parrot in the room this time. I don't like his...observations.

Parrot on Sam's Shoulder: Squawk, if you can't take the scathing recap, then get off my blog!

Angle On: Lady Samantha shoving the parrot's feathered face out of the room, and then divesting both her husbands of their tight, rather useless clothing. They spend endless hours pleasuring her in every conceivable way, in-between feeding her ice cream. The night culminates as Duke Danny and Pirate Sam Jell-O wrestle for the privilege of—

No! Noooooooo! I was ripped from the world's most amazing fantasy by some jackass banging on my front door. I pounded the bed in frustration and switched off Colin Firth.

They knocked again, tearing away the final wisps of my scenario of Danny and Sam wrestling. The winner would get to flip me over and —

Bang bang bang!

The real winner would have been me.

Full of horn-dog hormones, and vowing to get rid of this asshole so I could return to bed with Colin, Sam and Danny, I snatched up my robe and stomped to the door.

A split second before I opened it, I remembered that I was a public persona, so I probably shouldn't open the door and scream 'fuck off' to a British Girl Scout or something. I took a deep breath and peered through the keyhole.

Like a mysterious rash acquired at a discount gym, she was back. "Valerie," I said, my fists readying themselves.

"I can hear you breathing," she sing-songed. "And also saying my name."

"Just a sec! I have to get decent!" I ran to the kitchen and dove into my impromptu junk and/or electronics gizmo drawer to retrieve my tiny recorder. I hastily shoved it in the pocket of my pajama pants.

More beating-down-the-door bangs reverberated from the front. "Coming!" After a quick mirror-check, I answered the door, a genuine smile on my face this time. I'd have the advantage...unless she just killed me now. In that case, the prosecuting attorney would have the advantage.

She pushed through the door. "Hello, Valerie," I announced loudly for the benefit of my ponytail. "Shelley," I added.

Shelley slumped behind her boss, muttering a, "yeaaaaaaaaaaaah," on the way. She stood near a window and typed a no doubt important text.

The clock told me it was seven p.m. local. Too early for Scotch? Or too late? This film would send me to Betty Ford if it didn't send me to Hollywood Forever first.

"What do you want?" No need to pretend in my own apartment. I'd be damned if she'd get a warm reception here, in my lair.

Captain Taco jumped onto the couch beside her and began snuggling her leg.

Damn that cat.

"She's so cute!" squeaked Valerie.

Ha! I hoped Taco was suitably emasculated, although, personally, I do not believe that calling a male a female is an insult. Indeed, it is a compliment. But such musings were for another time—a time after I got rid of the evil female person infecting my couch with her cooties.

"What. Do. You. Want?" I stayed standing near the door and crossed my arms.

"Where. Is. My. Cape?"

I rolled my eyes. "Really? Ask Sam, unless his dick already told you through osmosis."

Her lips pursed, and I mentally kicked myself for having revealed such weakness. In a more musical tone of voice, she said, "His 'dick' does love to talk, doesn't it?" She sat back. "I don't care who grabs the cape, but I want it. One week—or else." She practically sang "or else!" like a demented Disney princess.

Shelley lifted her head when the threat rang out. She balled a fist and nodded, which I think I was supposed to take as an incredibly lazy threat.

"And by 'grab it', you mean 'steal it', correct?"

Eyes narrowing, Valerie shot me a withering stare. "Are you really this stupid?"

"I get it, okay? You're gonna kill me unless I steal the Mold Cape from the British Museum."

She shrugged. "There are many people in your life, any one of whom could have a horrible accident if, by some chance, I don't get what I want. Like this."

It was the way she said it. My breathing hit double-time as Valerie gestured to Shelley. The moron started for me, and I nearly bolted, but somehow, I stood my ground. *They need me, they need me*, I kept telling myself. I lifted my chin, too damn stubborn to cower before this horrid person.

She circled around behind me and waited. What the hell was she doing back there—texting her idiot support group? I gritted my teeth and stood firm, staring straight into Valerie's eyes, letting her know that I—

I screamed. I was suddenly on my knees, Shelley's fist in my hair, holding me up by it, my every root screaming in pain. She had a telescopic bat in her other hand, that was what she'd knocked me down with, and a smile of great joy on her face. Such an unexpected and horrifying expression. I struggled in vain, bent backward and unable to right myself, when a heat like fire seared across my head, and I collapsed to the floor.

The back of my scalp hurt, oh, God how it screamed, and my hands rushed up to cradle it while I rolled onto my side. Shelley held up a long, thick clump of my hair and grinned. She'd ripped it straight out of my freaking head. Hot and fast, the tears streamed down my face and fucking damn it, I'd have given anything to not cry right now.

Valerie leaned forward and said, "There's only one thing our lovely Shelley is good at, and that's torturing people. And it doesn't even show! Don't cross me."

My blood boiled and my stomach turned to acid. She was like a newscaster—delivering the most horrible of news with a half-smile and a lilt only suitable for speaking to furry animals. See? Taco loved it, as he'd now climbed completely into her lap and was receiving traitorous affection.

"Oh!" She held up a finger and wagged it at me. "And no cops—I'm watching you. Always."

I sat up and groaned, "Get out."

She stood, Taco in her hands, and thrust him into my arms. Which he immediately abandoned after scratching my wrist.

"Bye!" trilled Valerie on the way through the door. I had to actually nudge Shelley so that she'd look up from her phone long enough to follow—I guess now that the torturing was done, she was bored again. I slammed the door unnecessarily, locked and re-locked it, and threw open my windows to air away the stink of Valerie's over-zealous perfume. "You're getting dry food from now on, Taco," I muttered. "Fancy canned food is for loyalists to the cause."

I lifted my hand to my poor, poor scalp and came away with blood. Suddenly Shelley didn't seem so silly. Vain being that I am, I rushed to the bathroom to check the hole in my hair. The. Hole. In. My. Damn. Hair! Argh! But she'd snatched it from underneath so the damage was only obvious to me and my pain receptors.

Coffee. I needed coffee to wash away the memory of Valerie, psychotic princess and friend to fink cats.

While I held a towel to my bleeding head and stared at my French Press as if my eyeballs would make it brew faster, my phone rang. The phone in the apartment—I had to search around a bit until I remembered where it lived. "Hello?" I asked in a terrified manner.

"Why don't you answer your cell? I thought you'd been kidnapped!"

"Ellen," I nearly screamed into the phone. "Oh, I need to talk to you."

"You *have* been kidnapped. I told you!" She yelled that last bit away from the phone, so she must have been gossiping about me to Nicolette.

"No, no, I'm not kidnapped." Merely tortured a little. Torture-lite. Ugh. I rooted around for some pain medicine. "I may have lost my phone…"

"Is it in the toilet?"

"I hope not." But these things will happen.

My mouth opened to spill my heartache, but I bit the story down just in time. I'd vowed not to tell Ellen, or she'd rush back to London to help me, and I couldn't have her or Nicolette on my conscience again. "Nothing. Nothing's wrong. I just miss you. Where are you guys?"

"We're in the French Riviera! On the Riviera? I don't know, but it's spectacular and we look gawgeous in our bikinis."

We talked about her trip so far, and she gushed over Versailles and Paris and everything that was happy. Tears slipped from my eyes, and I swallowed them silently. How I dreamed of taking such a trip with Sam, *sans* bad guys. I mean Danny. But also without bad guys.

Ellen served as a good reminder of why I needed to play along with Evil Princess. I told my bestie I loved her, and we hung up. That's when I fell into a full-fledged crying fit, heaving and sobbing so hard and loud that Taco stalked closer to me and lay down a foot away, just watching, a sympathetic loaf of cat. I swooped him into my arms and held him while I cried it out some more, and he even allowed me to for five whole minutes.

Did I really believe that I would die soon? The fear — and the pain, dammit — forced me to do what she said, but still, in my heart, I knew I would never give up. I'd fight to the bitter end, and do my best to enjoy whatever time I had on this Earth, be it a week or a decade or five.

I don't know how much time passed, but eventually I flopped onto my back, my tear-stained face staring at the ceiling. There's an emptiness after a good cry that's unlike anything else. I floated in space, not thinking, not feeling. The neutrality was the most delicious thing I'd experienced in days.

Knock knock!

The door again. "Are you kidding me?" I asked the universe. It did not deign to reply.

Whoever it was could just stay in the lonely hall. Samantha Corp., a subsidiary of Where Did I Put My Vibrator, Inc., was officially closed for outside business. There were much, much better things to do, like revisit that amazing dream.

Although why I'd given Sam a mean parrot is beyond me.

"Samantha?"

I bolted upright. This new person was not Valerie, returned. The truth was a horror so unreal, so unexpected, I ne'er could have imagined its dark revelation.

"Mom?"

The hall echoed with the loud, distinct echo of a North Carolina drawl. "Did she send me the wrong apartment number? Just like her! She was always terrible at math."

Yup. Only my mother has enough confidence in my lack of abilities to think I don't know where I live.

Why the hell was she in London? I crawled to the door, banged my head a couple of times and eventually made it to my feet. The door swung wide and there she was, the NASCAR queen of Vegas, Suzie Lytton—model, spokesperson, supportive mother figure.

Her Pepto-pink lips frowned. "You look terrible! Well, that's what you get for spending so much time in Europe. Please tell me you're still shaving what you ought to."

I jerked her into a fierce hug. She smelled of powder and a perfume almost as assaulting as Valerie's. But she felt like Mom, and I suddenly needed her immensely, insults and all.

"Hi, Diego," I said when I finally let Mom go. My stepfather Diego was younger than me, but it was only creepy in every way possible.

"Young lady," he intoned with the authority of a middle-school guidance counselor. "Have you been crying?"

"Um..." I rushed them inside, taking a quick look down the hall to made sure I wasn't about to get any more unexpected visitors. "I was rehearsing! For my film."

"I thought it was a comedy," Mom said, perching delicately on the couch. "Those are what you do, not real movies. I mean, Nicole Kidman isn't in it."

I rocked that barb—a recent addition to her arsenal. If Nicole Kidman wasn't in the film, my mother usually wasn't interested. She considered the Aussie actress the perfect example of good taste and success. When I'd gotten my first big studio role, Sam had told me that Suzie would finally be proud of me. I'd known better.

I said, "There's an element of tragedy in every work of humor. You know—a delight of sorts when life beats the heroine down." I sat next to her. "It makes you feel better about your own life to see someone else flailing in theirs."

"I've never had that feeling, but then again, I work hard to be a winner." She shrugged, and her blonde hair fluttered in its attractive bob. "Anyway, Diego had the wonderful idea to surprise you with a visit! There's a dance troupe here in London he's always dreamed of seeing, so here we are."

Diego is a hot, blond, handsome professional dancer. Yeah, my mom got game. Too bad game ain't genetic.

I stood. "Let me get us some coffee."

"I've gone off coffee. Diego recommended I try green tea instead." Diego rushed to her side and kissed her hand. "It's so much healthier. Do you have any green tea?"

In my opinion, green tea tastes like boiled ass. The only thing it has in common with delicious, beautiful coffee is that they both exist in this solar system. "No, I'm afraid not."

"Mmmmmm. That explains why your teeth need to be bleached."

My hand flew to my mouth, and then to my crusty, aching eyes. Urgh, why even bother? "So, do you want to do something tonight? My whole evening is free!"

"No friends here yet? It was always so hard for you."

"But keep trying!" Diego added. "I'm sure there are some people who would be lucky to have you as a friend."

Perhaps Valerie would be willing to return and improve my evening by putting bamboo shoots under my fingernails.

A series of *knock-knock-knockety-knocks* thudded upon the door.

I take it back! I take it back! Jesus Lord, it was just a joke!

My mother observed, "Someone is here, Samantha." I turned panicked eyes to her, but didn't know what to say. "Diego, will you be a dear and answer it?"

Diego's muscles rippled a moment or two for the audience before he jumped to his feet to do his wife's bidding.

Was there an open house sign outside? "Come one, come all to the Samantha Lytton Shit Show! *See* a grown woman drool Cheez-It crumbs onto the carpet! *Hear* her cries of terrorized sorrow! *Experience* her inability to function like a normal human adult!"

Where were these people coming from? And why would no one allow me a moment to put on a bra and check my hair for blood?

"Did you order Chinese food, young lady?" Diego asked, the door open a crack.

My mother tsk-ed. "So salty. That must be why you're puffy. You've always been a bloater."

Puzzled, I pushed aside Diego. "Danny! Wh—what are you doing here?"

I pulled him inside while he gave the stink eye to Diego. My entire soul slunk into my feet — *Chinese food*. Even though the man carried no bag whatsoever and wore a suit and tie. Holy shit. Could this damn night get any worse? "I'm so sorry," I whispered before saying, louder, "Daniel Zhang, this is my mom, Suzie

Lytton, and her husband, Diego. They're visiting me as a surprise. Mom, Danny is the co-star of my movie. He is one of many people of Chinese descent who don't work in the food industry. Not that there's anything wrong with that."

This earned me a small, knowing smirk from my hunk. My heartbeat braked to a normal rate.

"Of course I know Daniel Zhang!" Suzie undulated to her feet, her hot pink pantsuit tight and her relatively new cleavage at attention. "You starred with Nicole Kidman in *Moonlight in Morocco*. I adore that movie!" She giggled and didn't stop. Diego's brow furrowed.

Danny's shoulders released from their angry perch, and he smiled. "Thank you very much." He turned to me, and his face relaxed even more. "I apologize for dropping in...unannounced." Slowly, his gaze roamed from my head — rat's nest — to my robe — old, tatty — to my enormous jammies — octopi/tacos, mismatched/stained. I remembered that I didn't have a stitch of makeup on. Surprising that he even recognized me. I guess the height gave me away. My mother tittered some more.

Danny continued, "But I couldn't announce myself, because I accidentally stole your phone this morning in the coffee shop." He handed it to me.

"Oh! I was afraid it fell in the toilet."

Everyone gave me a strange look for that.

"Thank you for running it by," I recovered, excellently. Mom fluttered next to me, her eyes so large on Danny's perfect face that I worried after her heart health. "Please give my regards to your grandmother. Although she has no idea who I am."

"Yes, she does." No one should be allowed to be that fine in a navy suit unless their brown eyes were twinkling all over me the way his were. "I told her everything about you."

Mom snorted and said, "You did?"

Bang bang bang! The door shook from whoever the hell this new freaking person was.

My neighbors were gonna think I was a call girl. I was going to have that door replaced by a steel one three feet thick.

"Well, aren't you a popular little miss tonight?" Diego sidled to the door while I plotzed in anticipation. He reached for the handle. He swept the portal open. "Look—it's Doctor Sam!"

Oh, *fuck*.

Chapter Twelve

The Ex Files

Sam burst into the apartment and stopped, frozen, shock suffusing his face. His regard slipped from Suzie and darkened into a black cloud directed at Danny. Diego said to Mom, "You remember Samantha's boyfriend Sam? The oncologist."

That was the lie we'd spun the one and only time Sam had met my mother in Vegas.

Well and good, except that our current lie said his name was Zack, and he worked as my assistant.

Danny's mouth hung open. His gaze ping-ponged from one of us to the next. Finally, he settled on Sam and said, "Good evening...Zack. You — are you — do you date Samantha? And cure cancer?" His brows tightened the more he spoke.

Sam glared at me. I stammered, "W — well... I don't think that anyone can actually *cure cancer*."

Crickets.

"Unfortunately."

Crickets.

My face went numb, and I searched Sam's eyes for the brilliant new fib that would disentangle us from the other fibs. He crossed his arms and dared me to get myself out of it, which was massively unfair. I'd never been forced to lie about a boyfriend before this asshole showed up.

"Sam is my ex." I said it to Danny.

Mom sighed and muttered to Diego, "I knew she couldn't keep a doctor. I win the bet!"

Bet?

I swallowed my rage...barely...and continued digging out. "His middle name is Zack, and that's what he goes by professionally."

"Professionally as what?" inquired Danny, whose arms were now also crossed.

This was the point at which Sam shook his head at me and jumped in to help. "I used to be a doctor, but I gave up everything to follow Samantha across the Atlantic and work as her lowly assistant in a last-ditch bid to work things out."

Nobody knew what to say to that. Mother appeared skeptical. Danny finally began to look at me like I was the crazy person I was. Good. These efforts to appear normal take their toll.

Captain Taco ran from the bedroom and straight to Sam. He scooped up the cat and clutched Taco to his chest, a man clinging to a furry piece of wood while adrift in a sea of falsehoods and competing men.

"Why are you here?" I asked Sam, although I knew the answer was to join the parade currently ruining my evening and/or life.

Sam jerked his head out of Taco's fur and glared at Danny. "I need to speak to you."

Danny started. "To me?" He switched into Robert De Niro mode. If he'd have been a porcupine, every quill would have been erect for attack. "You have something to say to me?"

"I meant Samantha. But I could say something to you."

My current flirtation inched forward. "I'd love to hear it."

"I'd love to say it." Sam put Taco down—I believe that's the fighting cat-lover's equivalent to taking off one's earrings.

"Go ahead, then."

"I will."

"Spit it out."

Sam took a step, his arms stiff, the cords in his neck vivid. "You don't want me to do that."

"Oh, I do. I bloody well do."

I needed to end this before we descended into full-on poo-flinging. Or, God forbid—truth-telling.

"Stop!" I wedged between them, barely, as they were so close they'd either begin shoving or kissing, and my luck wasn't nearly good enough to get the latter. "There's no need for this. Jesus, I don't even have makeup on, how can you possibly fight about my blotchy ass?"

Mom laughed. "Ha! I just said that to Diego. See, you can be funny."

Danny blinked, retreated from Sam and curled his lip at my mother. "She's so nasty," he whispered. He glanced at his phone and cleared his throat. "I must go. I apologize for...bursting in."

I grabbed his arm and walked him to the door. "I'll call you later, okay? I'm sorry about all of this—it's confusing, I know, and—"

"No, no." He took my hand and held it. "You told me you were in an unusual place. I can't be upset when it's true."

My guilt flowed free from my lying mouth to my horny lady parts. The fact that he behaved so gentlemanly, even in the face of my bullshit, shamed me. Fiercely. I smiled and waved while he shot a filthy look at Sam and left.

Whew. One down. Three to go. The dream of being reunited with Colin Firth, the lover who never lied or questioned your lies, was almost a reality.

"Sam," I hissed, "I am spending the evening with my mother, who has flown all the way across the Atlantic to see me." He ignored this and plopped himself on my couch.

"No." Mom primped with a compact and lipstick. "My modeling agent in Vegas got me into a party tonight with an agency here in London. It's models only, you know!"

I stared at the floor. "I am an actual film actress, Mom. Nobody is embarrassed to be seen with me, nowadays."

"I'll call you tomorrow — I want to visit your film set. I bet the director will adore me." She was already halfway out the door, Diego in tow. "I got to meet Daniel Zhang!" she squeaked as the door slammed.

Why the hell had she even shown up tonight? I told myself she was concerned about me, that was what the self-improvement "suggestions" were about. But no. I think I finally landed a movie interesting to her, and she was here to ride my short coattails. That's a kind of pride in me, right?

"If you're not careful, she's going to steal your part in that movie. She gave Zhang her card."

I turned to stare in amazement at Sam. "No, she didn't."

He nodded, the dimple peeking out, like a groundhog sniffing at winter. His face was drawn, tired—he appeared as rough as I felt. But I couldn't pretend that of all the people who'd traipsed through my apartment tonight, I was sorry that he ended up last. Hopefully last. There was no one else left, unless Parliament swung by.

At least I didn't have to pretend with Sam. Not in any way. There's a soothing freedom in being able to let your stomach loose after sucking it in for a long time.

"Want coffee?" I asked.

He nodded and took a deep breath, letting it out and unwinding a hair's breadth. Taco joined him on the couch, and soon Sam sprawled across it to play with the cat. The entire scene of normalcy overcame the flimsy walls I'd glued around my heart, and I fled to the safety of the kitchen to avoid a total collapse.

I'd just ground fresh beans when his voice startled me. "You really have moved on."

I knew what he meant by the hurt, defeated tone. "I just kissed him once." Twice. *Shh, stupid conscience!* "We do that much in the movie."

"Apparently, you do it on the street corner for the benefit of every single entertainment news show."

A flood of memories flung themselves around my brain. "Oh, shit!" I turned and ran to get my phone, which Danny had left on the living room coffee table. Yup—hundreds of messages in my inbox from agent, manager, publicist, gossip sites, journalists, on and on. "I'd totally forgotten."

Strange—I hadn't thought of that kiss at all since it happened, but apparently the gossip sites had.

"How could you forget that? And how could you—" He'd followed me into the room and squeezed his eyes shut as if having an internal crisis.

I threw the phone on the couch. "How could I what?"

His face fell into stark lines of grief. "Sleep with him? Really?"

I sat on the table, too tired to stay upright. "I didn't. I just told you that to be mean. I shouldn't have, and I'm sorry."

"I can't believe you're still lying to me."

"I'm not!"

He gripped the chair back with white hands, putting it between us. "You spent last night with him! I mean…today."

My eyes nearly popped from my head. "You're nuts. I came here, alone, and went almost immediately to sleep. Only to be woken up this morning, uh, evening by Valerie. And Shelley." I shuddered.

He slid out from behind the chair like a viper. "You were with him!"

"What is wrong with you? I was here!" Controlling the urge to kick him became harder and harder. So I stomped away, brushed past him and continued to make coffee. I splashed water into the electric kettle. Some stalker Sam is. Couldn't keep track of me for one freaking night. Maybe Danny had taken some other short redhead home.

Stalker… Damn him!

This time I actually did kick the cabinet. It bounced hollowly and banged me in the shin. I huffed back into the living room to dish it out to my stalker. "Danny accidentally picked up my phone in the coffee shop this morning. He took it home with him, where it stayed. All night. Without me." Sam's mouth dropped open. "That's why he came here this evening—to return it." I took a step closer. "But if my ex-boyfriend was tracking my phone, then the asshole might think I'd spent the day there. Which, frankly, I wish I had."

"Please don't say that." Sam ran a hand behind his neck and squeezed. "Zhang is not the primary reason I keep track of you. You know that."

I stuck my finger in his face. "The reason *you* weren't in my bed all day today is because you kicked yourself out of it." My voice rose to shrillness, and soon I was practically screaming at him. "You have no right to question what I do anymore!"

"I can't let you be with me while this shit is going on."

"But I am with you! Here! Now! With your psycho-thief ex threatening me!" I took a step back for my own health, because seeing him up close stirred in me a confusing mix of passions—part churning loins and part balling fists. "Wait, wait, wait—you can't 'let me'?" A tidal wave of rage swallowed me, and I stumbled to the couch and forced myself to sit. I twisted my robe over and over in my hands.

Finally, I comprehended what had been eating my heart out for the last week. "You decided for me. You resolved to end our relationship, rather than having me choose what I wanted for myself."

He barked out a bitter laugh. "You were on the verge of leaving me anyway."

"Don't tell me what I was or wasn't going to do! I love you!" I sucked in a breath and turned away. "Loved...you. And now I'm dealing with the same villains I would have otherwise, but my only ally is a vibrator." I put my head in my hands. "And my cat, but obviously—two different purposes."

Dumbfounded, he stood there, just staring at me. Taco meowed and wound around his legs. Sam picked him up and slowly approached the other end of the couch. He set the cat down between us, and sank into the cushions himself. "I thought if I made you go, you'd be out of danger."

I petted Taco to avoid actually facing his dad. The cat set his head on my thigh, and his silken fur calmed me. Or maybe I was just too tired to fight anymore.

In a low voice he said, "It was easier for me to rip off the Band-Aid than to anticipate the axe."

I chewed on my lip, the last few days whirling through my head. I let out the breath I'd been holding. "You're right. I mean, you tore out my heart, but—I understand your reasoning. Who the hell knows what the right answer is."

"Whatever it is, I never seem to find it."

Reaching over Taco, I took his hand and squeezed. He clutched it and stared glassily in front of him. After a minute or so, he patted my arm and carefully set my hand back on my side of the cat. An alluring mix of gentleman and scoundrel—that was my Sam.

"I'm still bothered by you tracking my phone," I said.

He sighed and searched my eyes for understanding. "Can you think of it…like a detective protecting his undercover operative? You haven't been speaking to me. She could have hauled you off to Russia, and no one would realize before it was too late."

There was a certain comfort in having one ally. Nobody else knew about the quicksand sucking me down, down. "Okay, but no more jealousy or bullshit. I'm free to do what I want."

"Yes! Yes. I shouldn't have come here tonight."

This was clearly my cue to throw him out, but…the idea of being alone filled me with a yawning ennui. I stayed silent, and he relaxed further.

In this moment, our friendship comforted me. We'd been such torrid lovers and fighters I didn't usually think of him as my friend. He was, though. Absolutely, in the best sense of the word. He knew everything about me, and I knew him down to the core. Sure, he'd hidden details when we'd first met—criminal, natch—but over time he'd revealed so much. He cries when Captain Kirk sacrifices everything for Spock. He delights in coming up with the perfect present unique to me. I know to order twenty chicken nuggets because he loves them as leftovers. Important things in a relationship. Was memorizing someone's middle name really more important than knowing they have recurring dreams about being lost, naked in the woods when they're stressed out, and understanding enough to rub their shoulders in the right place to help them fall asleep again?

He was my best friend, and I knew, I knew that despite everything he only wanted wonderful things for me. I traveled all over for my work now, and he delighted in my every success and listened when I cried about the failures.

Maybe I wasn't such a great friend to him—when the shit hit the fan, I usually jumped to the worst conclusion. Yes, he'd earned some of that distrust, but he'd also risked everything to try and be with me. Hot shame burned across my chest.

"What's your middle name?" I asked out of the blue.

His head popped up in surprise, but not unpleasantly. "Matthew. Biblical. Guess it didn't take."

"It worked some." My gaze dropped to the dusky green V-neck tee he had on. He'd worn one of my favorite shirts over here to argue with me. I couldn't help but smile.

"Do you have anything to eat?" he asked, bringing his full charm to bear with a lopsided grin that could shatter heaven and drop you down to hell, giggling as you fell. How I'd missed that cocksure attitude. Not to mention his actual cock.

"Fine, I'll feed you. After."

"After what?"

Heh. At least he wasn't assuming to get anything more than food. "You people keep interrupting my date with Colin Firth."

He sat up a little straighter. "How rude of us," he said, light as air.

I kept petting Taco. "I mean, you're here. And we're gonna die."

"If not soon, then at least some time."

"Right. So, in a completely uncommitted fashion, we could, you know, celebrate life." I'd used this reasoning when deciding to sleep with him the first time. If it wasn't sound logic, it was, at least, familiar.

I let my offer dangle, like a sexy carrot on a sexy stick. The hope flaring in his eyes began to smolder into full-on determination. He licked his pretty, pretty lips. "If it helps, I'll kidnap you. For old time's sake."

I laughed out loud at that. "I haven't been kidnapped in days. I would make a joke about missing it, but I don't think that would say anything good about me or the state of my life."

"This is a totally consensual kidnap."

I nodded and stared into his eyes—a luminous, mossy green. They matched his shirt, above which his soft brown chest hair peeked. My hand reached up to caress the notch in his neck quite of its own volition. Silken warmth greeted my fingertips. He took the cat, placed him on the floor and scooted closer to me as

Taco protested, loudly. We ignored him. Sam took my face in his hands and leaned forward to kiss me.

Oh, God. He felt like home.

He took his time, pressing his lips to mine slowly, again and again, barely opening his, just enough to tease me. After a minute of simultaneously driving me mad and bringing me completely to peace, he set his forehead against mine. His breath danced on my face like quick bursts of warm sunlight. We stayed like that for a while, his knuckles rubbing my cheek, my hands playing in his hair while I memorized the scent of his skin all over again.

"Would you like to be kidnapped to the bedroom, or stay here?"

He moved to nuzzle my neck, and the delicious sensations he brought to life rendered me temporarily speechless. Delicate kisses nibbled their way from behind my ear to my ear lobe, down to the shoulder and collarbone. With each one, he brought my skin to a new pitch of yearning. "Here," I managed to whisper.

"Mmm hmm," he agreed. Coming up for air, he pulled back, his face flushed. I leaned forward to really put the bloom in his cheeks, but he stopped me with a finger to my lips. "And would my unfortunate victim be more comfortable with me in or out of clothing?"

I giggled. "I prefer my abductors shirtless, but leave the jeans on. For now."

He spread a wide grin and stood up to perform the shirt removal for me. He slid it up over his adorable belly, past hairy pecs, and finally tossed it to the ground while his shoulders rippled. Hot, shirtless men in jeans are a particular weakness for me, along with my other three hundred thousand weaknesses, all of which Sam seemed to exploit.

"Would the lady enjoy being stripped?"

Six little words and I was wet. Although, to be honest, I'd been ready to throw him on the floor since the moment he walked in. Some of us board the train to disaster bedecked in ugly bathrobes. "I'm sure you would enjoy that. I know I'm an eyesore."

"No." He returned to the couch and took my hand. "Look, I like makeup and sexy clothes and, um, brushed hair as well as the next guy, but you're always beautiful to me." He pushed a lock of hair behind my ear and wound it through his fingers. "I really just want you to be comfortable. There's never a time I see you and don't think how lucky I am to do so."

Totally against the rules to make me love him all over again. "The feeling is mutual."

He dimpled at me. "You don't mind when I don't wear makeup?"

"You would look so pretty!"

One of his eyebrows cocked. "Is *that* what you want to do with me right now?"

I nearly rolled off the cushions laughing. He would have let me, too—his eyes held an unmistakable twinkle that said, 'Screw it, let's David Bowie this shit'. I crawled onto his lap, straddling him, and sat back on my heels. "Maybe some other time. Right now, the kidnappee respectfully requests that you divest her of her mismatched pajamas."

"These are kinda sad."

"It's hard finding octopus jammies."

"They're for children, aren't they?"

Of course they were, but I'd learned lying from the best. I shook my head. "I refuse to participate in this interrogation."

"That would be your right under the Geneva Convention, if it covered jammies, or octopi." His eyes locked on to mine while he unbuttoned my top, his fingers lingering on the flesh between my breasts. He traced the inner curves, his skin impossibly shivery on mine. I pushed forward. Laughing, he eased me back. "If you're too close, I can't unbutton." I squirmed over his lap, and oh, hello to you, too, wonderful penis. I reached down, my hand caressing us both through our clothes. He let out a breathy moan and rested his head on my shoulder.

Better do that again. I found his zipper and eased it down as leisurely as he'd been treating me. In retaliation, he teased my nipples—both of them, at the same time, the vile man. Lips, hands, palms everywhere. An intense devotion washed his face in bliss, and he closed his eyes. "You can say it," I whispered.

He blurted, "I missed them."

"You mean me."

"I mean all of you."

Hands on my waist, he lifted me off him and set me against the end of the couch. He removed my top completely and grinned at us in approval. I had to giggle—he faced me with the reverence of a pilgrim at a holy shrine. He probably would have prayed to my tits had I asked him. *Hail boobies, full of grace. Thine bra is off thee.*

His trance ended and he turned to other concerns. "The bottoms, Miss?"

"At your leisure, wicked Sir."

"Are you certain I'm not interrupting your evening?"

"Well, I could be viewing important cats on the Internet now, but I suppose these activities will do."

He got on his knees—mmmmmm—and crawled over my legs. "I'll try my best to fill your time." The way he purred this, I think he wanted to fill something else.

It took a moment or two for us to bounce my pajamas down my bubble butt, but we managed. He always loved this part. My view of his stretched back and his bottom bobbing in the air distracted me anew, inspiring me to run my fingers over my already-aching pussy. He tossed my pants aside and paused to examine my play. "Well, well," he said. "Were you anticipating a fake kidnapping?"

Apparently my black, lacy hipsters met with approval. I reached for him.

"No, no. As your kidnapper, I demand you keep touching yourself."

"Then inspire me."

His hand already stroked the bulge in his pants, and he worked himself for my edification until I began to squirm, his eyes never leaving mine.

"These are very nice"—he leaned forward and slipped a finger into the bottom of my lace—"but I bet you'll have more fun when they're gone."

"You first."

The dimple liked that. Sam reached into his open fly and took out his cock. The male member is not exactly pretty, no, but it is invigorating just the same. My blood pounded through every inch of me, and I could not look away. He stroked the shaft nice and slow, performing for me.

Out of sheer, charitable gratitude, I slid my undies down my legs and threw them aside. A flurry of movement and chastising 'mewr's told me I'd just thrown my underwear on the cat. Sam stopped his sensual stroking to lean back and guffaw.

"Whoops." I shrugged my shoulders and grinned.

"His therapist is going to have a field day with this."

I turned onto my knees, threw my arms around Sam and kissed him—hungrily, desperately. His grip landed on my ass and pressed me to his cock, stiff and hot between us. My hands slid down his spine to knead his marvelous butt. "Hey, hey," he whispered. "I gave you a different job to do."

"But I've been doing it for myself for days and days."

He groaned. "Tell me."

I sank onto the couch and teased myself, coaxing out my wetness. My head fell back, it felt so good and so nasty to be showing him at his demand. My eyes closed, I said, "I lay in bed, in broad daylight, frustrated."

"Go on." His voice sounded thin and higher. He leaned over me now, his cock in his hand, moving faster.

I redoubled my efforts—for him, of course. "So I rubbed my clit. And I got really wet."

He swallowed. "And what were you thinking about?" His eyes opened. "And it better be *me*."

"It was!" No lies—it was. "I thought about you. About your big body not being there." My pussy ached, and my hips arched up to meet my fingers. "When I close my eyes and imagine a big cock inside me, it's always yours."

With a breathy sound—happy or unhappy, I couldn't tell—he yanked me down until I lay flat and he entered me. I cried out, I was too tight. He held me there, for a moment, barely moving. He kissed my forehead, and I smiled. He returned it and gazed at me while I rubbed his waist, his ass underneath his still-clinging jeans.

He murmured, "I'm sorry I left you to do the heavy lifting, but you told a great story."

"Apparently."

He laughed silently and pulled out, achingly slowly. They always amazed me — the sublime sensations emanating from our joined bodies. He thrust in again, and I rose to meet him. "Samantha, baby," he said. I held on to him with my arms, legs, my hands pulling him into my body. I'd have given anything in that moment for him to never stop.

"Brawr!" Captain Taco leaped onto the tiny space of couch next to my waist — to save me, or Sam, I don't know. His fur tickled, and I started to giggle again.

"This damn cat." Sam grabbed him by the belly and deposited him on the floor once again. Taco leaped onto the coffee table and sat there, staring at us.

"Your cat," I said.

"Your cat — I gave him to you."

"After you taught him your perverted ways."

He drove into me with his hips, and hot damn, the pleasure nearly drowned me. Here's to perverted ways. "Like that?"

I gasped when he bore down on me, again and again, and I couldn't form actual words. I think he knew the answer.

Soon, our audience was completely forgotten while we made up for lost time, maybe all the lonely time we'd ever experienced.

Just when hot, sweet sweat began to trail down his back, he said, "I need to see you." I moaned my acquiescence—he had me so tight in the grip of pleasure that I'd have done anything he wanted. He pulled out and I protested, vociferously. That brought out his dimple—deep and smarmy. "Poor thing," he said unconvincingly.

He turned me onto my shoulder and climbed around me to stand and take off his jeans. He must have been the inspiration for the phrase "sight for sore eyes." Mine were sore from tears, and he was definitely the medicine.

Grinning, he squeezed in behind me. We barely fit on this tiny space, but that only served to force him to hold me against every single centimeter of his body. His legs teased the backs of my thighs, and I ground against him. "Damn, woman. Give me a moment to breathe."

"No."

He didn't sound too upset. He gripped my leg from behind, running an exploratory hand from my inner thigh to the back of my knee. That same hand returned the way it came, and by the time he reached my pussy, I held it there, slipping his fingers in. I needed some, any part of him inside me. He encouraged me, "Yes, yes," while I rode his hand, slippery and so damn good, but he didn't last long. He replaced his fingers with his cock and took me from behind.

Oh, and he watched me, as he adored doing. He played with my breasts and thrust into me without fail. I wound my arm around his head and grabbed him by the hair. His eyes were half-closed and so dark, and we saw each other—really saw—naked in every way possible. The love in his eyes was palpable.

A small smile preceded his fingers rubbing my clit in fevered circles, and my moans became high, breathy, guttural. I came with his hand on me and his cock never ceasing, while he bathed my face in a loving regard that overwhelmed me.

"Don't stop," I said. Sometimes he would, to let me enjoy my afterglow. But I wanted to shatter him as he'd done me. I took his hand and held it to my breast while he pounded me faster than before. Soon his eyes closed, and he reveled in his own orgasm, riding it out however he wanted. We collapsed against the cushions, his arm holding me to him.

I don't know how long we lay there, my brain drifting and my eyes closed. My scalp didn't even hurt too badly anymore. Orgasms cure everything. After a while, I felt him chuckle. "What?" I asked.

He pointed. Captain Taco sat two feet away from the couch, sitting with his back turned, shunning us. We both cracked up, laughing so hard that the cat shot a disdainful eye our direction as if to say, 'Do you not see me hating you? How dare you find this amusing!'

"Did I earn my dinner?" Sam asked while nuzzling my shoulder with his nose.

"Breakfast. And *yes*. Except I don't have any."

"Lazy."

"I've been too depressed to grocery shop."

He turned my face to look directly at me. "I'm sorry."

I kissed him, lightly. He smelled of sex and masculinity, and I wanted to bathe in him. "Take me out? Nowhere special, just...let's just go have fun somewhere."

"Yeah. Get dressed."

Reluctantly, I unwound my limbs from his and got up. I couldn't stay there forever and besides, food was one of my fervent lovers, too.

I threw on a T-shirt and jeans, and he came into the bedroom to get re-dressed, too. My hair stood out at impossible angles, so I attacked it with a brush. I couldn't hit all the major cities of Europe with sex hair. He held my pajamas from the other room and got a puzzled look on his face while he pulled something from the pocket. "What is this?"

I gulped. "Oh, crap. I recorded my convo with Valerie and forgot it was there. Hey, why are you going through my pockets?"

He slumped into one hip. "You're telling me you have the entire evening recorded?"

"Um...yup."

"Hmmm." He set the recorder on the dresser and didn't answer my question. Sigh—thieves. "Did she say anything incriminating?"

I went into the bathroom to find some mascara. He followed. "Well, I said things, and she didn't disagree with them. Then she threatened my family with 'accidents'. And Shelley—" No. I closed my mouth. I wouldn't tell him about that. It might make him stupid.

He groaned and sat on the toilet lid. "Valerie's gotten worse. Maybe she was always this cruel, and in my lusty, naive twenties I didn't see it." Peeking up at me, he said, "I was taught that ladies were ladies. Even non-Southern belles were different from men— kinder, gentler, peaceable, predictable. *Now* I understand that's just a hole men try and force women into to make them behave the way they want. It's an appealing lie, though, when you're a young, stupid dude and want to romanticize every skirt. And the prissy innocent act is something Valerie performs very well. It's what makes her such a great thief."

I regarded him with amazement. "What convinced you that women were actual human beings, and not a different race of giggling porcelain figurines?"

"Jane." He grinned. "Jane doesn't take patriarchal bullshit. If you treat her like anything other than your master and commander, she'll eat you alive." He ran a hand through his hair to tame it. I wasn't the only one with sex hair. "Funny enough, Jane has actual honor, not pretend-lady honor. Took me a while to spot the difference."

I paused swiping mascara into my lashes and asked, "Do you really think Jane would have killed us?"

One eyebrow cocked, he said, "I don't know. My heart says 'no', but I've proven I can be an idiot."

"Poor man. Beset by so many wicked women."

He came round behind me and pulled me close. "I prefer my ladies unladylike in my bed, or wickedly cracking zingers."

"Good thing for me." Our smiles met in the mirror. "Or not."

"Shut up and stop ruining the moment."

"Okay."

I finished making myself barely presentable, and we emerged from my cave to wander the neighborhood hand in hand. As if nothing untoward was happening in our lives. Slipping into normal, happy mode with him seemed perfectly natural. I guess I'd learned to live in the now a bit more since encountering Hurricane Sam.

We found a little pizza place and ordered, with frothy, yummy beers to start, because the now required both.

I asked him, "Can you call in any of the folks you got your immunity with?"

He sloshed his beer in surprise and set it on the table. He sighed, taking a pensive moment before answering. "No. My whole goal was to not rat out anyone else. If I give up Valerie, it'll be open season."

"Hunting season appears to have already begun."

His lips pulled into a grimace, but he didn't disagree. "I've only ever worked for Val and Jane. I suppose the minor players might be affronted."

"But none of them have actually waved a knife in your face."

"No."

I took a sip of the bitter, cold beer. It swished down my throat into my empty belly. "So it's Valerie between us and—"

"Us and what?" His eyes flickered, tired and concerned, in the candlelight.

I played with the tablecloth. "You were really doing all of this so you could"—I swallowed—"settle down with me?" Why was this a hard concept for me to embrace? *Because you're not the kind of girl who gets happily ever after!* said the voice in my head, which sounded suspiciously like my mother's.

He nodded, his brows drawing together. "What a great job I've done."

"You can't be held responsible for the actions of others."

"Yes, I can. If I wasn't who I was, you'd have never fallen into this mess."

I plopped the beer down and reached for his hand. "Sam, if you weren't who you were, I'd be a depressed secretary still. Yes, I would." The candle had nearly burned away in the little glass holder. His face got less stark the more the flicker waned. "I know who you are, and I started a relationship with you. I shouldn't hold your occupation over your head."

"No. No." He took his hand back and drummed it on the table. "I have spent my entire adult life as a criminal. If I have...issues regarding my profession, I deserve to have them. I deserve to deal with the consequences." He grinned, his eyes blazing and clever. "If I was a truly honorable man, I'd be in prison now, paying my debt to society."

"I guess you can take the boy out of the den of thieves, but—"

He nodded and laughed.

I continued, "I don't want you in prison. I'm not that lofty, either. Let's face it, a lot worse jerks than you get away with not paying their debts."

"At least I'm not a politician."

"Amen."

I held out my hand again, and he took it, pressing a kiss to the tips of my fingers. The pizza came, sausage and mushroom. You have to keep a man whose favorite pizza is the same as yours. I'm pretty sure Miss Manners says that.

I polished off my first piece and paused to wash my grease down with beer. "So, does this mean...what?"

"What?"

"*I'm* not asking *you*."

He licked a long piece of cheese from his lip. "Oh." Nodding, he wiped his fingers and folded them on the table. His face shifted into faux-serious mode. Boy, he gave good earnestness. "Miss Lytton."

I sat back. "Yes, Mr Turner."

"Will you be my official girlfriend again?"

"And?"

"And?" He cocked his head and rolled his eyes. "Just because *you're* wordy and overblown—"

I lifted my eyebrows.

"My dearest darling Ms Lytton. You're so wonderful that a rainbow would be jealous of your booty, and unicorns bow to your graceful charm."

"Do you really mean it?"

His eyes emitted a heart-melt ray similar to that of a puppy. "Yes. If rainbows were sentient and unicorns existed, it would be true."

"Thank you, Sam." He kissed my hand and lovingly caressed it. I shrugged and added, "I'll think about it."

He snatched his hand away. "You are such a pain in my ass."

"What? You broke my heart! I'm not just gonna let it go because you have a nice penis and a fancy way with rainbow compliments. For all I know, Daniel Zhang also has those things."

Sam's mouth turned hard and bitter. "Daniel Zhang. Urgh. *Ooh look at me, I'm a tall, handsome, rich, suave movie star.*"

Nodding, I said, my voice full of sorrow, "I know. What an awful person he is."

"Like hemorrhoids." He sloshed his beer on the way to his mouth. "You're my little, redheaded, painful hemorrhoid."

I snatched another piece of pizza. "Okay. You can quit with the compliments now."

"With nice tits."

I started giggling. I did enjoy the idea of myself as a loud-haired boil on the ass of humanity. With nice tits.

* * * *

"Samantha, stop! You're hitting me!"

I must hit him. I have to get away. I flailed and punched out in any way possible, sweat pooling in my lower back, my —

"Samantha, you're dreaming!" He shook me. "Ouch! It's Sam, it's me."

This time, he caught my fist and held it to his chest. My eyes opened. Sam's face. Sam's hands.

"What the hell were you dreaming?"

I squeezed my eyes shut and sagged against him. He held and rocked me. Flashes of terror still slammed into my eyeballs. I concentrated on his soft skin, his smell. On the now, which was warm and full of bliss. After a while, my breathing settled, and my adrenaline calmed to a dull roar. "What was that?" he asked again gently as he stroked my back.

I sighed into his chest. I hadn't ever told him about the nightmares. "I dream about Scott Coulter. Sometimes."

"Oh, no, Samantha..."

Scott Coulter was the asshole from Steak on a Stick who'd kidnapped and almost killed me and all my loved ones over a damn Picasso. He was currently serving many, many years in prison, thanks to me.

"I dream that he gets out of prison early and comes after me. Or that I'm in the trial again and no one believes what I say. Although it's not always me he hurts. Sometimes I find him attacking Ellen."

"Shhhhh." The panic crept up my spine again, and he stroked my hair until I stopped digging my hand into his shoulder. "Baby, I'm so sorry. Does this happen a lot?"

I shook my head. His fingers soothed my forehead again and again. "Not as much as before. It was bad, for a while." It had taken weeks to not worry over the trial every single day, to be able to combat that constant anxiety. I'd lost weight during that time, and everyone had told me how great I'd looked. Har de har har.

"Jesus Christ. I gave you PTSD."

"No."

"Why didn't you tell me?"

"I don't know. I didn't want to make it a big thing."

"Baby." He turned out from under me and lay on his side so we were face to face. A weak stream of sunlight from a gap in the blinds illuminated his eyes. He stroked my cheek. "It is a big thing. I'm supposed to be here for you, and I failed."

"We've been long distance. We can't—"

"No. No." He leaned forward until his forehead touched mine. "I'm going to do better. So that you don't have to be afraid anymore. You can tell me anything. I know I can be a bear, but usually it's…shit. It's because I get so fucking mad that I can't instantly fix everything that's wrong with you." He sniffled, his voice choked with emotion. "I love you so much."

I scooted closer and nuzzled his cheek.

"Do you still love me?" he asked, his voice small.

"Yes!" His face in my hands, I kissed him. He rolled us over and pressed his warm lips to mine again and again, seeking a reassurance I was happy to give.

I forgot my nightmare in his encompassing arms, his strong body. In the words of love he murmured over my skin. What a glorious mess we made. And how easily we could forget it.

Temporarily.

Chapter Thirteen

I Guess I'll Eat Some Worms

I paid for my joyous night of hide the salami. The next evening, my agent, publicist and manager chose choice words for me on the matter of my radio silence re Kissgate, but were all equally delighted that my relationship with Daniel Zhang had become international gossip fodder. I'd moved up at least three rungs on the celebrity fuckability scale!

Sam nearly ground his teeth to the gums when surfing the internet, so I took away his access and sent him grocery shopping for us while I dealt with real life. Danny left a voice mail for me that I didn't return because it would have made me feel guilty to speak with him. But then again, the guilt of not returning the call guilted me in a guilty way. I began to fantasize about going full *Cast Away*, where the only person I could disappoint was a volleyball with a bloody hand print on it. Meanwhile, my stomach churned, churned.

When Sam returned with glorious food, he hustled me to bed again where it seemed he was eager to prove who was the man in my life. Indeed, after his glorious turn in the sack, I honored him with the Oscar for Best Performance By a Leading Man With Bonus Colin Firth. I'm not even sure what to call what he did to me, except logistically impressive.

With such wicked thoughts in my head, we returned to film the following night. The moment I stepped onto set, I got hustled to a corridor in which stood Danny and our director, an up-and-coming British hotshot named simply JenX. She was the hottest funny lady going, having shot to A-list status when she directed Carrot Top into a Best Supporting Actor Golden Globe nomination in her first feature. If that doesn't lend credibility, then nothing does. "Hey, S," JenX said. "So, video. You and D. Hot. Nice. Paparazzi. Awesome. Sex on stone. Cool?"

Danny bit back a smile. I blinked from one to the other and said, "What?"

"Profesh, yeah?"

I nodded and flashed a half smile and shrugged—all the answer JenX ever seemed to require, anyhow. I was getting more used to her way of speaking. When she'd called me to offer the role, the entire conversation consisted of, "You. Jayde. Kill it. Nice." I'd called my agent afterward to figure out what the hell had happened.

JenX model-stomped away on her platforms, which appeared to be ten inches high. "Translate?" I asked Danny.

He stepped closer. "The producers have decided to capitalize on the video by adding a sex scene for us."

"What, are we gonna hump on a display case in the middle of the robbery?"

He handed me new script pages. "The Rosetta Stone, namely."

Sex on stone. Holy shit. "Ah. Well, at least it serves the story in a dignified way."

Laughing, he pulled me farther away from the whir of crew getting the set ready. I could feel Sam's eyes boring into my back from the darkness. Danny's perfect face peering down at me churned, churned my guts. "I'm sorry I didn't call you back," I told him.

His mouth twitched sadly, and the anxiety in my belly birthed anxiety babies. "I'm sure you were busy."

Busy learning about how fun the Hitachi Magic Wand Olympics can be. I nodded. He stayed silent, clearly waiting for me to say something. Better to come clean about my being dirty. "I got back together with Sam. Zack!" I pressed my fingers to my temples. "Zack Sam. I'm sorry, and I didn't mean to lead you on. You are insanely attractive and wonderful, and I feel lucky to have even smooched you in front of millions on the Internet."

His jaw shifted in annoyance. Maybe this was the first time in his life he'd ever been dumped, or at least thrown over for some dude with no name. He recovered and flashed a confident smile that told me, *somehow*, he'd survive the loss of me. "It was just a kiss. I'm glad you worked it out with..." He shrugged, and I did not gaze at his sexy shoulders. "It does make things a bit awkward in that everyone thinks we're dating now."

"Yes." A PA stopped by and shooed us toward makeup. We promised him we'd be right there and began walking. "Look, we can still hang out. The more we don't misbehave in public, the crazier they'll go. They'll think we're hiding something."

"Sure."

The conversation thankfully ended when a blur of people with brushes attacked our faces. *You are a shitty person,* I told myself. Myself didn't have any fast comebacks to the contrary. Churn, churn. My stomach ached enough that I skipped the craft services table in favor of resting before my first scene.

I was forced to lock myself in the bedroom of the trailer to get away from Shelley, currently slumping on my couch, smack-smacking away on her third gum piece of the morning. The sound of her saliva squirting might force me to commit evil acts. Like tearing out her stupid hair. My bitterness merged with my vanity and anger to create a brand-new emotion — vitterger. I was so vittergry at that woman I nearly blacked out.

No more than ten minutes later, PA Wayne knocked on my tiny bedroom door. "Hi, Samantha. Can you come out? Um…"

Something told me that this "um" was of the "oh, shit" variety. I scrambled to my feet and opened the front door. Wayne smiled halfheartedly and said, "Your mom is here and talking to JenX."

I squeezed my fists closed until my fingernails bit my flesh. "Witch!"

Wayne's eyes goggled, and he backed away. For good reason, for there appeared to be lightning sparking from my ears. I heard nothing but the whistling of my rage and the opening strains to the theme from *Jaws.*

I ran out of the trailer, and Wayne caught me up to lead me to the scene of the accident. I heard the Southern drawl oozing through the galleries before I saw her. "Ah've starred in the Las Vegas Players production of *Guys and Dolls* twice now, and —"

And then I died, only to return and haunt this old woman until her botox caused her face to mummify.

"Mom!" I screamed it, and everyone who wasn't already gaping in glee turned to witness the new goings-on.

Be cool, Samantha. Be the star you know you are. Or at least, the star you might be, someday. Be the kind of cool person who would be a star if they weren't you.

Oh, to hell with it. I squared my shoulders and glided to my mother's side. I wedged between her and Diego, who wore a shirt made of mesh that came from an *International Male* catalog circa 1986. "Mom, hi. How nice of you to visit the set."

JenX ran a hand over her blue fauxhawk. "So...why?"

I grabbed Suzie by the shoulders and swiveled her toward any direction away from JenX. Suzie being on set was definitely not "profesh, yeah?" "My mom's a big fan!" I called over my shoulder to JenX. "But she must go now."

Suzie squeaked and adjusted her silk pink capris. "Don't you think Jayde should have a mother?" she yelled to all and sundry. "Not that many would believe that I could be a mother to such an old—" I shoved harder. Diego trotted next to us helplessly, his mesh shirt no doubt irritating his razor-burned chest.

We passed Sam on the way outside. "Holy crap," he said. Suzie's sequined suit jacket was trimmed in hot pink ostrich.

I bypassed my trailer and continued yanking her by the arm all the way to the parking lot. Every time she wiggled I growled at her and, for once, she seemed to acknowledge my feelings by shutting the hell up.

I stopped on the sidewalk. "How did you get here?"

"Cab."

Pointing toward the street, I said, "Diego, please take her away."

"Samantha!" Mom fluffed up her ostrich and descended into full on Scarlett O'Hara. "How dare you embarrass me that way?"

Something inside me snapped. I felt it physically — a flick, a sharp pain, a loosening. My face tingled into numbness, and I took a deep breath. "Embarrass...*you*?"

"Samantha." Sam, behind me. Whispering and grabbing my arm.

"But I embarrass you all the time, don't I, Mom?" The echoes of a thousand cutting remarks slithered into my head. "I'm too fat, or too ugly, or too untalented, or too short, or expectedly single, or too poor, or too not-rich-enough, right?"

Suzie's jaw went slack. Her eyes roamed to a focus somewhere behind me.

"How dare you spend my entire life disparaging me, and then come into my job — my *job*, Mom — and...and try to..."

Sam grabbed my shoulders from behind. "Baby, don't. You have an audience."

I closed my eyes and sagged against him. My adrenaline rushed so hard, I heard little but a whirring noise.

"Suzie, leave." Sam did my talking for me. "Do not come back here. You two can discuss this later."

A few moments' silence. No one moved. "Discuss what?" said Suzie, light as air, before clicking away on her kitten booties. Diego shuffled off to Buffalo right after without meeting my eye. At least one of them was experiencing shame.

My eyes squeezed shut, I turned around and pressed my face to Sam's chest, peeping Toms be damned. I forced out every thought but the balming scent of his shirt. He held me for a moment before grabbing my hand and leading me away. I didn't even see where. Or care.

When I peeled my eyelids open, we were in a deserted stairwell on the first floor. "Do you think I'm fired?" I whispered. My hushed words bounced off the steel surrounding us.

"No." He rubbed my shoulders. "No, she'd only just gotten to speak with JenX. It wasn't nearly as bad as you're imagining."

"Oh, so I overreacted?"

"Whoa." He took a step back and leaned down more on my eye level to stare me directly in the face. "I said nothing of the sort. I'm telling you I watched the whole thing—I sent the PA to get you—and you have not lost your job, okay?"

My hands began to shake. My body was Vesuvius, and I was ready to reign terror upon the poor citizens of Pompeii. Right now, Sam was the only poor bastard in front of me. I clenched my teeth closed to avoid saying something I oughtn't, and that he didn't deserve.

Only one thing to do, if I couldn't erupt poisonously.

I grabbed his shirt front, slammed him into the wall and stood on my tip-toes to kiss him. No, I didn't kiss him—I devoured his mouth with mine, biting, sucking, tugging. He offered no resistance, but grabbed my face and leaped into the fray. The first yelp of pain came from me. My sore, throbbing bottom lip hurt damn good, and I pressed my hips into his so he would abuse me further. My hand inched downward to cup his hard-on through his jeans. His ragged moan reverberated in the tiny space. I teased his zipper downward.

His hand caught mine. "Samantha." His voice blended in an ego-boosting combination of shocked censure and aroused fascination. "We can't screw on the stairs."

I grabbed him by the back of the head and pulled him down to my mouth. "I wasn't going to fuck you. I was going to suck your cock."

"Jesus." In a flurry, he removed my hands from his hot, bulging places. He whipped his phone out of his pocket and said, "You need to be on set in ten minutes."

"Ugh." I paced away a few steps and turned to face him from too far away to grope. "Are you actually being my assistant right now?"

"Shameful, I know." He grinned, and the dimple told me that it, at least, was completely pro-blow-job. "You are so hot right now, and I can't begin to tell you how that dirty little jumpsuit with its dirty, long zipper has invaded my personal fantasy time, but"—he took a deep breath and moved his cock into a less obvious place—"rain check. Or not, but I don't want to get you fired for real. Someone needs to support the family when I'm forced to walk the straight and narrow."

Sam acting high and noble and correct should have sobered me...yet, all I wanted was to toss him on the cold ground. Especially when he threw around the word "family" willy nilly. I pictured a quiet night at home—him, me, Taco—watching old episodes of *The Dick Van Dyke Show* and then showering together. Maybe not the cat for that last part. It was the horniest, homiest thought I'd ever thunk...and it filled me with bemused bliss. My muscles began to ease. "I love you," I told him.

He melted me with his eyes, already a melty shade of chocolate. "You only love me for my body."

"The body is only seventy-eight percent of it. Your evil mind and admiration for my butt also contribute." He smiled and made wiggly eyebrows in my butt's direction.

I licked my lips and took a steadying breath. We were alone, and I couldn't not ask the question anymore. It haunted my brain like the specter of unflattering pictures on the Internet. "What is the plan, Sam? We only have four, five days until V—her deadline. We can't just—yank the thing out of the...thing. Because I'll bet there are things that will...counteract...when things are thinged."

He gave me a thumbs-up. "Good code wording there."

"Thank you."

He climbed a few stairs to peer up the square, circular staircase. Squarecular? When satisfied that we were, indeed, alone, he said, "I am waiting for...a thing. Equipment. It will help. But I can't do anything until the thing arrives from...the place."

I nodded as if I understood any of the words.

"Look, what is she going to do to you if you miss her deadline? Nothing." He began to pace. "She can't touch you while you're filming." His eyes focused on mine, then slipped away to stare at the wall. "You're safe in production."

Safe. The bald patch on my head tingled. Safe. "What about you?" I asked softly.

He only hesitated for a moment. A second long enough for me to imagine every worst scenario. Belatedly, he laid a reassuring smile on me. "She knows you need me for this."

"And what about Ellen? And Nicolette? And even horrible Suzie? If anyone is going to end my mother, by great Caesar's ghost, *it will be me.*"

"Enough." He closed the few steps between us and swept me into his arms. His kiss brimmed with the kind of desperation usually only found in movies about vampiric teenagers. He pawed my body, pressing it to his own, and we fell against the wall.

"Yeeeeaaaahhhh," came Shelley's voice a split second before the metallic screech of a door opening. "They're in here."

Thump thump thump sounded Shelley's heavy UGG-footed steps. My legs were still wrapped around Sam and his hands helpfully supported my ass, when who should follow Shelley...but Danny.

Sam froze at the sight of Danny, who glared first at me, then at Sam. A wide grin split my lover's face, and he cocked his head in a pure asshole kind of way. Danny crossed his arms and stared Sam down. "A little help, please?" I asked. When Sam didn't reply, I helpfully tweaked his nipple.

"*Ow.*" That moved his hands.

I nearly slid to the floor, but Danny lunged in to slow my progress toward a certain bruising. "Thank you, Danny. What a gentleman—"

Sam snipped, "Do not even—"

"What can I do for you, Danny? I'm very sorry about...this."

Danny narrowed his eyes at Sam, both still too engaged in their dick-measuring contest to respond.

I left. The smack of boots behind me told me that my time apart from Shelley had come to an end, and that of all the people I would want following me, I got her instead. I smoothed my outfit and jumped into makeup for a lipstick refresher—whoops—and ran into JenX. "So, right. Your scene. Running. Danger imminent. Danny. Where?"

Shelley removed her gum. "Yeah. Samantha has a massage now."

"What?" I will not punch Shelley. I will not punch Shelley. "I have to start work now, Shelley."

She didn't immediately reply, but stared at her wadded-up blue goo before depositing it back into her maw. "Yeah. I have to talk to you, and give a massage. I'm your massivity."

JenX said, "So...schedule, yeah?"

"Yeaaaaaaaaaaaah, no. I'm massuring her."

"Shut up, Shelley!" I stepped between her and my director, who was now disturbed enough that her giant designer headphones were off. If she was forced to remove her sunglasses, I was in deep shit. "Shelley is an idiot. I'm totally ready. Running. Danger. Profesh!" We were set to film a chase—our group running from and foiling security. I smiled, yet JenX did not return her headphones to their usual position.

Danny joined us then, thank goodness. He said, "You sure you don't need some time to boff your boyfriend? Maybe we could all take lunch while you snog in the stairwell, and Shelley gives you a massage." Damn. And also ouch. Danny had stepped up to the plate, batting a nasty shot straight over the pitcher's mound.

I smiled. At least, I grimaced, teeth grinding. "You're getting funnier, Danny. This comedy thing is rubbing off on you."

"Speaking of rubbing off..."

There could be no good end to that sentence. When did Danny get so snarky? And since when did horrible Shelley want to 'talk' and 'massivity' me? The idea of her massaging me struck me right in the cold sweats.

JenX pushed up her aviators and said, "So, focus, right? Mum. Boyfriend. Weird gum girl. What is it?" She dropped the glasses again. "I need hot thieves. I need sexy running. I need box office."

"Right," I replied, my heart pounding. To hell with all these jackasses. I nodded, lifted my chin, and sailed onto set, ready for work like a responsible actress.

"Not ready for you yet!" hollered a deep male voice.

"Right!" I continued sailing out of the crew's way like a responsible actress. I hid myself between two giant, warm generator things and ducked when Shelley came wandering around in the lowest-speed chase ever. Danny spied me, but kept his distance and began flirting outrageously with a startled-looking middle-aged makeup artist. I hadn't meant to lead him on. I'd been dumped, and he was hot, and geez, it was only a little kissing, anyhow. The guy probably got as much action just by setting foot outside his house—that mother of four was ready to jettison her eyeshadow brushes and commit adultery on the spot.

When my actual job began, happiness disrupted the worry smothering my soul. I could deal with drama so long as the magic flowed through me while we filmed, and it did. Even my co-star warmed to me once we began work.

Early the next morning, they were done with me, and instead of dealing with my people like an adult, I ran straight to my trailer, Sam on my heels. He was the only one I wanted to see. Or hear. Or grope. "Come here," I said, and he obliged me. We made it to the couch, me atop him, his hands everywhere. Sex is the best way to avoid real life—that's a life lesson for the masses from yours truly.

I sat back on my heels, facing him, and he pulled me deeper into his lap. His fingers played with my zipper pull. "Ah, jumpsuit," he murmured. "We meet again for the first time."

I giggled. The jumpsuit jiggled. His dimple flashed. With two fingers, he tugged, the zipper unlocking tooth by tooth. His smile got wider the more cleavage he revealed. He opened his mouth, and my breasts tingled, anticipating his warm, tender assault.

The door opened. "Dammit!" growled Sam, loud, the frustration piercing my eardrum.

"Yeeeeaaaahhhh."

Sometime before all this was over, I would punch Shelley. Punch her full in her stupid, yeeeeaaaahhhh-ing, gum-popping mouth.

I didn't move. If she wanted to speak with me, she could talk to my bum. Bum is a fancy British word for ass, which Shelley could also kiss. "Spit it out, Shelley." I turned. "No, not the gum! Lord love a duck. What do you need to tell me?"

Shelley sat right beside us on the couch. Sam's hands tightened on my waist, and he stared into my face with crazy eyes. I massaged his shoulders to keep him calm. "Yeah. Valerie says you need to steal the thing already. She doesn't like, ya know, waiting."

"Shelley," I yelled over Sam, who'd started to speak in tones that sounded very much like a rant, "she gave me a week. We need that week to work on our plan. Valerie isn't going to get the cape if I'm caught stealing it, is she?"

This argument elicited a flicker of understanding in Shelley. Her face rippled with an unusual happening—a thought.

"Now get the hell out. Your shift is over. Valerie can have me watched tomorrow night, but the day belongs to me."

Shelley shifted to her feet and shuffled toward the door. "Yeah, someone else has day shift. It's boring, anyhow." She left. The door clicked closed behind her.

I bit my lip in an effort to keep my swell of emotion at bay. My eyes stung and my stomach churned, churned. Jesus, it was like I was making butter in there.

"Stop, baby." Sam collected me into his arms and cradled me against him.

"I don't know what I expected," I said in a high, breathy voice. "Of course I'm being watched all the time."

He took my hands and stared me down. "Not for long. I'll make this right."

I managed to smile for his benefit. After all, I believed that he believed that. But wasn't there a saying about good intentions? Ah, yes. The road to hell is paved with short redheads.

Chapter Fourteen

All That Glitters is Not Mold

*Ext: The Set Of The Reality Tv Show Thief Island —
night.*

Angle On: Samantha Lytton *sits on a stump in the
center of a beach camp. The Fire of Judgment sparks beside
her. The other contestants on the show,* Sam, Danny,
Valerie, Shelley, Jenx, Suzie *and* Diego *sit on logs in a
circle around her.*

Angle On: The charming host of Thief Island, Captain
Taco, *approaches Samantha. He wears a little lavaliere
microphone on his collar, and yes, it's insanely cute.*

Captain Taco: Samantha, your fellow campers here
on *Thief Island* have chosen you as the worst thief of
the episode. You failed to eat the live grubs in the
team challenge, and to steal the Mold Cape from the
British Museum. In fact, you didn't even try. You just
cracked a couple of stupid 'mold' puns and
complained a lot.

Samantha: Thanks.

Captain Taco: That's a bad thing on *Thief Island*.

Valerie: Duh.

Valerie giggles. Sam scoots away from her.

Samantha: *Me?* Nobody wants to vote out Psycho McGhee here? She tried to kill Diego!

Angle On: Diego, grimacing and clutching his crutches.

Captain Taco: Valerie is very annoying, but she smells kinda like catnip, so I'm conflicted.

Angle On: Captain Taco begins to climb off his hosting cat perch toward Valerie, but after a dirty look from Samantha, he licks his butt like he meant to do that all along.

Shelley: Yeeeeaaaahhhh, make her do the thing on the thing.
Captain Taco: Yes! It is time for Samantha to take The Walk of the Civilians.

Angle On: Samantha's brow creases in worry.

Samantha: What's The Walk of the Civilians?
Danny: Haven't you ever watched *Thief Island* before?

He sneers.

Danny: I guess you're not a *method* thief, like I am.

Angle On: The camera sweeps across the fire pit.

Captain Taco: You, Samantha Lytton, shall walk across the fire, barefoot, and steal the Oscar sitting in the center of it.

Angle On: The golden statuette standing upon a pedestal in the middle of the fire, which is ten feet across.

Samantha: Fuck no! I'm not walking on fire for you people. And I'm pretty sure that Oscar is about two hundred degrees at this point. It's starting to list to port.

JenX pushes her headphones off her ears.

JenX: So, fire. Hotness. Flame. Blaze. Heat. Searing. Combustion.
Captain Taco: Thank you, JenX. Lots to think about there.

JenX puts her headphones back on.
Angle On: Samantha stands.

Samantha: Screw this island, I want to get off.

Angle On: The gallery of thieves.

Sam: Damn, baby. In front of all these cameras? Okay.

Sam begins dancing and taking his shirt off, which is distracting for several of the other contestants. Diego shoots Sam a dirty look and begins making his pecs jump. He is already shirtless.

Suzie: She never could win a contest. You should have seen her at the Little Miss Junior Tarheel

Competition. They awarded her 'Worst Use of Vaseline'.

Angle On: Valerie stands and starts toward Samantha with determination.

Valerie: I want to see you burn!

She begins chasing Samantha around the fire.

Samantha: Aaaaaah! Sam, help me!

Angle On: Sam struggles in the sand with limping Diego, who has challenged him to an involuntary wrestling match. Diego pushes Sam's face in a salty puddle as Suzie cheers.

Samantha: Heeeeeeeeeeelp!

I awoke after yet another anxiety dream, the wisps of it clinging to my mind like kudzu. Sam stirred close by and soon his hand began roaming all over.

At least I wasn't dreaming that Sam was in cahoots with my enemies anymore.

I swept the sleep from my eyes and poked Sam. "Please tell me what the plan is. I'm sick with it." I bunched the blanket around me like armor. "I don't want that cape to be destroyed. I don't want to steal it." The tears slipped down my face, and for the first time in a while, I let them. A crying jag can only be kept at bay for so long before it comes roaring out at an inappropriate time, like when you're naked and post-coitus and ruining everyone's sleep. "My life finally got good, and now it's screwed up again."

Sam sat cross-legged beside me and handed over a tissue. His brows formed an annoyed V while he yawned and checked the time. Two p.m., i.e. the middle of the night. "I can't have you privy to it. If something goes wrong in the middle, you have to be the innocent patsy who knows nothing."

"I do know nothing!"

"Then what's the problem?"

I picked at the blanket. "How many times do you think me playing dumb will keep me out of jail?"

Silence. Not what I wanted to hear. What the hell good is being with an accomplished liar if he can't lie when it will help? He rubbed my back and said, "But you're very good at playing dumb."

And that was when the real sobbing commenced. Every single negative, hurtful, fearful emotion splattered across the duvet, and I fought to keep from dry-heaving. Sam emitted a low, keening noise of distress. Tears were his undoing and flailing his only response. With stiff hands he patted my shoulders and 'there, there'd' me.

I used my out-of-control emotions to my benefit on set the next morning—my snippy fight with Danny's ex-husband character went beautifully, and JenX finally seemed to have forgotten about the incident with my mother. It had been nearly a week since I'd heard from the evil witch, and that was fine with me. Even Shelley was staying mostly out of my way.

If I squinted and tilted my brain to the left, everything in my life almost seemed normal. Having Sam back at my side, and on my side, and humping my side made everything so much better.

Only one more personal matter to attend to.

As everyone packed up for the morning, I pulled Danny aside. "Can I speak with you?" I turned on my most charming smile, and he nodded and let me tow him gently to my trailer. A quick peek told me that Shelley was wonderfully absent for freaking once.

I gestured to the couch, and he sat. I grabbed his favorite kind of sparkling water and handed it over. You can't butter up health-conscious actors, but you can hydrate them.

"I've treated you shabbily, and I'm sorry," I began.

He shook his head. "No—"

"Yes. Look, you are so amazing. You're kind and funny, and were I not previously attached, I'd be on you like hot butter on pancakes." My stomach rumbled, which elicited a laugh from him. Damn, all these butter thoughts were getting me in trouble. "I don't usually run around kissing men and leading them on and then dropping them again. I'm sorry."

His face lifted into a wry smile. "You never promised me anything. But"—he scratched his chin—"is it unmanly to admit my feelings got hurt?"

My heart cracked in half and oozed like an egg. Boy, I needed dinner. "Shit. I'm not that great, anyhow. I'm kind of a pain in the ass."

"Yes."

I cocked my head, waiting for more. Nope. Damn— tough crowd. I cleared my throat, swallowed my pride and said, "Well, I just wanted to clear things up. I adore you, and I want to be friends—both for the sake of the movie and for my sake."

I held my arms in the universal invitation for 'let's hug it out', and he obliged me with a strong, warm squeeze that held me tight. Very tight. Firmly. He pulled me practically into his lap. His hands smoothed down my spine and kept drifting…

"Okay, great." I pulled back and took a steadying breath.

"Sorry," he murmured. "You have a lovely ass."

I laughed — a feminine giggle full of sauce.

He winked and stood up to leave. "Thank you for speaking with me. And now, if you'll excuse me, I have a date."

Only the tiniest twinge of jealousy nipped at me. "Good of you to let me know."

"Too bad for you."

"Obviously."

Chuckling, he left. I sagged onto the couch, feeling good. It wouldn't take too much convincing to get Sam to take me out for pancakes with butter, and eggs. Where was he, anyhow? I glanced at the clock on my phone. Holy crap, it was late. The crew would be done packing up by now — they were hard-working, burly magic. After they finished, the museum's cleaning staff would sweep in to fix whatever was left. Only a few hours before opening time.

I lay down to wait for Sam. The trailers were tucked away at the back of the property, and nobody seemed to care when we came and went.

My phone rang, and I lazily fished it out of my pocket. Mom! Hell, no. Not ready for that conversation. Or non-conversation of me talking and her pretending the things I said weren't English.

I set the phone on the table and closed my eyes again, a blanket snuggled around me.

I'd just begun floating in the bliss of almost-sleep when I heard the door click open.

"Hi, baby," I murmured. "Are you hungry?" 'Are you hungry?' was our special code for 'Samantha is hungry, so feed her'.

"Yeeeeaaaahhhh, get up."

Ugh. I turned away from Shelley's voice to face the back of the couch.

Something hard pressed into my head. "Get up and come inside. You gotta do the thing."

I peeled my eyes open. The something hard felt suspiciously like a gun.

The door banged open. "Shit!" Sam, rescuing me. "Everyone, just stay calm."

"Get *up*," Shelley repeated.

I knew the drill well enough to obey orders from gun-wavers and/or hair-snatchers. My stomach fell, and fell, and fell. Tingles suffused my fingers with stiff energy. I swung around and sat up in one motion, and raised my hands for good measure. Shelley had adorned herself with a ski mask.

"She imprisoned the cleaning crew and guards," Sam said.

"What?" Bile rose in my throat.

"Yeah, time to take the gold thing. The moldy coat." She threw a duffel bag at my head. "Now," she added with a helpful gun shake.

"Shelley," Sam said, gently, like you speak to a squirrely-looking dog, "Samantha doesn't need to participate. We're the experts. Let me go in with you, and I'll have it stolen in no time."

Shelley reached into her sweatpants, which said 'hottie' on the butt, and pulled out another gun. The couple who's imperiled together, obeys together. And that's how all of us ended up inside the quiet British Museum main atrium, ready for burglary.

We both knew where it was. Sam grabbed my hand and held it as if we were on a beachy stroll. Shelley followed, leisurely, gun pointed, her phone in her other hand. Not even a grand larceny attempt would tear her away from whatever the Internet had to offer. Who could blame her? I'd rather read the moronic

Tweet stream of my least favorite politician than be where I was.

Sam pulled me closer and grabbed my bottom. "Is now really the time for this?" I hissed.

What he whispered in my ear wasn't a tender nothing, but a tender recounting of his plan. His butt-grabbing was a distraction. Literally. Every ten feet or so he'd stop talking, continue fondling, and I'd have to poke him to continue. No wonder all his crime bosses were women—men were far too easily distracted for this sort of thing.

My belly gyrated anew, and a wave of dizziness wound through me like a tornado of horror. This was really happening. I would be that girl who was once sorta a movie star, but finished in a British prison because she screwed the wrong dude after he screwed the wrong gal. Maybe I'd sell my story and use the money to pay a larger woman in the clink to beat up people on my behalf. All of my butt-fondlers in the future would have to be female.

I don't even remember the walk to the Ancient Europe gallery. I blinked, and we were there, Shelley absentmindedly pointing the gun, Sam taking me by the shoulders and giving me a hard look in the eye.

"I love you," he mouthed to me.

"I love you, too," I said out loud.

Sam approached the case containing the cape. It was mounted on a pedestal inside it, so the golden wonder appeared to be floating inside the Plexiglas. Two lights were directed toward it, and they cut through the relative darkness of the rest of the gallery. Oh, how it shined. Breathtaking. Or maybe that was my inability to catch my breath.

He worked his way around the case, examining, deciding where to start. Finally, he stopped between Shelley and the case itself, blocking her view of me.

I took out the heavy, metal object he'd handed to me on the way. I slipped it through my knuckles, the weight of it somehow putting my thoughts into stark relief.

"Yeah, let's go," Shelley said, her nasal voice drawing out every syllable into a misshapen mess.

Let's go, I thought. I closed my fist and turned, keeping my hand out of her view from every angle. The closer I got to her, the more my teeth chomped together. I raised my arm. She glanced down at me, her eyes unfocused. "Yeeeeaaaahhhhh," I said as I clutched my brass knuckles and punched that monster in the fucking jaw.

Bam! Her eyes widened for a hot moment before the force of the punch spun her backward and sent her splatting across the wooden floor.

Sam fell to his knees beside her. "She's out cold! You're amazing!"

"I don't go to the gym for my health."

I dropped the knuckles and swayed on my feet. Sam stood and said, "Are you okay?" I tried to nod, but suddenly everything went pink and hazy, and I clutched my stomach. Then my mouth. But nothing could stop the tidal wave of vomit that poured from me. Sam leaped out of the way, so I threw up all over Shelley's hottie pants. And her shoes. And—

"Dammit, you threw up on the gun!"

I spat the last of the grossness out of my mouth and wiped my hand across my lips. "I'm sorry."

"Sit down." He gave me an un-gentle shove, and I landed on my butt. Nose squinched, he turned Shelley by the shoulder and yanked her other gun from the front of her pants.

"You okay?" he asked.

I nodded. And burped.

"That's my girl." He crouched beside me. "I have to do my thing now. Shelley was always the least of our problems. I have some jobs for you, okay?"

"Okay." Holy crap, did I feel better. I'd flattened horrible Shelley, and my stomach seemed happier than it had in a week. *That's for my crowning glory, yyeeeaaaahhhhhh.*

"One, tie up Shelley. Two, check to make sure the cleaning crew and guards are still on ice."

"Holy crap — they're dead?"

"No, I mean, tied up. She said something about stashing them in closets. But for God's sake, don't let them see you."

"What if they've gotten free? Do I knock them out? No, I can't — I did a PSA about not falling asleep when you drive. Knocking people out is just plain against my platform."

"Wha — what?"

I huffed a breath and squeaked. "Sam!"

"Ugh." He backed away and stood. "Sorry, but you smell like —"

My hand flew up and covered my mouth. "Oops, sorry."

He waved his hands. "S'ok. Just bind dorkus here, and check on the people. I'm not asking you to hurt anyone. You know me better than that." Black leather gloves appeared on his hands as if by magic. He probably had them stashed them on his person at all times. "Here." He tossed something to me.

I sucked in a breath and caught the small bundle. "Gloves of my own?"

"Who loves you, baby?" He pulled me in for a kiss, but turned away at the last moment. "Maybe you could find breath mints, too."

I nodded and took off toward where I knew one of the curator's offices to be. After a quick search around, I found some shipping tape and a pack of gum. I'd grown an aversion to gum since I met Shelley, but this was an emergency.

It gave me a glowing joy to bind Shelley's hands and feet with the tape, even though she reeked of my stomach problems. However, I considered that she was partly responsible for my likely ulcer, so she deserved what she got.

Then, I ran to the main entrance with its high, rounded white ceiling. A diamond pattern criss-crossed it, and it make me feel like I walked around the inside of a Faberge egg. The grandeur of the surroundings was marred by the thumping and muffled voices I heard coming from a closet marked 'private' on the edge of the room.

Upon closer inspection, it appeared that Shelley had sealed the door shut from the outside using a screw through the door edge and into the wall. They were safe in there. I said a little prayer of well-wishing and continued on my way.

I had no idea where the guards hung out, so I jogged from gallery to gallery, down the stairs, through the offices. This place was huge—my agent would be proud of me, getting real-life experience for my role *and* exercising at the same time.

I discovered two guards imprisoned in a pantry off a break room, next to the security room. A uniform shirt hung on a chair in the kitchen, so I figured they'd just begun their shift. Again, I left them inside and stayed quiet—couldn't have them knowing I was out and about during the robbery. On the break table sat the screw gun and screws in a plastic bag. I grabbed them and ran.

When I returned to the cape's gallery, Sam stood in front of the object of our desire. Still on its pedestal. Inside the case. "What the hell have you been doing?"

He turned to me, his dark brown eyes glinting wickedly. "We're not stealing the cape."

"What about Valerie?"

Taking a step toward me, he said, "Is that gum in your mouth?"

"Yup."

He grabbed the back of my head and pulled me in for a brief, intense kiss. "Do you trust me?" he asked.

I pressed my lips together. At some point, I needed to decide to become a part of the team. I mean, if he was willing to make deals with foreign governments and put himself in harm's way with every criminal in the hemisphere just to spend nights in front of Mel Brooks movies with me, then I needed to take a step toward meeting him in the middle. "Yes, I trust you. What's the plan, thief-man?"

His grin glowed in the reflected light of all that gold. He looked like a devilish angel. He whipped out a small piece of metal from his pocket. "Take the tape off Shelley. Put this on her."

The object glinted in the light. "Oh, my God! You broke the cape?"

"Just a little." He shrugged, but his forehead fell into lines of guilt. "They pay people to restore this sort of thing."

I trust him. I trust him.

I unbound Shelley, minding the vomit, which truly reeked. Then, I eased the piece of precious gold into her hand and wound her fingers around it. The tape and roll went into Sam's bag.

I looked up to see Sam kneeling beside the display case and knuckles deep in the wires and electronics of it. "You're disarming it?" I asked.

"I already did that. Before, when I took the piece off."

"Oh. What are you doing now?"

"Arming it again. But it won't go off until I turn everything back on in the security room."

"What? I thought you didn't go in for this sort of gadgetey, technology-based thieving."

He cocked an eyebrow. "I didn't choose this mark, did I? Serious museums have serious shit."

I twisted my hands together. "What do you want me to do?"

He told me the rest of the plan. Damn, it was good.

I hoped so, anyway.

We put the brass knuckles on my fist. I stood near Shelley. "Catch you on the flip side."

Flashing me a crooked smile, he chucked me gently on the chin. "You're a helluva broad, Sam." He whipped out a small water bottle and leaned down to put Shelley's hand around it. Fingerprints, you know? Then, he handed it to me.

I lifted up the bottle. "Here's to getting away with it," I said, and drank the whole thing. He held out a ziplock, and I dropped the bottle into it.

"Sit." I did so, and we rested together for a few minutes. My hand fidgeted with nervous energy. It seemed weird to take a break in the middle of the thieving and do nothing. But after about ten minutes, everything seemed...better.

"Hey, Sam," I whispered.

"Hey, baby. Feeling good?"

I wiped my nose. It itched. But it tickled, too. Holy shit—the cape was so sparkly. "No, no." Sam caught my hands on the way to touch it. Suddenly, I wanted to touch him. A lot of him. Everywhere. I ran my fingers down his chest to grab his gorgeous dick. "Whoa. Tempting, but nope."

"Let's have sex on the—the—thinging thing. The languages. Did you know it has three? We can screw in three languages!"

Sam laughed and eased me onto the floor. He brushed the hair away from my forehead the way I loooooved him to do. It felt so good, and he felt so good, and he was so warm. I lay there and watched him do whatever he had to do. The ceiling spun around and around. This part of the plan was the bestest part. Except I really needed Sam to take off his pants. I tugged on them, but he just laughed and walked away. After a while, all I wanted to do was sleep. Screw and sleep. And sleep. And…

Chapter Fifteen

And the Award for Best Performance During a
Double-Cross Goes to…

"She's waking up."

My head was made of cotton. Someone groaned, and after a minute, I realized it was me.

"Samantha? You're in the hospital."

I didn't recognize the voice. My eyes opened a sliver and the sterile white and beige of a hospital room did indeed greet me. A lady in a white coat stood over the bed. "We think you were dosed with GHB, and it knocked you out. How do you feel?"

"Tired." What the hell had happened? Last thing I remembered…

Ski mask. Sam. Some sort of plan…

I closed my mouth, afraid I might say something in my grogginess that we might regret. The doctor lady left, anyhow. My room smelled like a florist's shop. Nearly every surface was jammed with bouquets, stuffed animals and balloons. *How kind of everyone*, I thought. The generosity warmed me, and I closed my eyes.

"Samantha, the police are here to see you."

My lids popped open. Crust surrounded my lashes—I had no idea how long I'd slept. "Hello," I croaked.

"I'm a huge fan!" said the tall, skinny woman in a pink button-down and no-nonsense black pants standing beside my bed. Her accent sounded Indian and British both, and her praise was wonderfully melodious. A man who appeared to be her partner was also there, in a terribly-fitting brown suit.

I tried to sit up, but everything went haywire and I fell back.

"Let me help." A nurse hurried to my bedside and pressed a button on a white remote. The head part of my bed slowly elevated me into less of a recline.

"Thank you," I said to the lady detective, who continued beaming at me.

"I've never seen you in anything," said the dude cop. He sounded skeptical that he even should have looked at me in a film. "Can you tell us what happened to you?"

"I—I don't remember." Shit, I'd better get my act together. Wisps of cobweb clung to my brain synapses. I did know I'd been drugged. When Sam had found the GHB in Shelley's bag, it was a blessing straight from the lord. Or the devil. But it was a blessing. One of the side-effects can be memory loss.

Flashes began returning to me—the cape room, throwing up.

Here goes. I took a deep breath. "We finished filming for the day. Night, sorry. I went to my trailer with Shelley, one of my assistants." I shrugged and shook my head. "And then I woke up here?" I gasped, awake enough now to enjoy my role. "Is Shelley okay? Was she drugged, too? Why?"

"You poor dear," said the female cop.

Her partner said, "We found you with your assistant next to the item she was attempting to steal."

I recoiled in horror, clutching my thin hospital blanket to my bosom. "Steal? Item?" Really, this performance should earn me a daytime Emmy, at the least.

Copper long legs leaned in. "That Shelley woman drugged you!"

"No. I don't believe it."

"Yes. She knocked you out and tried to steal the golden cape." Her eyes took on a distinctly conspiratorial shine. "But you tried to stop her by punching her! And"—she broke into a chuckle—"it appears you threw up on her. From the drug, you know. That's a common side-effect."

"I did?" I looked from one to the other of them, my eyes so innocent Bambi should be ashamed. "How mortifying. Was anyone else hurt? Oh, I hope not."

"No." The man cop clipped his answer before Officer Big Fan spoke. "She also drugged your other assistant"—he referred to his notes—"Zackary. He's recovering in the next room."

My head turned toward the wall he'd indicated, as if I could see him through it. My body unclenched just a little. We'd made it this far.

"Ms Lytton, did Shelley strike you as an intelligent girl capable of single-handedly carrying out the robbery of a museum? She even disabled the cameras, but got tripped up by the alarm."

Bless Sam. "Well, no. Shelley always struck me as an idiot. But maybe she was acting. Maybe everything she ever said was a lie." Perhaps I could convince them that Shelley was the most brilliant actress of all time. The more she played dumb and denied knowledge, the more they wouldn't believe her.

"How did you come to employ Shelley as a masseuse?"

My heart slammed into my throat and stayed there. That had been a very good question. One that I did not have a good answer for. I licked my lips and tried to swallow.

"Do you need some water?" asked Ms Detective.

I nodded and smiled up at her gratefully. How had I met Shelley? How had I met Shelley? I couldn't mention Valerie—I had no good reason to know her, either. Gaaaaaah. "She showed up on set one night. Said she was sent by my agent to help me relax." I swiped a hand across my face. "Yes, I know I'm spoiled, and that a personal masseuse is a little obnoxious. So was Shelley. She never so much as touched me."

"Then why did you continue to employ her?"

I shrugged. "I've found in the Hollywood game that it's usually better to just be grateful anyone wants to do anything nice for you. Go with the flow."

Man Cop put his hands in his pockets. "Why were you at the museum so late?"

"Just dawdling in my trailer. I was waiting for Zack."

"Your boyfriend. Or ex-boyfriend?"

I smiled. "Boyfriend, then ex, then boyfriend."

My biggest fan tsk-tsked. "I thought you were dating Daniel Zhang. He's such a hottie!"

"Well"—I played with my blanket—"Danny is amazing, but I've been dating Zack a while. You can't fight love." I pinned a star-filled gaze on her, and she practically sighed before nodding.

Her partner actually elbowed her in the ribs. She swallowed and referred back to her notes. "You foiled another art theft a year or so ago, Ms Lytton?"

"Big coincidence. You and art thieves." The male cop was not having any of my shit. I took a deep breath in, and let it out. I just had to pray that Valerie had threatened Shelley enough to scare the idiot into taking the fall alone. "Shelley says you were supposed to help her steal the Mold cape."

I laughed and put my hand over my mouth. Taking a beat, I glanced from one to the other of them, reading reactions. She didn't believe Shelley—not one bit. He did, because why wouldn't he? I was a big non-coincidence.

Finally, I gasped and let my face settle into innocent mode, with a hint of incredulity. "That's...that's insane." I spluttered for a moment in alarm, and the lady cop sat on the side of my bed and took my hand. Yes! "I didn't like Shelley. She got me in trouble with my director the other day by acting the fool. Why—" I laughed at the sheer preposterousness of it all, wait one, two, three beats... "Why would I help Shelley do anything, much less steal something so...so..."

"But the Picasso—"

"I put my life on the line to help law enforcement recover that painting!" Tears welled in my eyes, and I turned away to find a tissue.

"That's enough." My doctor to the rescue, exactly as I'd intended.

The woman detective patted my hand and rolled her eyes at her partner. "I think we're done here. Thank you for your time, and we're sorry we had to trouble you further, Ms Lytton."

"You're just doing your job," I said with a piteous sniffle.

She stood to leave. "This Shelley has a record as long as my arm. She bit off more than she could chew this time."

I shook my head, too overcome by my pretend-horror to comment. They left. I let out a long, long breath. My doctor told me to rest and vamoosed as well.

"Wow," came a voice from the doorway. Sam. He turned to check that the hall behind him was clear and shut the door. At my bedside, he whispered, "That was a thing of beauty. You're the Meryl Streep of bullshit."

"I have no idea what you mean, Zack." A sneaky smile played on my face. "Are you okay? They said that terrible Shelley drugged you, too."

"I'll survive." He sat on the bed and stroked my hand. "You really okay?"

"Yeah. Just kinda foggy."

"Me, too."

"What time is it?"

"It's the next day." He looked at his phone. "Nine-thirteen a.m."

My jaw dropped. "We lost an entire day?"

"Most of one." Leaning close to my ear, he said, "Your agent is not going to have any idea about Shelley."

"I know. They'll just think she lied to me to get on set." Oh, shit. I squeezed his hand in my suddenly sweaty one. "But why didn't I say anything to my agent about her?"

"Right."

"Shit." We considered this story hole for a moment.

"How 'bout this..." He licked his lips. "You asked me to send some flowers to your agent to thank him for sending a masseuse, but I totally forgot."

I grinned. "You're such a crappy assistant."

"I'm good at the things that matter." He winked.

"Zack." I pulled him closer. "They're already pulling up your passport info and stuff, right? What are they going to find?"

"My deal with the Brits includes an identity that checks out to a high level. I'm pretty much an informant for them. They'll divert any attention and protect me." He swallowed.

"Even now?"

He ran a hand behind his neck and grimaced. "I'm meeting someone after the hospital discharges me. They're gonna want the truth."

"Are you going to give it?"

"I don't think I have a choice. My immunity deal is for past crimes, not current ones."

I set my forehead on his warm, solid arm. "You'll send them after Valerie?"

"I'm pretty damn tired of her. It didn't have to be this way, but she forced the issue." His muscles clenched and he squeezed me close. "The minute she began harassing you—"

"Samantha?" A knock sounded on my door—accompanied by Danny's voice.

"Yes, hi!"

Sam stood just as Danny and JenX came in the room. They barely glanced at Sam, but hurried over to me.

JenX cocked one hip. "So, amazing? Punching. Foiling robbery. Badass, right? Publicity." I couldn't see her eyes because of her shades, but she almost sang that last word, and I'm sure her peepers sparkled with the promise of box office receipts.

"The press is calling you Sherlock Samantha." Danny grinned and leaned against the bed. "Did you really lay her out with brass knuckles?"

"I don't remember it." I shot a quick look at Sam, who blinked prodigiously. "But, yes, I carry around brass knuckles for my protection. In the US I carry Mace, but it's not allowed in the UK."

JenX smiled, nodded and patted me on the knee. "So, rest. Recover. Interviews." She pointed. "Star." And with that, she bopped out of the room.

"Production is shut down because of the police investigation," Danny explained.

"You're good at speaking director."

"I like the way JenX does things," Sam said. "Simple. To the point."

Danny deigned to glance at Sam. "They said she drugged you, too?"

He shrugged. "I'm totally fine. It was Samantha she dragged into the museum to take hostage."

My eyebrows lifted. Danny turned to me in concern. "I don't remember anything." It would be my mantra until the end of my days.

"She needs her rest." Sam set a concerned hand on my shoulder. Oh, brother. They were gonna measure dicks again, but it never turned literal, dammit. "But thank you for coming by, Danny."

"Of course I'm going to come by. The rest of the cast wants to, too…"

"I'm sure they'll let me out of here soon." I smiled at both of them. "We can all get a drink or something. Please thank everyone for the flowers and stuff."

Danny turned to leave, and was beset by a tall, brown-haired whirlwind. "What in the actual *fuck* is going on here?"

Yay—Ellen!

Oh, shit—Ellen!

She stopped dead and pointed an indignant talon at Sam. "You," she nearly spat.

"Ellen, you remember Danny." I yelled it too loud, and my head throbbed.

My tone seemed to bring her out of her rage stroke, and she uncurled her lip. "Hey, Danny. Long time, no see." Nicolette had followed Ellen into the room, and she now waved at everyone while also taking the time to frown at Sam.

"I'm so tired!" I gasped, putting a hand to my forehead and doing my best semi-swoon.

Danny made polite noises and hurried himself out. None of my other compatriots felt the need to leave. Sam hurried to the door and closed it.

Ellen plopped herself on my bed. "Are you okay? What did this devil man do to you?"

"Nothing! And I'm fine, thanks. He saved us both." My BFF's face screwed up into the precursor of a tirade, so I continued, "That's all I can say right now. Dig? Later. Somewhere else. But I'm totally okay."

"You don't call. You don't write. I have to see the fucking newspaper to discover that 'Sherlock Samantha' Lytton is in the hospital—"

I threw my arms around her. "I'm sorry!" Over her shoulder, I said to Nicolette, "I'm sorry to you, too. I'll make it up to you. The rest of your vacation is on me. I'm so sorry."

"You don't have to do that," Ellen said.

"Yes, she does." Nicolette always knows what's what.

My nurse came in then to give me another examination before they would let me go. My people all left with promises to meet me at my place—I gave the keys to Ellen. When everyone was finally gone, I sagged back in relief.

Had we really done it? Turned the tables on our nemeses?

"Will I play the violin again?" I asked the nurse.

She put her hand to my forehead. "Are you confused? Do you know what day it is?"

Having been working nights, I didn't actually know what day it was. I guess bad American jokes like me don't translate too well.

* * * *

That night—actual night, not morning night, this was seriously the worst jet lag in the history of jets or lags—Sam, Ellen, Nicolette and I yakked over pizza and beer in my apartment. Before we began, Sam swept for bugs, stole my hair recorder and powered off every cell phone in the place. He made Nicolette swear on Ellen's life to never reveal what we spoke of in that living room. Ellen insisted that she'd not leave the room without the full story. Nicolette did it for Ellen's sake. The fact that Sam/Zack wasn't in jail told our lovely cop that he must be in league with the Brits, so that lent him some credibility.

My sneaky gut suspicion told me that Nicolette considered our adventures interesting, anyhow. Her eyes shined, even as she directed shady looks to Sam.

"Let me try and get the machinations of Sam's devious mind straight," began Ellen whilst lapping up a long string of pizza cheese.

"If you can," said the devious mind deviously.

"After filming finished, you skulked after Shelley, because she was gross and not to be trusted."

"Skulking," I said, scooting closer to him on the couch. "That's hot."

He waggled his eyebrows and squeezed my thigh on the way to his beer bottle.

Ellen continued, sounding very much like the YA adventure writer she was. "You observed her donning a skeevy ski mask outside Samantha's trailer."

"Shifty," added Nicolette.

"Even on the slopes, ski masks are shifty. Upon realizing that Shelley was about to force the issue and undertake the devious robbery, the first thing you did was bolt to the security room—whereupon you found that the guards had already been locked in a closet—and turn off the system and the cameras."

He smiled. "Yes."

"You did not check on Samantha, who might have been shot by Shelley."

I turned to him, frowning. "Hey! Yeah."

He repaid my massive frown with interest. "Shelley had no reason to shoot Samantha. Samantha was worthless unless she was alive and inside the museum."

"Worthless? These terms of endearment touch me greatly, darling."

Massive eye roll. "I'm pretty sure Valerie's plan involved using Samantha's near-unfettered access on set to get Shelley inside when the museum shifted from filming personnel to the cleaning/normal overnight guard staffing, which was more minimal and, frankly, not as diligent as they are during the period when the museum is closing to the public. What? I'm trained to observe these things. Samantha's second purpose was to serve as the patsy for the robbery because Shelley intended that she be filmed inside the museum."

"I changed my mind. I'm glad you went for the cameras." He made a face at me. I ignored his antics in favor of the pizza.

Nicolette's eyebrows quirked. "How did you do that, by the way? Shut down the electronic security?"

"After Valerie told me I'd be robbing the museum, I put out feelers to buddies and learned whatever I could about the security. Not the first time it's been broken into."

Her eyes got wide, but she shook her head and didn't ask for any more information.

"He learned how to be prepared at Thief Camp," I told her.

The dimple smirked and said, "I got a merit badge in Pissing Off Authority Figures."

Ellen gave him a round of applause. "I am always pro-fighting The Man." She finished her beer and waved the bottle at me. That was our special signal for, 'Skank, get me another beer'. So I did.

"To continue," Ellen continued. "The security cameras are off. Sam joins the two ladies, and you three proceed into the museum. Sam tells Samantha to bust Shelley's head, which she is only too happy to do."

I held up a semi-impressive bicep.

"Then, you both stage a scenario in which Samantha has been taken hostage and fights back, allowing Shelley to be caught when Sam sets off the alarms on purpose and then drugs himself. All the while, leaving the cape there, but slightly busted."

Sam nodded. "I left the Plexiglas slightly off the display case so that when I reset the alarm, all hell broke loose."

Nicolette chuckled. "I admit, that's pretty nice. But aren't you worried that Valerie is still pissed and out for blood?"

He took my hand and squeezed it. Such a nice gesture, even though it interfered with me grabbing the last slice of sausage, which Ellen stole, the wretch. Sam said in a low voice, "Yes, but we're hoping that Scotland Yard picks her up, and soon. I've told them everything. At least I think I have. I spilled my guts to a man in the park who knew a lot about me."

Nicolette frowned. "You two had better go somewhere else. She's been to this apartment?" I nodded, my heart thumping. "Yeah, y'all need to jet."

"Yes, this was stupid of me." Sam downed the last of his beer. "Pack it up, starlet. Let's put you in a penthouse somewhere."

I clutched my chest. "This is so much better than the first time you kidnapped me."

"I'm gonna barf." Ellen stood and wiped crumbs off her pants. "Have a care for my blood pressure."

"Ellen." Sam shot to his feet, his expression shockingly earnest. "Everything you know about me is terrible, I understand that. But I will tell you, though you have no reason to trust me, that I love her." He hid his eyes toward the floor and breathed deep. "I love her more than I've loved anyone save my grandparents. And I will work the rest of my life to make her happy and safe."

A sliver of softness broke through Ellen's gaze, and she nodded at his obvious emotion. "'Cause if you don't, I'll kill you and use Nicolette to conceal the crime."

Nicolette's head popped up. "What?"

"Deal," replied Sam.

* * * *

We stepped into one of the suites of the Stafford London about an hour later, registered under the assumed name of Sonny Malone. British country elegance greeted us from every angle. Sam tipped our bellhop and flashed me a dimple-riffic smile. I nearly knocked him over with the force of my hug and kisses. He immediately hurried me to the bed.

"I guess you like the hotel," he said, scooping me onto the soft blanket.

"What I like is you telling my best friend how fabulous I am and how you're devoting your every moment to my happiness." I grabbed his T-shirt and yanked him down to my face, which is where his face needed to be.

He pulled back. "I don't remember saying that exactly."

"Yes, you did." I ran a finger along his collarbone. "You said you worship me in every way and live to serve me, like a sexy slave. I believe you mentioned how you'd like to wear some sort of gladiator loincloth in my presence."

The dimple twitched. "Funny how we remember things differently." Despite his obviously shoddy memory, he pulled me into his embrace, and I settled in for a long, horizontal snuggle. His lips brushed the top of my head. "I really do love you, Lady Pain in the Ass."

"Good. Because I lied to the cops for you again."

Knock knock. He sat up on one elbow, his head cocked. "Are we expecting anyone?"

Knock knock. "Hello, Ms Lytton? It's the police."

The lady detective!

We both sat straight up. Sam swooped in close to my ear, his breath hot on my lobe. "I'm not here. I went out for food." After driving the point home with a finger to his lips, he ducked into the bathroom off the living room, leaving the door open a crack.

I was the pain in the ass? He was the one who'd just abandoned me to my lies and the cops who disbelieved them. With a sloth in my step, I answered the front door. "Hello, officers."

"May we come in?"

"Of course!" Of course, nothing to hide here. Just the enormous fiction I already related to you, and my criminal man candy hiding on the toilet. I swept my eyes along the thankfully-empty hallway, shut the door behind them and locked it. "How did you know I was here?"

"Internet," she replied, taking a seat on the couch. "At least two different people snapped photos of you checking in."

"Sherlock Samantha," said the male cop flatly. Still a fan of mine.

I graciously handed them each a ridiculously expensive bottle of water from the bar and sat in a chair opposite the sofa. "How can I help?"

"Do you remember anything else about the robbery?"

I took a moment to stare off and search my memory before responding. "No. I've been trying, but it's all a mush."

He sat beside his partner. "Because Shelley insists that you were in on it."

"I wasn't." I put my hand to my chest and leaned forward. "Why on earth would I risk my entire—life, career, on such a stupid thing to do? I'm not really hurting for cash. I've been very lucky."

He snorted. "We found your fingerprint on the inside of the case."

I couldn't hide my shock. My brain rewound at a hundred miles an hour, replaying the thwarted robbery while I tried to catch my breath. No way. I'd never touched the inside. I'd worn gloves the whole time. "That's impossible," I said one hundred percent confidently.

He was fishing. I saw the frustrated shift in his eyes. He thought I was lying, but had no idea about what. Or maybe he was just under a lot of pressure to get such a high-profile investigation right.

"Who is Veronica, and why hasn't anyone else on your staff ever heard of this 'publicist'? You have a different publicist, correct?"

My mouth opened into a round O. I licked my desert-like lips, my mind, so full a few moments ago, a barren wasteland of 'LOL nope'.

He stood. "I think we need to keep discussing this down at the station."

I laughed and stood as well. "I'm happy to help, but this is bordering on harassment." *Dammit dammit fuck aaaaahhhhh!* "If you're going to continue treating me like a criminal," I shot eyes at the woman detective, still awash in sympathy, "then I must have my attorney present." This was not an empty threat on my part—my brilliant attorney, Deborah Diaz, Attorney to the Stars, had hopped on a plane the moment the story broke. She was already in London.

The cops agreed with me, and that was how I found myself getting ready to slog to a police station. Ha ha, no, not for the first time. But for the first time on this continent! I was an *international* embarrassment.

I ducked into the bathroom Sam occupied before we left in order to consult with my Chief Evasive Officer. I yanked on the door to the shower and froze.

Sam was gone.

Chapter Sixteen

Worth My Weight in Gold

How cosmopolitan it was, branching out into a new country's penal system. Deborah met me at the police station, all sassy chestnut pixie cut and 'stab a bitch' black spike heels. Her going rate of obscene dollars/hour was so worth it.

My unfriendly neighborhood detectives ushered us into a little room with a mirror—definitely not two-way, wink wink. Deborah and I smiled at one another, but said naught besides her advice of "Don't say a word about anything."

We waited. And waited. Thirty minutes went by. I guessed this was to make me sweat things, but, per usual, the cops were the least of my problems. Where the hell was Sam? He'd crawled out the freaking window and shimmied down a drain pipe like Spider-Man. I couldn't blame him, because, you know, *criminal*, but I felt abandoned just the same. What if Valerie had gotten him again? Deborah patted my sweaty, cold hand, and I told myself that as long as I said exactly nothing, I'd be okay for now.

After another twenty minutes or so, the male detective entered the room. I sat up straight, but Deborah maintained her air of "I'm already vacationing in the south of France, that's how sure I am this is all going away."

"I'm assuming you've wasted enough of Ms Lytton's valuable time?" Deborah intoned. Sure, my valuable time—eating pizza and humping. I had important business to be out of jail for!

But what if this was it? What if my unlucky luck had finally run out? They knew everything. Hell, maybe Valerie had told them everything, and they'd throw me in jail for not coming to the police, for allowing the cape to be damaged, for letting vile persons walk around the movie set. I'd be fired, and sued, probably. By the museum, the production. Me in prison, Sam in prison. Everything wonderful in my life ripped away in an instant. My heart ran so fast I nearly spun myself out of the chair. My eyes hurt, and I reached out to grasp Deborah's hand, and my forehead broke into a fever, and—

"She's free to go."

What? I slid sideways and collided with Deborah, who put a firm grip on my arm and squeezed. Hard.

She rose gracefully, like a ballet-dancing pit bull. "I trust this will not happen again? I'd hate to have to tell the international press about the Metropolitan Police and their incompetent detectives. You have a red-handed thief in custody, or don't you remember? Have you lost her?"

He seemed to possess no good reply, so we left the interrogation room. Air whooshed into my chest once again, and my sticky, gross feeling fled the farther away from the little room we got. Why the hell had they dragged me down here just to let me go?

We sailed out of the building, Deborah snarling sweetly at all in our path, and me trying not to look like I'd gotten away with something. I hugged her in the cab, and she asked me if she should know anything.

"Do you want to know?" I asked.

She laughed and held up her hands. "Not unless I must. I have to say, Samantha" — she leaned closer — "you're definitely one of my most interesting clients. More fun than keeping an A-list drug addict out of the news when he shows up naked in a stranger's house wearing a tin foil condom."

"No!"

"Yes."

"Who?"

Smiling, she replied, "I don't spill secrets."

"That's why you make obscene dollars per hour."

She smoothed her cashmere skirt with diamond-bedecked hands and nodded.

I dodged the photogs in the lobby of the hotel by going in through the service entrance. A helpful waiter showed me the way, and I tipped him enough to make him grin and, hopefully, be quiet.

I trudged into the room and threw my handbag on the couch. "Watch it," said the couch.

"Sam! You abandoned me! I—"

"Samantha, meet James." My paramour removed the purse from his legs and pointed to a tiny man standing beside a potted plant. He was one of the most distinguished men I'd ever seen, his medium-brown skin contrasting beautifully with his gray suit, his hair perfectly salt-and-peppered.

A spook, of course.

Sam said, "James is my buddy from Her Majesty's Government."

James waved jauntily. At least he was a friendly spook. Were all spies in Britain named James, after Bond?

"You're more beautiful than even in your films," James exaggerated.

Finally! This was how I expected to be treated by law enforcement. What was the point of being a rich American movie star if you were forced to pay for your crimes like some schlub?

I poked at Sam's feet until he made room for me on the couch. Quietly, I waited. I'd learned enough about Sam's world to know when to shut up and let someone else speak. Besides, my fib bank tilted dangerously toward empty.

James obliged me. "The police will not question you about the unfortunate business at the museum again."

Thank you, British Jesus. Relief flooded me almost like an orgasm. I nodded my gratitude and remained silent, which earned me a sneaky smile from my lover.

Spooky handed me a card with a phone number on it. Only a phone number. "Call me if you are bothered by the police again. Thank you for thwarting the robbery attempt."

I smiled and shrugged. Sam began laughing, his eyebrows up. James shook his head. "Charming." With that, he picked up Sam's suitcase, which I just noticed had been sitting at his feet, and left. Sam didn't seem to mind.

First thing I did was get my ass to the minibar and screw off the top to a tiny bottle of Scotch. After a nice, long pull, and the fire in my throat that came with it, I said to my darling one, "Spill it. And if you don't tell me everything, so help me, I'll divorce you."

"We're not married."

"I'll marry you only to divorce you. That's how serious I am."

He reached toward my Scotch bottle. "No way," I said. "I earned this." I took the second—and last, dammit—pull of Scotch and bent to examine the other offerings. "You can have merlot, vodka, tequila or beer."

"Beer, and come here. I recount stories of my brilliance better when I'm within boob-grabbing distance."

Me and my helpful titties sidled to the couch and plopped down. One hand on his beer, one down my shirt, he began. "I'm sorry for running out on you, but I knew I had to do something before they poked more holes in your story than a Swiss cheese."

"I don't think they poke the holes in Swiss cheese. They form because of gas or something."

I received a boob squeeze for that science fact. "I called James, who has been helping me get straight with the British authorities in exchange for information about stolen art buyers. He agreed to make the police drop you as a suspect."

Uncurling myself from his arms, I said, "But why would they do that?"

"In exchange for the Mold gold cape."

"But...the cape is in the museum. It never left."

"The cape has not been in the museum for several days. It just left this hotel room in that suitcase."

I leaped to my feet. "What?"

He grinned, his hair flopping over his forehead like a naughty puppy. "I stole it the day before Shelley pulled her bullshit."

My breaths came so fast and heavy, he actually got up and guided me back into a sitting position. "You okay?" he asked, his voice full of laughter.

"You bastard! You stole one of the most—you fucking stole from the British Museum! How did you do that?"

"Well"—he brushed a lock of hair behind my ear— "I've stolen from the BM before."

"What!" I pushed him away and took a hard, incredulous look at him. He didn't appear unrepentant in any way, shape or form. In fact, pride glowed from his skin like an unholy light. "Wait—you didn't *just* learn how to break into the BM. You already knew."

One boob grab.

"Do they know you stole something else?"

A head shake *no*. A smirk. Another boob grab.

"So…what you were waiting on…was…a copy?"

A third boob grab.

"Holy shit—the copy was made of real gold?"

He nodded and heaved out a breath. "It physically hurt me to pay that much money. Do you have any idea how much gold is an ounce? Not to mention my metallurgy forger. She don't come cheap, especially for such a famous job at a rush. She made her own alloy to mimic the ancient composition."

I fell backward onto the arm of the couch.

"Why? Wasn't there another way?"

"Maybe." He ran a hand across the back of his neck and sagged into the cushions. "But I was breaking my word to the British authorities, endangering everything I'd spent a fucking year trying to fix. Valerie kept threatening you—"

He shuddered, and I realized guiltily that whatever Valerie had said to me, she'd given Sam a lot more detailed threats. I pulled his hand into my lap. He squeezed mine and gave me a look with such soulful green eyes that I turned to mush. "I knew I needed a trump card, and I figured having the actual cape would save us in the end, one way or the other. And it did." He made a wry face. "If we never had to give anyone the real thing, I thought we could buy an island with it."

Wow. Wow. "You traded the real cape for my freedom?"

He blinked. His lashes were wet. I threw my arms around him. "I don't know what to say."

"Say you'll give me a chance to make everything up to you."

"Sam." I pulled back, my own eyes pouring freely by now. A wave of love swelled in my chest, almost hurting. It was wonderful. "No. You don't need any more chances. You have nothing to prove to me. I love you, and I'm never letting you go."

His lip curled, and he stared at his hands. "Really?"

And then we were both crying and hugging and kissing. Truth be told, it was all a little snotty, but wonderful just the same. He gave me such a feeling of peace, after the trials and tribulations. They were worth it, if I got this crazy man in the end. I think I'd needed a bold man of passion to break me out of the doldrums of my life. I could have walked away a thousand times, but I didn't. He was in my blood, in my soul.

He was my soul.

I planted a soft kiss to his brow and he held me. After a while, I put his hands on my boobs, and he soon forgot his high emotions. Boobies heal — that's just a fact. "Please tell me they're going after Valerie?"

"Yes. I've sicced James on her. He's given us a security detail in London until she's caught."

"Yay!" I squeezed him around the neck until he made chokey sounds. "Are they going to give you the fake cape back?"

He gave a shout of laughter. "No fucking way."

"… At least I'm rich."

The dimple gave me a wink. "That's what I'm counting on. Why else do you think I'm here?"

Chapter Seventeen

Maui Owie

"Pass the sunscreen, please."

"No."

I sat up on my elbows and peered at my darling lover. He sprawled out next to me, his tanned skin glowing in the sun like a pornographic Coppertone ad. "Do you want me to turn into a sunburned blob? It will clash with my hair."

Sam scooted closer to me on the giant blanket guarding us against the hot sands of a Maui beach. "Of course not. But I take my job as Rubber of Sunscreen very seriously."

Well. Who was I to deny him his job? Especially when he'd so recently abandoned his life's work on my account.

I took a quick peek around to make sure there were no camera phones pointed in our direction—I didn't know if I was vain, paranoid or realistic, probably all three—and lay on my back to give him access to everywhere my bikini wasn't covering. It would probably take him twenty minutes to apply the sunscreen, so I settled in for a long, titillating rub down.

After Super Hero Sam rescued me from the London police, flying in to save the day arrayed in a golden cape, the craziness in our lives just stopped. Production resumed, and I was able to think about my role in the film unfettered for the first time. A boring life is highly underrated.

I even made up with Danny, who, as tabloids revealed, had been dating a professional gymnast and a famous literary author whilst also snogging me. Cool, cool — we most certainly had not been an 'item'. The press, however, took my side in the whole thing, as I was the It Girl du jour for a couple of weeks.

All in all, I came to consider my brief flirtation with *People* magazine's third sexiest man alive a solid win. We'd agreed to be terribly flirty during the eventual press junket when the movie opened. JenX approved of this plan, saying "So, speculation. Sexy, right?"

Filming finished, and I think it'll be a damn funny movie that also makes a statement about the current state of financial hardship for the ninety-nine percent the world over. I'd come from the ranks of the plebes, and hoped I represented us well.

Sam's hands now began to wander around the lip of my bikini bottoms, and I don't know if it was the freedom, the heat or the complete inappropriateness of his actions in semi-public, but I lowered my sunglasses and said, "Wanna go back to the bungalow?"

He grabbed my hand and yanked me up to standing faster than you can say, "beach boner."

We'd rented a bungalow of such beauty, we now fantasized constantly of moving to Hawaii. Everyone probably does that while under the influence of a warm ocean, spectacular views and Mai Tais. Funny thing was—we could. We could do anything. I was a lady of some means now, and Sam...

When Sam finally laid his cards on the table and was honest about his financial portfolio, my eyes goggled at all the zeroes. Yes, it was ill-gotten. Yes, I felt guilty. But at least we'd helped put Shelley behind bars. And we were going to set up a charitable foundation to give away bunches of it.

Sam might even consult for different governments from time to time when a big art theft went down. They reserved the right to use him in exchange for him not being locked in solitary.

Whoops—not Sam. My darling was officially in witness protection, which meant he would not be able to appear in public with me until all the baddies after him were caught. His full name, forevermore? Zachary Samuel Ballitch. Pronounced Bale-itch. Uh-huh. Sure.

The Feds definitely got the last laugh. I had only to call Sam "Mr Ball Itch" when pissed at him to receive the Hulk in response.

Today, I harbored no ill feelings for my sexy, sun-kissed man. The glow he gave me melted my bones, and also my underwear. What can I say? He's got a good butt for brief swimming trunks. We ran, hand in hand, up the private beach and straight to our bedroom's sliding glass door, like a couple in a movie, except only doing one take. He unlocked the door, and I grabbed his arm to yank him to the bed. We tumbled, laughing, onto the palm-frond pattered comforter.

My cell phone rang.

"Urgh," said Sam.

Since I was still a witness in an investigation, I was forced to at least check the caller ID. I leaned over the bed and fished it out of my bag to glance at the face. "My mother," I muttered. I dropped it back from whence it came.

He hitched his fingers into my bikini bottoms and started to yank. "Don't say that word when I'm about to—"

"Please don't. I just ate lunch," said a saccharine voice.

I screamed and fell off the bed. In response, Valerie giggled. Like a politician who can't seem to stop texting dick pics, she was back. *Again!*

She held up a gun, which stopped Sam mid-lunge. Her pistol contrasted sharply with her 50s housewife dress drenched in shades of pink and yellow. She looked like a very special episode of *I Love Loony*.

Valerie stood in the doorway between the bedroom and the rest of the cottage—she'd been lurking in our bungalow for who knows how long. Her eyes sent daggers in Sam's direction. "You said you weren't dropping a dime of any of your co-criminals. Only on the buyers."

He hurried to his feet and moved in front of me. "That was before you came after her. All bets were off after that, and you knew it. This innocent act is wearing really fucking thin, Val."

"What do you expect? Parading around with that?" She pointed. I was "that." "You think nobody's going to notice? In the old days, you'd have leaped at the chance to pull off something like the Mold gold cape. You took pride in your work."

Sam made an exasperated noise. "I can't do this forever, Val. You get older. You get slow. You get caught." He put his hands on his hips. "I don't want to rot in a jail for the rest of my life."

"Neither do I!"

"And I never was okay with hurting people. That's why I left you in the first place."

She seethed, her hand flexing on the gun. The initial shock had worn off, and anger stiffened my muscles. Valerie and Sam continued debating, but I could hardly hear over the roar of blood in my ears. I didn't give a shit what she said, anyhow.

I was done being screwed with by June Cleaver.

I stayed crouched behind Sam and tried to put a scared look on my face, but I was moving beyond fear, into a dark and angry place that made my heart pound and my vision tinge red. Against the wall, just beyond my reach, leaned a fishing pole. I'd asked Sam to move the wet thing out of the bedroom to no avail, and I'd been too lazy to do it myself.

But now… I thought I'd go fishing for some evil ex-girlfriend.

I darted out from behind Sam and launched myself toward the pole. Movement began above me. I concentrated on grabbing the handle while I slammed into the wall with my back. With a mighty, screaming heave, I flicked the tip toward Valerie. The hook launched into the air. She screamed and reared back. The gun went off.

Sam yelled and hit the floor.

"No!" I ignored Valerie and crawled furiously to Sam, rolling and clutching his side.

I pried his hand off the wound, and he began hollering a string of curses the likes of which are still floating in the atmosphere, sullying everything they hit. A huge chunk of his flesh had been torn and burned away, but there was no actual hole. More of a giant trench. A bleeding, blackened trench. I hugged him in joy, and he sagged against the carpet. "Don't fucking squeeze it!"

Oops, right.

My brain stepped away from the edge of panic, and I remembered that Valerie was still at large, and about five feet away from us. She'd sat up, blood pouring from her forehead. With a short scream, she fished out the spangly green hook. I'd hooked her in the face!

In.

The.

Face!

I pointed and said, "Awesome!"

She didn't appreciate that at all.

She dropped to her hands and knees and started for the gun, which she got to just ahead of me. I punched her in the throat, and she doubled over, still clutching the weapon. We grappled for it. She made choking noises, still disoriented, but had about ten inches and quite a few pounds on me. I was quickly losing the fight when Sam jumped into the fray. The gun dropped to the floor.

A couple of guys pulled the drapes aside and ran into the room through the open sliding glass doors. I heard, "Is everyone okay?"

Valerie kicked Sam in his wounded side, and he crumpled like a demolished building. She bolted past our would-be helpers, taking the gun with her.

The two surfer dudes gaped open-mouthed at what they saw. Sam croaked, "Call nine-one-one."

I stumbled to the corner where my running shoes were. Sam followed me with his eyes and gasped, "Don't you dare!"

"I will dare. That woman needs to learn that you *do not fuck* with Samantha Lytton!"

The other guy asked, "Is that Michelle Williams?"

"That hair does nothing for her," said the first.

I bolted through the open door and down the concrete path. I reveled in every bit of blood splatter I found—first on the path, then in the grass. I spotted her ahead of me, and I burst into more speed. Folks were jumping out of her way, probably because her face was covered in blood like freaking Carrie, and because she waved a gun. She possessed longer legs than mine, but I had on the proper shoes. She couldn't run in five-inch heels. See? That's why no adventure heroine in the world should ever wear high heels!

She tripped on a curb leading into the street and splatted, her crinoline flying like a be-ribboned tumbleweed. I jumped atop her and grabbed her wrist to keep the gun pointed away from me. She spat at me—it landed on my chest.

Now I was double extra pissed.

I stepped on her gun hand, pulled back one fist and yelled, "Don't you know who I *am*?" That punch to her stupid face was even better than the one I'd delivered to Shelley. My hand hurt like blazes, my fingers feeling like they would pop off, but I just did not care.

My satisfaction was brief. She came up, fast, and head-butted me. A burning agony flashed from my forehead to my face and I fell backward off her. I scrambled to my feet, my brains reeling, but she delivered a kick to my stomach, and I spiraled and slid into the asphalt street.

Pain seared across my side, my arm, my leg. A car screeched to a halt close to my head. The toxic exhaust seared my nose and eyes. Everything went topsy-turvy and I scrambled to move past the screaming spasms in my body so that I could stand. I crawled to my knees. She was on her knees, too, still holding the gun in one limp hand, her head in the other.

Finally, I regained my balance and got into a defensive crouch. She peered at me through terrifying, dripping red eyes. Her mouth split into a smile and she giggled. That's the last thing I heard before the explosion of the gun.

I felt punched in the gut by a demon the size of Iowa. I flew sideways and smacked into the roadway, my head bouncing on unforgiving spikes of pavement. The sunlight blinded me, and people were screaming. I couldn't move my left arm. But I knew it was still there. A terrible pain unlike anything I've ever known exploded across my chest.

I'm dying, I thought. *I'm dying, and people are taking cell phone pictures of it.*

A woman dropped beside me and started talking. I caught bits and pieces. "Gun." "Ambulance." "Sherlock Holmes lady." The woman yanked the cardigan from around her waist and pressed it to my body. "You're hit in the shoulder," she yelled. "I'm a nurse. Stay awake, you'll be all right."

The sun made spots of my vision. Her face floated above me, shining and kind.

"Samantha!" I heard Sam before I saw him. He came down on the other side of me.

My nurse said, "Shit, this one's bleeding, too. What the hell is going on with you people?"

"I don't know," I whispered. "His dimple got me in trouble."

Someone said, "We tied up the woman with the gun." Applause broke out. Camera phones clacked and snapped. The ambulance came screeching up.

And that is how you use a motherfucking fishing pole to foil the villain. FYI—I recommend a more straightforward method. My way hurts like a son of a bitch.

* * * *

Make a sex tape. That's how you should rise to fame the easy way. I was being accused of being a publicity whore by some in the press, and it stung, but not more than my recovery from surgery did. No matter what you do, never hump an art thief to get ahead.

Only hump an art thief out of love.

I enjoyed my time recovering from my gunshot wound—so metal!—to the shoulder. Well, as much as one can. They gave me good pills and great doctors, and I was holed up in a different Maui bungalow having Sam wait on me hand and boob. I'd donated a huge chunk of money to the cancer charity of choice on behalf the wonderful local nurse who'd leaped into action to save me. Damn, it was the least I could do.

Local youths had wrestled Valerie to the ground after she shot me, and *ha ha fucking ha* she was finally in jail! Every time I thought about her in prison, sipping toilet wine with flat hair, I grinned and sang "Xanadu." Every time I did that, Sam begged me to stop.

Poor Sam. He currently limped around the bungalow trying to make me a sandwich. He kept running into doorways and tripping on nothing because of his eye, and it's my fault. See, I'm a witch whose dreams come true, because when I woke up after surgery, Sam greeted me with an eye patch on. Some of the helpful local youths had thought *he'd* attacked me, too, and enthusiastically put a beatdown on him, including throwing a heap of gravel in his eyeball. I'd turned him into an actual pirate, albeit temporarily. He didn't help himself by carrying Captain Taco around on his shoulder a lot, but at least the fiendish feline couldn't talk.

Sam set a laptop on the table in front of my couch. "A new video of your fight with Valerie has sold to the press. The best one yet." He quirked one eyebrow, which really made him appear piratical. Super hot. "The post is called 'Actual Charlie's Angel Samantha Lytton Captures Criminal Wearing Itsy Bitsy Bikini'. Wanna see?"

I hid my face in my hands. "Do I want to?"

He sat down next to me gingerly. "It's amazing." He sighed. "I love you. You're crazy, but I love you."

"She shot you! The woman needed to get told."

"Okay, okay, calm yourself. You'll bust a staple. Watch."

He clicked play, and I materialized into view. The camera person had caught the last moment of me chasing Valerie, and her tripping into the street. I launched myself at her like a pro-wrestler woman. "Whoa!"

"Body slam!" Sam pumped both fists in glee.

We wrestled. I punched her. It looked totally badass. Although thank goodness my embarrassing 'catch phrase' wasn't picked up by the audio. It had felt good at the time, however. She kicked me, and I splatted into the street. My torn-up skin hurt even now to watch it—half my body was raw and scabby from asphalt burn. "Oh, shit, no," I moaned.

"Yeah, sorry about that. Your ass looks amazing, though."

My ass hanging out of my bikini bottom. When I'd hit the street, half of my already-brief bottom had smushed itself into my butt crack. From then on, it was cheek, ahoy! I tore my eyes away from my pasty white wedgie and watched myself struggle to get up, my hands clawed and my expression ferocious. Valerie raised the gun and shot me, and three different people tackled her. I hit the deck, blood gushing. I had to turn away then. Even my bottom recoiled in horror—it was now covered in a spectacular array of bruises.

Sam was still grinning like an idiot. "Look at the comments."

"Never look at the comments on the Internet! I bet half of them are about how my body is ugly or my bikini is unfashionable."

"Well, yeah, there are some trolls, but consensus is that you're a totally awesome babe."

I scratched at my shoulder wound, which was really starting to sting again. "Really?"

He turned his head to peer at me with his good eye. He can put more censure into half a glance than most people can with a whole. "Yeah, dummy."

Totally awesome babe. Maybe I should have business cards made up.

Soon he brought us sandwiches and settled beside me to eat. I kept telling him I was glad to help, but he shushed me and insisted on doing everything, even though he himself was still wounded, too. The cat jumped between us, always eager to act like a puppy and beg for food, the downtrodden animal. It didn't help that Sam slipped him little pieces of bacon.

Sam flipped on the TV and we munched and chilled out. Maybe it was all the narcotics floating through my system, but a sense of peace and well-being settled over me. Sam had sworn that nobody else would come after us. He'd even made a point to call Jane and reassure her in case she got twitchy again—he threatened that I would attack her in a bikini if she misbehaved.

I'd just finished my last bite of my BLTA when my cell rang. "It's Mom, again." I leaned slowly — ouch — to put it on the table.

He snatched it up again. "You answer this. Every time you ignore a call from your mother, someone points a gun at us."

Holy crap, he was right. My mother — genteel harbinger of pink doom when ignored.

"Hi, Mom."

"Well! Finally!" Exasperated breaths and flutterings. "I thought you'd lost your phone!"

"No." I took a deep breath and swallowed my rage. Sam offered me a pain pill with a smile. I laughed silently, but tamped it down to say, "How have you been?"

"I've been horrified to see that my daughter was shot! I had to call your father to find out that you were okay."

"Aren't you really horrified at the unflattering angle or the videos of me, or the fact that I didn't lose ten pounds before I ran around in a bikini?"

Silence. I put the phone on speaker so I could take my pain medicine. I needed it. Finally, she said, "I know I'm hard on you, Samantha."

I waited for a 'but'.

"I just want you to be as great as I know you can be." She sighed into the line. "Diego and I agree that it was amazing the way you fought that disgusting woman. A true lady doesn't run about pointing guns. Although I liked her outfit."

I burst into laughter.

"It's true!" There was a pause before she said, "I love you, Samantha. I'm proud of what you've accomplished. I only bother pushing you because you're capable of anything. You just have to believe. You gave up on yourself for a long time."

That last bit struck me straight in the heart, it was so true. I hadn't known she was that perceptive, as the one-sided advice column she'd perpetually spewed had never changed, it only became more intense. My heart brightened with joy, and happy tears sprang into my eyes. This was the first time she'd ever, ever told me she felt any pride for me. The knot named 'Mom' in the dead center of my chest unwound a little. Even Sam appeared to be moved. He made a 'wow' face and stroked my hand gently.

"Thanks, Mom."

"Are you really going to be okay?"

"Yes." I wiped my nose. "It was a clean through-and-through shot. I'm sore as hell, but with time and physical therapy, I'll be okay. Sam is okay, too. She wounded him in his side."

"Just a flesh wound," supplied Sam.

"Okay. I'm glad you came to your senses and begged him to come back." Sam smirked at this, and I was forced to kick him. "Well, you rest. I have to go on the Internet now and leave some comments for idiots who don't understand how brave you are."

"No!" I nearly screamed it. "No, please don't. My, um, publicist will take care of the haters." A lie, but the last thing I needed was for my mom to go on Facebook and start slinging insults to "help" me.

"Hmmmmmmm," was the response before she hung up.

I hung my head. Sam said, "Hey, at least she's not one of the haters anymore."

I started to lean over to rest my head on his shoulder, but everything hurt, and I groaned instead.

"What are you moaning about? It's not like you got shot or something." He propped three pillows that I didn't need around me, but the gesture was so cute I just snuggled in.

"They're going to put Valerie away, right?"

"Four different people filmed her shooting you. She'll go away for that, at least. And I called my personal spook—the British have her, not the local authorities. She'll go down for the robbery, the kidnapping, etc."

"I hope they ship her off to Area 51."

"That's in America."

"Area 51?"

He grimaced. "That's the same place except with a British accent."

"I know. I don't really care what happens to her, as long as it involves iron maidens, and fleas, and maybe the ghost of Richard III." I warmed to the idea of her suffering and imagined a horrible dungeon complete with big, fat rats with a fondness for eating flipping hair.

"Area 51 is for aliens."

"Good, because she's from the planet Asswipe, in the Buttface Quadrant."

He didn't argue any further, but kissed my hand fervently. "I love it when you get all elegant and shit." He rose to take the plates back to the kitchen. A moment later, he hurried back out to the living room, a package in his hand. "Crap, I forgot that something came for you when you were asleep earlier."

The overnight envelope was thick and fairly heavy. "Feels like a script to me." Always good news, when *they* send *you* a script, and I wasn't expecting anything. I pulled it out and read the note from my agent on top first.

Holy.

Effing.

Shit.

I read the cover and squealed in excitement. My mouth dropped open and my throat got dry. Oh, my God! This was the most amazing thing in the world!

"What is it?" Sam sat beside me on the couch, and I handed him the note. "Wow. Wow, baby."

Apparently someone at Universal liked what they saw in the press this week. I'd been offered a *superhero movie franchise*. There are almost no women superheroes — or super*heroines*, more like — with their own franchises! I was legit gonna be Sigourney Weaver or something!

Aaaaaahhhhhhhhhhhhhhhhhhhh!

Sam cracked up next to me while he examined the script. "The Ovarian Hellion."

I bounced up and down with unmitigated glee, well, as much as my injuries would allow. "She avenges people who identify as women who've been done wrong. She seeks justice for rape victims, and goes after stalkers and cheating CEOs who don't pay their employees equally. Oh, my goodness. Oh, my goodness! My agent says it's super-duper funny. It's a spoof, but she really does kick ass and take names."

I flipped to the middle and burst into laughter. "She wears baggy pajamas with embroidered ovaries on them as her heroine outfit."

It's the role I was born to play, baby!

Sam threw his arms around me. "You're going to be amazing."

"And comfortable. The Ovarian Hellion doesn't wear platform boots like a schmuck."

"Do you want me to take you outside to read the script? It's another gorgeous day."

I looked him over, tan and adorable in his baggy shorts, V-neck tee and rumpled brown hair. "I miss sex."

That brightened his face in surprise. "Me too."

"My pill will kick in soon. Maybe when our pain medicines coincide, we can fool around?"

He squeezed my knee and laid a warm, panty-melting kiss on my mouth. "I'll do it for science."

"Can we play pirate?"

"Okay. But who will I be?"

"You can be the Ovarian Hellion."

He blew kisses at me. "It would be my honor."

My goofy, in-love grin could not be contained, and why would I want to? He was here. He was mine. And we had no expiration date!

A tickle of worry flitted around the back of my brain...what if he got bored? What if real life was too normal for him? I squashed these angsty questions with a metaphorical shoe.

I'd work very hard to keep him, just like my mother always told me to.

I walked fingers up his shoulder. "You feeling less ouchy yet?"

"Getting there."

Turning was difficult for him, as his wound area, exactly on his side a few inches above his hip, seemed to be where every part of his body connected together. I'd have to get on top, and take care to avoid it. I shifted for him, toward him and my bad arm. Leaning as much as I was able, I kissed...his shoulder. That's as far as I reached. No kissing for now.

"Good try."

"Don't make me go badass bikini chick on you."

He started toward me, a quick gasp of pain stopping him.

"Let me." I scooted to the edge of the couch and used my good hand to undo his fly. We managed between the two of us. His cock was already slightly hard by the time I liberated it from his shorts.

His head fell back onto the couch. "Don't hurt yourself," he said.

"I'm only gonna hurt you. By being so sexy. Ouch!" My free hand flew to clutch my shoulder, still aching dully.

"Nope. It's too much, too soon." He made a move to remove his parts from my clutches.

"I need sexual healing." With renewed caution, and renewed lust, I stroked the beautiful dick I'd missed so. After a few minutes, he didn't protest any more. The poor man kept bucking his hips, then groaning because it hurt him.

I grabbed his hand and used it for leverage to disentangle myself and stand. "Let's try the bedroom. I need room to maneuver."

Slowly, our horny, pathetic train made its way to the room with the soft, comfy bed. We'd been given the honeymoon cottage by an admiring hotel manager, so the room was a crazy mix of pinks, reds and tropical decals. I pointed Sam toward the bed, and he sat down gingerly. "Bottoms off," he said.

Yes, much easier to do standing. I gingerly eased my pajama bottoms down until finally gravity won over the pull of my butt, and they fell to the floor. Sam cheered—pants off is always a wonderful thing. He took my good hand and helped me climb into the bed.

"Lose the shirt," I ordered.

"You first, ya bilge rat."

I cocked my head. "'Bilge' better be a fancy word for 'beautiful'."

"Um...yo ho ho, ya beautiful rat?"

I tsked. "You were a way better pirate in my dream."

"Dream?" He threw his T-shirt off the bed. "What dream?"

Oops. I decided to distract him by sexily removing my pajama top. I got all the buttons undone, eventually, but couldn't get it off either arm by myself. All the while, I smiled and fluttered my eyelashes suggestively. He just sat there and watched, his hand over his mouth suppressing his laughter very poorly. "A little help?"

"Wench, leave the shirt on." Reaching out with one arm, he pushed aside my top and caressed my breast with the palm of his hand. I immediately felt heavy and tingly wherever he touched. It had been days and days since I'd felt his skin on mine, even though he'd been by my side every minute. I leaned into him, ready to get this show on the road.

With a minimum of laughing, we worked his shorts off him and down his legs. I wanted to give him a moment to rest from his painful bending, so I slipped my hand around his cock again and played lazily with him until his breathing got faster, and he made the most delicious little moans. I started to fluff a pillow behind his head, and he said, "Wait. Come here."

"Where?"

He held out a hand. "Sit on my face. It's doctor recommended."

I got a little swoony—all the blood in my whole body rushed south. I ached so much for him it almost hurt. His rock-hard arm balanced me while I gingerly maneuvered myself next to his head. "Wait—what doctor have you been going to?"

"Don't worry about her."

"Her?"

He started to laugh, and then groaned a little, reaching for his side. "Stop making jokes and give me that pussy."

I leaned my arm against the bamboo headboard and said, "*You're* making jokes."

"Then shut me up."

Yes, sir. I climbed across his smiling face, and he craned his neck up immediately to deliver a long, slow lick from my lips to my clit. It felt so amazing, I lost my balance. His arms landed on my hips to hold me in place. He took his time, moving slowly, lovingly across my naked sex, his tongue gentle and demanding all at once. His hands slid up to my breasts. I leaned into them. He moved his lips to kiss and suck on me, and I moaned into the warmth of the morning sun. On and on he went, caressing my ass, my hips, and fucking me with his mouth. I rubbed myself over him, and the more I bucked, the more fervent his response.

When I couldn't take it anymore, when I had to have him inside me, I moved off him and shifted to his hips. I moved onto his cock, thick and warm inside me. "I love you," he groaned as I slid down, my hand on his shoulder. I took care to avoid his bandaged area.

"I love you," I said, sitting back, easing my pussy around him. "Now, don't you move. I'll do all the work."

He groaned and bucked his hips. "I don't care if it hurts. I need you."

I slid upward, and he sighed into the duvet, his eyes closed. He braced my working arm with his, and I relied on him to be able to move high up on his cock, and slide back down again. Pure delight, pure desire pulsed through my body, flowing from where we joined. My injuries were soon forgotten, and I reveled in his fullness inside my body. He thrust his hips into mine, apparently not caring, either, about our limitations. I rode him, working his cock, my entire sex pulsating and wet and feeling unbelievably good. I wanted it to last forever, but we'd been too deprived of one another, too ready to screw each other's brains out.

He jerked up one more time and cried out, coming inside me, the warmth of him flooding me. I leaned down over his chest and ground my clit against his body, almost there, a shattering bliss building up and spilling over as I convulsed around his cock. I almost fell on him in my shuddering pleasure, but remembered to hold myself just in time. His hands braced themselves against my stomach, and I stayed upright, my head dizzy, my body still fluttering with the last of my orgasm.

Gingerly, I slid off his cock—mmmmmm, a pleasure in and of itself—and lay down beside him. He took my hand, both of us breathing hard. "Are you okay?" I asked.

He pressed against his giant bandage. "I'm fantastic. Jesus, I needed that."

"Me, too." My arm throbbed from all the blood pumping though my body, but I willed myself to relax. My head spun from the sex, and from my medicine, truth be told. I couldn't say that I minded. Relaxation was a welcome change from a constant state of 'aaaagggghhh!'

The sun shining through the sheers and the heat from our bodies warmed us into a sleepy state. "Sam?"

"Yeah, baby?"

I licked my lips, my mouth worrying over the question. "Do you really think you can be happy this way?"

He turned his head, concern furrowing his brow. "What way?"

"Not criminal-ing anymore. Just, you know, playing house with me?"

Grunting a little, he pushed himself up to sitting. "I make my own choices. And I've chosen a different way to live. With you. Not only because of you, but because of me, too." He crooked one knee and shifted more toward me. "I loved stealing. I'm sure I'll miss the thrill, forming plans, getting away with it." He shrugged one shoulder. "But things change in life. I've found you, and I love you more than my old career."

My eyes welled up. "Really?"

"Yes. I decided this a year ago." He grinned, the dimple sneaking out just for me. "I don't want to rot in jail with a life mate named Lockpick Larry until I'm an unemployable senior citizen. Not that there's anything wrong with prison husbands named Lockpick Larry, but he's not my first choice. You are."

"Aw, you want me more than poor, hypothetical Larry?"

He nodded and pointed his non-injured eye in my direction. "Although you have worse taste in music."

I managed to get into a sitting position and grabbed his hands. "You're my first choice, too. I couldn't really ever stay away from you, even when it was good for me. Because, I guess, you're good for me. Thank you."

"For what?"

"I—" There were too many things to list. My heart swelled, and I gazed into his beautiful eyes, er, eye that could change from green to brown to grey. A lady could never tire of staring at such peepers. "For always being on my side, even when I'm an idiot and don't realize it."

A shy smile flitted across his face and he stared at the duvet. "North Carolina folks gotta stick together."

I smiled. "Do you want to drag our banged-up bones out to the beach to soak in the sun?"

He pushed a stray strand of my hair out of my face and tucked it behind my ear. "Soaking with you is one of my favorite things."

Something told me that Sam and I wouldn't be sitting around idle for long, but for now, I'd enjoy it.

Or maybe this was the end of the craziness in our lives. Maybe we'd become a couple whose biggest concern was making sure all our Tupperware had lids.

I shuddered. Maybe…not.

* * * *

What Could Go Wrong?
by
F. Langley

Final Draft

Ext. A Beach In Bora Bora – Day
Angle On: Jayde Loving *sips a piña colada on a chaise next to her partner in crime* Chase Dakota.

Jayde Loving: We got away with it, my darling. We cleaned out the British Museum and walked away unscathed.

Chase Dakota: Yes, and we also were able to reconcile so that our days are full of sunny splendor, and our nights full of sexual exploration under the stars.

Jayde Loving: I have the sand in my crack to prove it.

Chase pulls off his aviators in a sexy swipe and plants a fond stare on Jayde...one might even call it loving.

Chase Dakota: What shall we do now? The possibilities are endless. As long as the possibilities happen in a country that has no extradition agreement with the UK. We could climb mountains. We could comb the depths of the ocean for treasure.

Jayde Loving: I don't know. You want to get some enormous hamburgers and watch a *Misfits* marathon?

Chase Dakota: How did you know?

Jayde shrugs.

Jayde Loving: I'm super smart, and also super hungry.

Chase Dakota: Maybe we could knock over a bank on the way to get the food.

Jayde Loving: We have eighty million dollars!

Chase Dakota: That's not the point. I enjoy the notion that we *could* rob a bank whenever we wanted to.

Jayde Loving: Well, anybody could do that.

Chase Dakota: I know.

He sits up and kisses her hand.

Chase Dakota: That's the fun of life, isn't it?

Jayde Loving: How about this... I'll race you to the Burger Hut. If you beat me...

Chase Dakota: Which I will.

Jayde Loving: …then we can play cops and robbers.

Chase Dakota: You brought your sexy cop outfit?

Jayde Loving: With the tear-away bullet-proof vest.

Chase yanks Jayde out of her chair.

Chase Dakota: What are we waiting for?

He sprints across the sand and out of the shot.

Jayde Loving: Hey, wait! That's cheating!

Jayde, laughing, runs after Chase. One might even call it…chasing. She glows with renewed love for him – once a scoundrel, always a scoundrel. And she wouldn't really have it any other way.

About the Author

Lucy Woodhull has always loved le steamy romance. And laughing. And both things at the same time, although that can get awkward. Her motto is "Laugh and the world laughs with you, cry and you'll short-circuit your Kindle."

That's why she writes funny books, because goodness knows we all need to escape the real world once in a while.

She believes in red lipstick, equality, and the interrobang. Lucy daydreams in Los Angeles with her husband and a very fat cat who doesn't like you.

Lucy Woodhull loves to hear from readers. You can find her contact information, website details and author profile page at http://www.totallybound.com.

Totally Bound Publishing